This edition published in 2014 by
Oak Tree Press
www.oaktreepress.co.uk

Oak Tree Press is an imprint of
Andrews UK Limited
The Hat Factory
Bute Street
Luton, LU1 2EY

Sweet is revenge – especially to women

—*Lord Byron*

The *Malleus Maleficarum* meaning "Hammer of the Witches" in Latin is a treatise on the prosecution of witches written in 1486 by Heinrich Kramer a German Catholic Clergyman.

Witchcraft had been denied by the church in earlier centuries and they had specifically outlawed the old practice of witch burning since witchcraft was originally viewed by many early medieval Christians as a pagan superstition

However by the 15th century, belief in witches was once again openly accepted in European society. Persecution of witches became more brutal following the publication of the *Malleus*, with witchcraft being accepted as a real and dangerous phenomenon

The main purpose of the *book* was to prove that witchcraft exists and to discredit those who expressed skepticism. It also claimed that witches were more often women than men, and it's purpose was to educate magistrates and officials on the procedures that could find them out and convict them. It offered a step-by-step guide to the conduct of a witch trial, how to initiate the process and how to interrogate and torture the accused.

Foreword

I have once again teamed up with my good friend and mentor Ken Scott on this, my first attempt at a novel. My God! First an autobiography and now a bloody novel, what would those teachers be saying right now? Crissy Rock the author and now Crissy Rock the novelist!

I'll be honest with you; this was not an easy project to complete. When I worked with Scotty on my first book it was difficult. I was a total novice and at times I struggled to bring my demons to the surface or at least to a level where I was able to transfer those painful words on paper. He coaxed me gently at times and put a foot up my arse when I needed it but the words were always there, deep inside me, yes, but they were always there in my head and I knew they needed to come out.

So when they did come out everything flowed and although at times we shed many tears and I felt like throwing in the towel, I knew the book was taking shape and more importantly that there were enough words in my head to make up the word count the publishers were looking for.

Writing a novel is a somewhat different concept because the words are not there, they have to be dreamt up, created, the plot constructed and the characters invented. This was something very new to me, especially when it came to the characters and in particular the heroine Samantha Kerr.

I once read somewhere, 'write about what you know.' So that's what I tried to do. Sam had to come from Liverpool where else? I decided to build a little of my character within her and tried to get inside her head wondering what I/she would do when faced with impossible decisions. So I gave her a chequered past and a multitude of problems, but at the same time I wanted to make her strong enough to face up to those problems and not let it affect her life too much and of course I gave her a determination to overcome anything her enemies threw at her.

I'll be honest, I nearly gave up several times, wondering wtf I was doing trying to compete with the likes of Patricia Cornwell and

Lynda La Plante, but Scotty was always there and finished several chapters when things just weren't happening for me, they call it writers block.

I'll happily admit that this book is as much his as it is mine and he deserves an enormous amount of credit for lifting me mentally and bodily over the finishing line, he is truly special to work with.

I enjoyed the journey with Scotty again, but I'm not sure my career as a novelist is cast in stone. You, the reader will determine that with how successful this book becomes and I will read the reviews with interest.

I enjoyed the plot construction and being able to kill people at the stroke of a pen (just kidding) and for those of you who don't know, I am in fact a witch myself so I felt comfortable with the subject matter and have a good knowledge of what it is I was writing about.

One of the most rewarding aspects of constructing a novel is the research needed to progress the plot. I couldn't quite believe some of the things I discovered about the mediaeval witch hunts and the inquisitions or how much many of our modern churches still disrespect and yes, even despise the female form even to this day.

At times I felt the plot was a one woman mission to bash the Catholic Church but that was not my intention and that concerned me a bit because when writing a novel it's easy to confuse fiction with fact, if that makes sense?

I was brought up a Catholic as a small girl and experienced a particular horrific incident at the hands of an evil sadistic nun and those of you who read my first book will understand why I am now a lapsed member of my church. But I am also sensible enough to realise that there are bad apples in every barrel and most of the employees of all churches worldwide are genuine, decent people with no other agenda than to help the poor and their fellow human beings.

And having said all that, we mustn't turn our back on history or ignore it, and if I have offended anyone by bringing up that dark period then so be it but it's not Crissy Rock's fault because that history is all there to read and explore at the touch of a button and there are literally dozens of books that give a concise history of the mediaeval inquisitions orchestrated by the church.

It's a fascinating, but at times a disturbing subject to read up on and to be able to construct a fiction novel incorporating this material was once again a rewarding experience. I'm improving as a writer I know that, but still don't feel comfortable enough to be let off on my own. Does that make sense? I need a ghostwriter and in Scotty I feel I have found a good one because his overwhelming concern is to improve me as an author and make sure I learn my craft. If you haven't read my first book you may not know that I am dyslexic and couldn't read or write until I was in my early thirty's. My spelling is crap, my grammar shocking and my sentence construction not perfect. I have another problem in that I write as I speak, with a dialect that is not spoken in correct English and it is more difficult to pull a chapter together than someone who was educated at Eton or Harrow and talks proper!

But I have a great mentor and *spellcheck* and a built in thesaurus and a dictionary and an editor who is truly educated (not like me and Scotty) and I know that if I have determination and belief in myself and I can dream and keep stimulating my imagination then anything can happen.

I learn new words every day; I sit at the computer and find if I right click on a word it brings up synonyms. They are words of a similar meaning and more often than not I replace my word with one of the computers and I feel good that I can *cheat* this way.

With the technology at our fingertips these days there has never been a better time to write your own book. I'd love to think my two books have stimulated just one person to sit in front of a keyboard and give it a go, and if you feel you need a little help then why not drop Scotty a line and I'm sure he will look at what it is you have to say.

Enjoy my debut novel, I'll be watching for those reviews.

Crissy xx

REVENGE IS SWEETER THAN FLOWING HONEY

One

But (and this is remarkable) when on the next day the other witch had at first been exposed to the very gentlest questions, being suspended hardly clear of the ground by her thumbs, after she had been set quite free, she disclosed the whole matter without the slightest discrepancy from what the other had told. MM.

The priest bowed his head as he knelt. He spoke as if there were tears in his eyes but they were strangely dry.

"Father I have committed a grave sin, forgive me. Your mysterious ways are indeed strange to me for you made me the way you did and guided me from childhood in my quest to join your order. I have no one but you to confess to for I dare not disclose my actions to a living soul. I am sorry to burden you Father but have no alternative but to turn to prayer. Hear me Father and forgive me for I repent and I plead with you to hold the child's tongue."

The priest gazed skywards and crossed his chest.

"I have thought about taking my life Father but I know I must carry on your good work until I am no longer able to do so. I beg for a sign Father, a sign that you wish me to continue your work, a sign that you understand and I promise I will sin no more. I know not what this sign will be or in what shape or form you will deliver it but I have faith in you for you have created me the way I am. I have respect and love for you and I dedicate my life and know that you will show me the error of my ways and forgive me."

The priest stood and wiped at a solitary tear in the corner of his eye. He held onto the pew in front of him and genuflected to the huge cross once more. His knees weren't what they once were and he almost cursed to himself as a stabbing pain shot through his left meniscus. He almost cursed but then remembered where he was.

He stepped to the side and looked up at the gold leaf encrusted figure of the Lord suspended on the cross.

Such extravagance.

He made the sign of the cross once more, turned and walked through to his office in the far end of the church.

Cardinal Barberini was trying to find a word that would describe how he was feeling at that present time. Concerned, anguished... either could fit the bill he supposed but then again it was best not to jump to conclusions. Not just yet anyway. The Church has always had enemies who would do their utmost to strike at the heart of the Vatican and the secret of survival was simple, you had to be stronger and more powerful than your enemy. Conflict and wars – they were an inevitable part of life and it was important to hit first and ask questions later.

Cardinal Barberini laid the ancient tome on his desk and opened it at a chapter titled *Aragonese Crusade*. He gave a wry smile. *Crusade's* he thought. Lord, did the Church know how to organise a crusade or two and how the masses flocked to receive the Papal Blessing and absolution from all their sins if they simply boarded the ships to The Levant and waged war with the Muslims.

The 1st Crusade, the 2nd Crusade, the 3rd 4th 5th 6th 7th 8th and 9th Crusades, Crusades from the north, Swedish Crusades, Wendish Crusades, Alexandrian and Mahdian Crusades and incredibly even a Children's Crusade. Thirty thousand poor mites who marched in the name of their Lord to convert the Muslim heathens to Christianity.

Cardinal Barberini laughed inwardly as he read on. The Aragonese Crusade was ordered by Pope Martin IV. It was estimated that 25,000 people perished in that particular Crusade though some groups would inevitably claim a much higher death toll, always ready to criticise his beloved organisation. Atheists, Protestants, Jews and Muslims all ready to stand up and be counted when it came to criticism of the Catholic Church.

He stood and walked over to the corner of the room and poured himself a drink. Cognac... Remy Martin. He took a mouthful and allowed the beautiful tasting liquid to linger on his tongue. He held it there for a moment then tilted his head back slowly as the gravity pulled it to the back of his throat and to the receptor cells in his taste buds. Truly an exquisite experience.

He swallowed and breathed out and the strong alcoholic aroma seemed to fill the room.

The inquisitions. Another exquisite experience. How he wished he could have been alive when the Catholic Church was at its most powerful. True, there were barbaric times, bloody and murderous but the underlying purpose was justified. The heretics and non-believers were misguided and they needed to be saved. If they couldn't be saved they were eradicated. It was the way it was back then; a sign of the times. The world was a better place because of the Crusades and the Inquisitions he thought to himself with a smile. The Catholic Church had saved the world from Islamic domination. Just occasionally it would be nice if that were recognised by the liberals. There was always some individual ready to stick the knife in.

The telephone rang. He took the call and listened carefully. It was the Bishop of Place Vendome in Paris. He was expecting the call and he listened as the Bishop spoke. Suddenly he felt the urge to take more cognac on board. He thanked the Bishop for the information then bid him goodnight. He replaced the receiver.

He began to tremble involuntarily and reached for his glass again. He drained it quickly and wiped the surplus from his lips as he gulped in large quantities of air. He hadn't even tasted the fine cognac this time; he'd taken it for effect only.

He reminded himself not to jump to conclusions. He was getting paranoid in his old age.

Two

There is also, concerning witches who copulate with devils, much difficulty in considering the methods by which such abominations are consummated. On the part of the devil: first, of what element the body is made that he assumes; secondly, whether the act is always accompanied by the injection of semen received from another; thirdly, as to time and place, whether he commits this act more frequently at one time than at another; fourthly, whether the act is invisible to any who may be standing by. And on the part of the women, it has to be inquired whether only they who were themselves conceived in this filthy manner are often visited by devils; or secondly, whether it is those who were offered to devils by midwives at the time of their birth; MM.

The girl's thoughts were more lucid than they had been of late. She had no anger now. That had dissipated. Today she had a sense of well being and pride at the way she had carried out her third killing.

Her business was doing well. She was good at what she did and was turning down the smaller jobs and concentrating on the wealthier clients and high-class projects to the extent that she began to take on specialized employees and charged quite ridiculous fees for her services freeing up considerable time to concentrate on killing, which she was also very good at.

The girl was heading for New York, the Manhattan apartment of an 'A' list actress. She'd worked on her new London holiday home 18 months prior and her latest role in a Hollywood blockbuster persuaded her to splash out a six-figure sum on a five room renovation across the pond.

Little did she know as she sat in the airport that another opportunity would present itself in New York.

On the aeroplane somewhere over the Bay of Biscay she took a light breakfast of scrambled eggs and smoked salmon, lightly sprinkled with a dusting of paprika. She accepted the steward's suggestion of a half bottle of Don Perignon, figuring it would help her sleep. She'd been up at a ridiculous hour that morning and had slept badly as she always did.

Three hours into the North Atlantic Ocean her eyelids were growing heavy and she allowed herself to drift off into another world... a troubled one

The girl awoke covered in a cold damp sheen. The airhostess informed her the flight was just a few hours from New York and she tried to compose herself a little.

The spirit was back again taunting and demanding action and she craved another death.

The plane arrived at JFK airport fifteen minutes ahead of schedule. The girl gathered her hand luggage together and prepared to disembark. She tried hard to push the images of the dream into the recesses of her mind, for the time being at least.

As the girl collected her luggage she experienced first-hand the infamous American customs official who kept her waiting for a further fifteen minutes examining her suitcase and asking her at least a dozen questions on her profession and how long she intended to stay. Before long she was clear of customs and in one of the famous yellow cabs en-route to the city.

The hotel was situated in Manhattan with majestic views across Central Park and the rooms were luxurious and spacious with a gigantic flat- screen TV built into the wall. She unpacked her luggage as an involuntary shiver rippled down her spine. She looked out of the window and could see her beaming, toothy, childlike smile reflected in the glass. She was living the life of a normal person for a while at least. She knew Maven would come calling soon.

The girl awoke and showered, skipped the hotel breakfast and headed straight out into the streets.

She was in awe of the massive buildings that seemed to rise up from the pavement. Floor after floor after floor of highly polished glass, the upper floors split into tiny square centimetre blocks. At first she wanted to count each level but found it almost impossible for her eyes to take it all in.

The girl loved the noise and the hustle and bustle that went perfectly with the atmosphere of this incredible city and she was so glad to be a part of it. She tried to put a finger on what it was she loved about New York so much and then it came to her. Anonymity. That was it. It was the sheer anonymity of the place, walking past hundreds and thousands of people who didn't give her a second glance and she loved it.

She blended into the masses of people around her almost as if she was invisible. It suited her just fine. She stopped at a café for coffee and although it was a little chilly she was determined to sit out on the pavement and drink in the atmosphere.

The girl found herself scribbling some notes on to a napkin and looked at the words as they appeared as if my magic, not her words, the words of another hand. Maven was taking over.

She looked across the street and noticed an old church sandwiched between two huge skyscrapers. It looked so out of place, like something from a different era and yet something about it seemed so inviting. She needed to resist the urge. She hated churches. Don't go.

The attraction was growing stronger. No don't go.

She drained the last of her coffee and her eyes were once again drawn to the church building. She settled the bill and stood and took a hesitant step forward.

She wandered across the busy street almost oblivious of the cars and trucks wondering what was pulling her there. Surely a quick look inside won't do any harm she thought. Churches and cathedrals did little for her as a child nor did she get any great comfort from them in adulthood when she attended an odd wedding, a funeral or a christening. And yet this was strange. A magnetic draw she couldn't resist.

At the bottom of the stone steps she looked up at the dreary imposing building. The church doors stood open like a great big mouth waiting to swallow her up. She took a deep breath as she climbed the stairs one by one and reluctantly stepped inside. It's coming – the horror show will begin soon.

The pews in the church lay either side of the aisle like rows of giant shiny ribs. The ancient stone walls were adorned with statues of saints and Popes from yesteryear, all looking down at her and the cold almost hostile stares followed her every footstep. The altar was strategically placed in the very heart of the building with a huge cross supporting the broken body of a gold leaf encrusted Jesus Christ complete with fake blood oozing from his hands and feet and seeping from his forehead beneath his crown of thorns. She suppressed a smile.

The girl's footsteps echoed with each step and she found herself conscious of the noise, gently easing onto her tiptoes in a vain attempt not to disturb the worshippers. A few people were scattered around their heads bowed deep in prayer. She pitied them. She pitied the brainwashed ones.

Time to get out of there and enjoy the early morning sunshine, she'd been in there long enough.

As she walked over towards the door a voice behind her spoke. He asked if she needed help.

She turned around quickly to find herself looking at a priest and she at once realised this was the reason she had been called.

"Are you new to this parish? " he said.

The girl lowered her head, said she was visiting from England and was just a little curious to see the inside of his church.

"And you're more than welcome," he said with a smile. He introduced himself, "I'm Father O'Neill."

It was a smile she'd seen a thousand times before. A flirtatious smile, a certain natural glint in his piercing handsome emerald green eyes and she thought of the ridiculous rule the Catholic Church imposes on the poor priests.

Their dialogue continued as the priest tried to make polite conversation. She felt compelled to run away and yet something kept her in there. Maven was very persuasive. She felt her anger building and she could do nothing about it. She wanted to run but Maven ordered her to stay. There is work to be done she said.

As the priest guided her towards the door he gently placed his hand upon her shoulder and her whole body seem to shudder. She stepped back shocked and alarmed as her breathing increased slightly and she felt the hairs on the back of her neck stand on end.

The girl ran.

It was a relief to get outside. She tried to shake the feeling. She was being silly she reminded herself. It was only a church.

Maven told her not to worry. She would be seeing him again soon.

It took the girl only twenty minutes on her laptop to find all she needed to know on Father O'Neil. There were news stories and even a dozen images on Google search. Father O'Neil had been a naughty boy. How the fuck was he still working for the church? She couldn't shake the skin crawling feeling she had inside the church when the priest had touched her.

The girl took off her shoes and lay on the bed closing her eyes. She felt sleep creeping over her and there was nothing she could do about it.

She was walking through woodland. The heat of the sun warmed her skin as she collected herbs on the floor of the forest placing them into a wicker basket. She heard a rustle from the trees behind her. It startled her and she turned. There was a group of people... fourteen, fifteen perhaps more and a lone priest. A young woman was pointing at her and said something that the men seemed to take notice of. Three men came towards her. Something didn't feel right. They meant her harm. They wanted to hurt her. It was that priest, O'Neil. She could see his deep green evil eyes. She dropped her basket, turned and ran. She ran as fast as she could with a determination she had never felt before. She ran fast but the men were getting closer and closer until she could feel their presence almost upon her. A hand grabbed at her hair pulling her backwards onto the ground and they were upon her like a pack of wild hyenas.

And then the girl awoke with a start and the familiar perspiration covered her from head to foot. These dreams were coming to her far too often. It had felt so real, even her head was aching where they had pulled at her hair. She rose from the bed and tried to shrug it off. She ran a bath, undressed and stepped into the hot water. What was wrong with her? Her body was aching? Perhaps the jet lag was kicking in she told herself.

After a long soak the girl stepped from the warm water and began towelling her hair. As the towel touched her shoulder she recoiled in pain. She went across to the mirror and noticed what looked like a large welt mark across her shoulder. Where the hell had that come from? She couldn't recall bumping into anything. She looked again and ran her fingers across her skin. The flesh was raised and starting to bruise like she had been hit with some sort of belt. This didn't make sense. Had she fallen out of bed during one of those recurring violent nightmares?

Were they coming after her? Do they now know?

The girl looked in the mirror smiled and whispered quietly to herself. "Bring it on. Bring it on you motherfuckers."

She was enjoying her stroll through Central Park, the early evening breeze caressed her weary body and strangely refreshed her too and she stood still for a moment with her eyes closed. The coolness of the air tugged and pulled at her skin and she decided it would be a good idea to walk the few blocks back to the hotel. It would blow away the cobwebs she told herself... clear her mind. There was nothing like a good walk to do that.

The girl took a slightly different route to the one she was used to and before long she realised that for some strange reason she found herself directly opposite the old church. How could that be? She didn't want to go there, hadn't planned it. The route she took should have taken her away from the church. She was more than a little confused. Tiredness, it had to be.

All of a sudden her legs felt like lead and her head started to spin so much so that she steadied herself on a shop window.

No, she wouldn't walk. She'd take a drink or two and call a cab. She made her way across the road to a small bistro and sat down at a table outside.

The girl ordered a half bottle of chilled white Chablis. It wasn't long before the wine had arrived and as she placed the glass to her lips and tipped it she felt the coolness line her throat. It was a pleasant feeling and before long the alcohol kicked in and she felt herself slowly unwind. It was good to be alive she thought and this wonderful city was growing on her by the minute. The girl felt at home.

"I hope that's just medicinal," a familiar voice said.

She looked up as she placed her glass onto the table. It was the priest from the church. "Let the fun begin," said Maven.

She didn't know where the sentence came from. It was as if it wasn't hers as she asked the priest to join her. He came on to her, there was no other way to describe it and the girl thought the bastard had dug his own grave because he asked for it. It wasn't her fault or Maven's it was the priests because yet again he showed his hypocritical leanings and opened himself up. He forgot all about his vows and his promises and had no intentions of even attempting to quell his manly urges.

The girl and the priest became quite drunk.

As the darkness drew in the priest looked at his watch and said he'd better be going. He raised his almost empty glass and said his farewells. Their glasses touched and he looked straight into the girl's eyes with a steely stare as his hand brushed against hers.

It was unmistakable... quite deliberate. The girl hadn't misjudged his actions. The man of the cloth wanted her. He was a fraud and without a shadow of a doubt he had hit on her.

Maven said she would have him soon.

The girl persuaded him to stay. It wasn't difficult. She ordered another bottle of wine. He was so easily led, no willpower whatsoever and the conversation notched up to another level. They talked about celibacy and sex and they giggled like two children in kindergarten.

The priest was struggling to compose himself, conscious of his clothing and the many prying eyes that surrounded them. But this was New York and it didn't matter. So what if a man of the cloth was acting a little flirtatiously and enjoying a glass of wine. Who cared? He removed his priest's collar just after ten o'clock.

That was the moment she knew she had triumphed. She read him like a book as he sat back in his chair, placed his hands on the table and grinned smugly. The girl was enjoying leading this priest a merry dance. It was the thrill of the chase, the great taboo of awakening the sexual feelings of a man who was programmed not to entertain such thoughts.

Later they took a yellow cab over to Queens. They had dinner in an Italian restaurant on 73rd Street. The priest said he liked the Queens district of New York, he liked the ambience he said but she knew they were there because no one knew him. He was a fraud and a charlatan; he was lying through his teeth.

The girl had dinner with Father Michael O'Neil on two separate occasions before Maven came calling and she killed him.

The nightmares were becoming progressively worse and the attention to detail remained with her long after she had woken. She wrote everything down and found what she was looking for quite easily in the bizarre backstreet sex shops and flea markets of the Big Apple.

Make no mistake the girl thought, New York is one fucked up city.

$\sim$

Father Michael O'Neill was originally from New England of Irish descent. His ancestors had settled in America after the potato famine and through the generations had built up a very successful import and export business. He was a Catholic and the church had never been far away despite all the shit that life had thrown at the Irish over the years. The big man hadn't exactly looked after the Emerald Isle and yet they still followed the church like little lost sheep.

Michael was destined for the priesthood from an early age and took up his post at the age of 25 in a parish in Oregon.

It was not difficult to find why he had been moved on so many times during his short career. He was tried in Oregon under a severe sexual assault charge on an 11-year-old girl but the case was found to be not proven. In Washington DC the girl unearthed a similar story, this time the accusations had come from two teenage boys.

Reading between the lines of the newspaper reports, the young boys' families had been paid off and Father Michael O'Neill moved on yet again.

The priest had invited the girl to his apartment for dinner. She knew it was time and she would feel no guilt only pleasure.

He greeted her with a smile as he opened the door to the apartment. He kissed her. The kiss didn't linger it was almost fleeting. Ever the fucking gentleman thought the girl.

During the course of the dinner she guided the conversation to where she wanted it to go. They talked love and sex but they also talked repression and torture and how his church had used barbaric methods to extract confessions from ordinary women across Europe many years ago. The girl described the detailed words of the Malleus Maleficurum; the manual used by priests and the church to torture and extract confessions and he was genuinely surprised at how much the girl had read up on the subject.

There were denials and excuses and he was clearly uncomfortable with the subject matter as they dined on a fine piece of Chateaubriand.

The girl's excitement was building for now she knew it was only a matter of time. The girl had planned well... she was clever.

The good thing about killing abusive priests is that the church tends to cover it up and occasionally even pay the police off to do so. She knew it was unlikely they would look too hard for her.

Even so, the slight possibility that she would be caught pleasured her greatly.

She took his hand as they dried the dishes together. He turned to face her and she leaned forward and kissed him. He didn't resist, she didn't expect him too and as her tongue probed gently between his lips her hand slipped down to his groin.

He was hard. He was ready.

She took a step back so he could see her clearly and she slowly undressed right there in his kitchen allowing her clothes to lie where they fell. She turned and walked away.

"Where are you going?" he shouted after her.

The girl picked up her handbag as she walked into his bedroom and he quickly followed.

Her commands were firm and he obeyed her without question.

"*Strip.*"

"*Onto the bed.*"

He was putty in her hands.

He grinned as she pulled out the handcuffs and she shackled him to the brass headrest.

The girl climbed onto the bed and her head went down to where he wanted it to go. She lingered there breathing heavily, teasing him as he groaned and begged her to take him in her mouth.

He would make a noise as the girl tortured him, she knew that and she had come prepared. She reached into her bag for the mouth gag, a hard plastic ball on a chain with an adjustable strap.

"What's happening?" he mumbled.

He grinned as the girl forced it into his mouth and buckled it behind his head, thinking it was all part of the bizarre game.

And now the girl had him in complete control, she had him where she wanted him.

She grabbed his face with her hand and jerked it towards her.

She knelt down so that her face was only inches from his and she whispered quietly that she was there to rape and torture him like his predecessors had raped, murdered and tortured innocent woman during their witch-hunts. She told him his church had murdered her sisters for over three hundred years. "Your church is evil," she said "and you work for no one but the devil."

He wasn't so sure now, wasn't so sure it was just a game.

He shook his head and struggled for the first time.

The girl reached into her bag, took out the dog's collar and pulled it around his neck. The collar was strong leather with a row of stainless steel spikes facing outwards. The makers of the collars designed them to make the dogs look tough. It was perfect. The girl grabbed roughly at the priests hair and pulled his head back working the collar onto his neck with her free hand. It was a little awkward but she persevered. The collar was not meant to be worn this way, with the spikes facing inwards towards the wearer. It was loose at first but she tightened it gradually hole by hole until eventually the first spike pierced his skin and a trickle of blood eased from his neck, ran down his back and spilled onto the crisp white sheets. What a beautiful sight thought the girl, a beautiful contrast in colours and her excitement reached new levels as the victim began to whimper, plead and beg as he quickly began to realise she'd overstepped the mark of normality.

She reached down and tightened it further.

So much blood. So nice, so pretty.

He was breathing hard now, beads of perspiration mingled with the blood and she reached down and placed both hands in a small pool above his shoulder blade. She smeared the blood over her own face and onto her naked breasts.

"You tortured my sisters in public for no other reason but to sexually abuse and humiliate them and to satisfy your own carnal lust."

She straddled his face and squeezed his throat with her thighs feeling the warm blood flow over her.

It was all true, every word. The perverted priests and bishops and cardinals and torture masters and inquisitors would take great sexual pleasure in all of their deeds and convinced themselves that such desires emanated not from themselves but from the girls they attacked. They ripped out their vaginas and breasts with red-hot irons and pincers and would not stop even after they had dragged out a confession.

O'Neil was somewhat paler in complexion now and his erection had diminished completely. The tightness of the collar was bringing him ever nearer to unconsciousness. That was where the girl wanted him and she notched up the pressure one more hole.

Three

Now the wickedness of women is spoken of in Ecclesiastics xxv:
There is no head above the head of a serpent: and there is no wrath
above the wrath of a woman. I had rather dwell with a lion and a
dragon than to keep house with a wicked woman. MM

NYPD Upper Manhattan

The two police detectives had worked together for many years. An envelope with explicit colour photographs lay on the desk in front of them, their contents partially spilled onto the work surface.

Ed Flynn was an experienced homicide veteran and he lifted one of the photographs from the desk. It showed the dead priest, naked as the day he was born, hooked up and suspended by several ropes. He positioned his dated bifocals on the end of his nose and shook his head as the image came into focus. "The warped perverted behaviour and depravity of my fellow human being never fails to surprise me."

His partner Ken Nugent spoke. "We have to keep an open mind on this Ed. You know what they say; everything you see isn't necessarily black and white."

Flynn exhaled. "I hear what you're saying but from where I'm looking, this has sex written all over it. Our friend the dead priest had a little previous in case you've conveniently forgotten."

"Nothing was ever proven," said Nugent.

"The church moved him on that's good enough for me."

"He wasn't ever convicted of sexual abuse."

"But he didn't exactly deny it either Ken, and never mind this abuse shit, let's tell it how it is. He was raping little boys and girls not abusing them. He was raping little children while introducing them to the good Lord and the Holy Ghost, hymns and psalms. He wasn't the first priest in the world and he won't be the last."

Nugent didn't have the stomach for the fight. He picked up another photograph and studied it. "You think it was a sex game?"

Flynn walked around the desk and placed a hand on his partners shoulder.

"The only doubt in my mind at this moment is whether the priest was pleasuring himself or if he had a playmate."

Nugent stood. "I'm going to take a wander over there now are you coming with me?"

Flynn placed his hands on his hips. "Any particular reason?"

"Not really buddy, but it's our job remember?"

Flynn looked at his watch. "I'll come with you. I'm seeing his Bishop at four o'clock so that gives me plenty of time." He picked up a photo. "Nothing has been touched?"

"Just the body Ed, everything else is just as the cleaner found it."

"Poor bitch," said Nugent.

"My sentiments exactly."

The New York traffic was thick but Ed Flynn resisted the urge to use the siren. Not these days. There was always some bastard ready to complain or point a finger. It wasn't like that in the old days. They'd use the blue light for a coffee break or sometimes just for the hell of it.

Procedure. Everything had a procedure nowadays and even if you farted on duty someone wanted a form filled in. He would be glad to get out in little over 18 months with full service and a good pension. They would move out of their New York apartment and move up to Newfound Lake near to the White Mountain National Park and enjoy the peace and the quiet and the solitude. Weather permitting they'd be out on the boat most days. Corinne would pack lunch while Ed packed his fishing kit and they'd never tire of the nothingness of it all. Catching fish didn't matter, that was a mere excuse. Corinne would take the wheel and they'd complete the fifteen or sixteen mile circuit of the huge lake enjoying a beer or a glass of wine and enjoy the sunset before heading back to the cabin. Jesus he could almost taste it now. The kids could have the New York apartment as a weekend home. They were welcome to it and young enough to enjoy what they called the greatest city in the world. Not for Ed it wasn't. He'd seen enough of the Big Apple to last him a lifetime and he was telling the truth down at the station, New York could still shock and surprise him. Despite nearly thirty years he wasn't completely desensitised... not completely anyway.

Nugent paced the floor of the church owned apartment staring up at the ropes hanging from the ceiling. The blood that had pooled onto the floor hadn't been cleaned up and was beginning to let off a slight nauseating smell. He held a handkerchief over his nose.

"What gets me Ed is how good sex actually is. I mean why the fuck do the gays have to start stuffing foreign objects up their arses? Let them screw and blow each other to their hearts content. Ain't that good enough for them?" He pointed up at the ropes. "I mean what the fuck is this all about? What makes them get outa bed in the morning and say I think I'll tie myself to the ceiling today and stick a chair leg up my backside?"

Flynn couldn't help laughing. "It takes all sorts partner, it takes all sorts."

Flynn took a hold of the free hanging rope and pointed to the heavy oak table. "This is the only piece of loose rope, the rest has been used to tie the dead man's arms and legs and suspend him to the chandelier. Forensics said it was tied to the table over there while he gyrated up and down on the chair leg."

Nugent spoke. "And it broke loose and he fell onto the leg."

Flynn nodded. "What a way to go. The poor bastard, you think he'd have learned to tie his knots better than that."

Flynn looked at the end of the rope. Nugent couldn't help noticing the puzzled look on his colleagues face.

"What is it Ed? What's up?"

Flynn fingered the end of the rope. "I'm not sure." He studied it for a second or two. "When you tie a tight knot in a rope and then loosen it, it generally leaves an impression right?"

"In what way?"

"You know, it kinda wrinkles up, has a bend or two in it."

"Yeah I know what you mean."

30

Flynn held up the end of the rope. "Only this hasn't."

"No?" Said Nugent looking rather puzzled.

"It's straight as a die."

Flynn walked over to the table holding on to the end of the rope. He kicked at the heavy table.

"The rope is long enough and the table is heavy enough to support his weight," he said, "but I'm telling you this rope has never been tied."

He bent down and fingered at the nearest table leg. "No marks, no friction burns nothing."

"So what are you telling me bud?"

Flynn stood. "I'm not telling you anything I'm simply wondering if our friend the priest had himself a playmate holding that rope and if he had, as seems likely, where the hell is he now and why hasn't he come forward to help us with our enquiries?"

Bishop De Genelli had requested a home-based appointment at his residence in Lexington Avenue. That suited Ed Flynn just fine, always too happy for an excuse to get out of the police station he was growing tired of by the day. An hour with the Bishop, maximum and then a twenty minute ride back over home to North Bergen. It was Wednesday, midweek break day as Corinne called it that meant a quick shower, no phone calls or catch up on paperwork and a night out in one of the many restaurants nearby. Strictly no driving on Wednesdays. A walk there and a cab back.

A long walk holding hands reminiscing about the old days or planning their well-deserved retirement. Italian, Chinese or Indian it didn't really matter such was the restaurant choice in that part of the city. Chinese thought Flynn; he'd suggest a Chinese meal. Then he laughed inwardly as he remembered they usually changed their minds a dozen times anyway. Never mind he'd go with the flow... leave it up to Corrine or wherever their shoe leather took them.

The Bishop spoke, interrupting his thoughts. "A nasty business detective. Father Michael was a good man."

This was the point in proceedings that Flynn never looked forward to. The church and the family had been informed that Michael O'Neil had died. He met with an accident as the official line stated. It was true, at this stage that's all it was, an accident.

"Exactly how did it happen detective?"

Flynn paused. He'd planned his strategy in the car on the way over and prepared to hand over the envelope of photographs. That was probably the easiest way out. He still had the image of the tied up dead priest fixed in his head.

"It's not pleasant Bishop. In fact it's rather tragic. At this stage we are not one hundred per cent sure of exactly what happened but we believe Father O'Neill was engaging in some sort of sexual activity, let's just say a little out of the ordinary."

Flynn handed the envelope to the Bishop. "I think it's best if you take a look at these but I warn you they are a little gruesome."

He took a step nearer to the Bishop. "Father O'Neill was no stranger to homosexuality. I checked the files on computer back at the station. For the life of me I don't know how or why these people get off on something like this but as they say, it takes all sorts."

The Bishop accepted the envelope and took out the photographs. Flynn was aware of both hands visibly trembling as the colour drained from his face. The Bishop was shaking his head. "But I don't..."

"I wouldn't even try beginning to understand," said Flynn. "The fact is that people are always trying to push the boundaries a little further when it comes to sex, looking for the ultimate taboo. I've been a cop for more years than I care to think about and you wouldn't believe some of the things I've seen."

The Bishop replaced the photographs back into the envelope and handed it back to Flynn.

"At this stage we believe Father O'Neill was probably playing his little game solo," Flynn said. "That is, we're not sure he had a partner. The apartment was clean, no prints, no real sign of a struggle."

Flynn decided to hold back on what he had discussed with Nugent relating to the rope and hoped the bishop may be able to shed more light on Father O'Neill's lifestyle. He took the photograph out of the envelope again and pointed to the top of the picture.

"He was wearing a dog collar. Quite a common accessory in sadomasochism and bondage and he was wearing it in reverse with the spikes digging into his neck. The collar was hooked up to the chandelier attached by a thin wire with just enough pressure to cause a little pain and bruising. But as the rope came loose the collar ripped into his throat. Look here."

The Bishop nodded then quickly averted his gaze.

"There were several puncture marks in Father O'Neill's neck hence the rather dramatic flow of blood."

"Yes Detective," the bishop said. "Yes, I see what you mean; but I've seen quite enough thank you very much."

He palmed the photograph away and took a deep breath. "What will the poor man's parents say? Will they be shown this photograph?"

Flynn walked over to the large window that looked across Central Park and spoke.

"Not necessarily. That's up to the boys in New England. Don't get me wrong they will need to be told exactly what happened but at this stage I think we can spare them the visual effects."

"I hope so Detective. I certainly hope so."

Flynn turned around to face the Bishop as he spoke.

"You're sure there was no one else involved Detective?"

Flynn shook his head. "I'm not saying that. I'm saying there was no real evidence of any one else that's all. There was nothing left behind, no evidence of any drinks or a snack or two beforehand. No cigarettes, no pubic hair, no personal possessions. Father O'Neill kept a tidy house and very much lived alone. At least that's what we think."

Flynn took a glance at his watch. "You aren't aware of any relationship Father O'Neill was having are you Bishop?"

The Bishop looked slightly affronted. "He was a priest Mr Flynn and those sort of relationships as you know are strictly forbidden. If he was engaging in any sort of sexual activity I would be the last person he would tell."

A more worrying thought seemed to enter the Bishop's head as he spoke. "This isn't going to make the papers is it detective?"

Flynn explained that it was unlikely. There was a murder in New York City nearly every day and the press and the media tended to concentrate on those. At this stage Father O'Neill's death was being treated as accidental. It had a sexual angle off course which always interested the hacks but no, the NYPD would not be releasing any details to the press nor did they require any help from the public at this stage.

"I'm glad to hear it detective," said the Bishop. "There is always someone ready to have a go at the Catholic Church."

"Quite," said Flynn.

The Bishop offered the detective a cup of coffee, which he politely declined and lied as he said he had a mountain of paperwork to catch up on. He gave the Bishop his card and told him to call him if he remembered anything that may help with the enquiry.

As Flynn made his way along the long corridor towards the lift he sighed inwardly. He'd bury the file tomorrow in the huge pile of unsolved accidental deaths that had grown over the years. Perhaps O'Neill's lover, if there was one would make an appearance at some stage. As the lift doors opened he laughed to himself. He may well do just that. But rest assured the Bishop and his cronies would make sure that the man or woman whoever it was would be hushed up and moved away.

Ed Flynn was a practicing catholic, never missed a Sunday Mass or a weekly confession but there were some things about the church that really bugged him.

Four

What else is woman but a foe to friendship, an inescapable punishment, a necessary evil, a natural temptation, a desirable calamity, a domestic danger, a delectable detriment, an evil of nature, painted with fair colours? MM

The Bishop poured a generous measure of whiskey and carried it through to his study. He sank into the large leather desk chair and took a gulp of his favourite poison. He gasped as it stung the back of his throat bringing a tear to his eyes. Medicinal he told himself, purely medicinal. He picked up the phone and punched in the number. It was answered after four overlong rings.

"It's me," he said.

"Bishop. How are you?"

"Not so good to be quite honest."

"Why? What is it?"

"We have another one, right on my doorstep this time, here in Manhattan."

"You are sure?"

The Bishop nodded, his action lost on the voice at the other end of the phone.

"The Judas Cradle this time."

"Surely to God no."

"On one of my priests."

"Holy Mother of God how many more?"

"I wish I knew Cardinal. I wish I knew."

Five

A woman either loves or hates; there is no third grade. And the tears of a woman are a deception, for they may spring from true grief, or they may be a snare. When a woman thinks alone, she thinks evil. MM

The priest had suffered at the hands of the girl.

When he had eventually regained consciousness she was waiting, still naked, still covered in the blood she had smeared over her entire body

She had dragged him through to the lounge where she had rigged up her device. He had been out for around an hour. Plenty time enough.

The girl had built a crude reconstruction of what was known as the Judas cradle.

In mediaeval times the Judas cradle generally took the shape of a large sharpened pyramid, the victim suspended above it by robes and pulleys with the point of the pyramid pushed up into the vagina or the anus. The torturer would gradually lower the victim inch by inch after each question or accusation. The pyramid was always oiled and as the torture progressed the point of the pyramid was forced deeper into their bodies ripping and tearing them apart. It was a slow and excruciatingly painful death.

It had been quite impossible to locate a large wooden pyramid big enough for the purpose even in New York so the girl had made do with an upturned sharpened chair leg, still attached to the chair which she had bolted to the floor. She had rigged up a series of ropes and pulleys to the large ceiling chandelier that the priest hung from handcuffed and gagged. With the help of a jar of smelling salts he gradually came round. The point of the chair leg was already inserted two inches into his rectum. He could feel it as soon as he came round and his eyes filled with horror as the girl explained the exact way in which she would torture him and how he would die. He was educated enough to realise he would suffer massive internal rupturing and severe blood loss.

Pain beyond comprehension.

The girl adjusted the pulley and his body dropped two more inches. He arched his back upwards as the sinew and tendons in his wrists and arms stood out from his blood covered skin as he desperately tried to lift himself clear. Incredibly he held the position for about four minutes before his strength gave out and he succumbed to the inevitable. He let out a muffled roar as the chair leg was forced into him even further.

The girl laughed at that point. She enjoyed laughing at them.

After another twenty minutes she was growing weary of the spectacle. The chair leg had ripped up through the rectum tearing through the colon and small intestine and the tip had pierced the pancreas.

The priest's entire body was contorted in an adrenaline ridden agony and the girl once again marvelled at just how much pain the human body could endure. Incredibly he was still conscious. Just.

"You can go to your God now Father." she said

Still he fought for life and there was sheer terror in his eyes as he shook his head back and forth. His neck and chest was covered in a large blanket of blood and yet even now he found strength to struggle. She shook her head and grinned and he knew there was no mercy to be had.

"Take him a message Father; take him a message that came from his so called good book."

His eyes closed as she grinned and spoke, an evil vacant look painted across her face.

"And thine eye shall not pity but life shall go for life, eye for eye, tooth for tooth, hand for hand, foot for foot."

She reached for the main rope that held the priests weight and brought it into contact with the blade of the knife. He begged with his eyes as he whimpered like a day old puppy. She watched for some minutes until she grew bored then sliced through the rope with the knife.

O'Neil hit the floor with a dull thud. The leg of the chair was no longer visible.

He made no noise other than a muffled hissing noise that came from deep within his broken body as the leg punctured his lung and he died instantly

She raised her arms towards the sky and called out. "So mote it be."

The girl was confused. She had no idea where those words had come from or what they meant.

She placed the severed end of the rope in her bag and proceeded to clean the apartment from top to bottom taking care to wash away any trace of her person. Preparation and forward planning never fails she whispered and chuckled to herself.

After her work was done she took a shower in O'Neil's bathroom, masturbating as the hot water coursed over and cleansed her body. Oh what delight – an orgasm of the most intense kind. The girl stepped from the shower towelled herself dry, dressed and then left.

Six

Others again have propounded other reasons why there are more superstitious women found than men. And the first is, that they are more credulous; and since the chief aim of the devil is to corrupt faith, therefore he rather attacks them. The second reason is, that women are naturally more impressionable, and more ready to receive the influence of a disembodied spirit; and that when they use this quality well they are very good, but when they use it ill they are very evil. MM

The church had survived far worse. It was a thought that comforted Cardinal Angelo Barberini somewhat. He stood and paced wearily towards the window overlooking the Basilica di San Pedro. His favourite spot in Vatican City, arguably the finest completed work of Renaissance Architecture in the world. One must always take the positives from life he reminded himself. Granted, he was more than a little concerned and perhaps it was time to turn over what they knew to the Papal Ambassador but it was only three priests after all.

Best not get too carried away. It was the work of an unbalanced lunatic who would be quickly apprehended. Bishop Montserrat's tone was more than a little dramatic during the telephone conversation and yes, it had unnerved him but then again he was more than prone to a little exaggeration.

He turned away from the window and walked over to the ancient wooden cabinet and opened the doors. The impressive display of fine wines, brandies and liqueurs from across the globe had always been intended for entertaining purposes. The Bishops and Archbishops and Cardinals and even the Pope were frequent visitors to his quarters and they seldom refused an offering from Cardinal Barberini's much famed facility.

Not today, not this evening.

He reached inside and pulled out a French cognac, reached for a crystal tumbler and poured himself a generous measure.

Beautiful... simply exquisite. The smooth flowing liquid caressed his throat and within seconds the powerful alcohol had managed to calm his anxious state. He needed to think, needed to think rationally.

Just three priests he kept reminding himself.

He drained the remainder of the brandy and poured himself a refill before moving over to his work desk and switching on his computer. It booted up quickly and he clicked on the icon. The scanned documents and photographs lined up like small dominoes and he clicked on the first icon.

It was the Police report from Paris.

Father Ubriq had originated from Biarritz, entered the priesthood in his early 20s and worked all over the world even spending two years in Calcutta working for the Sisters of the Poor with Mother Teresa. His dedication to the church was unquestionable and despite the offer of promotion within the organisation he had always claimed he wanted to work at grass roots level in the communities that he felt needed him the most. It was somewhat of a surprise when he wrote to the Vatican from his posting in Mumbai and asked to be considered for the diocese of Place Vendome in Paris located to the north of the Tuileries Gardens and east of the Église de la Madeleine.

Or was it? Father Ubriq had always kept his nose clean apart from that one minor discretion with a house boy in Calcutta. Was it so wrong that in the autumn of his years he wanted to finish his working days in comfort in his native homeland? The huge house was undergoing major renovations at the time with designers flying in from all across Europe and even one from the States. Father Ubriq had taken great pride in overseeing the project and apparently enjoyed every minute until his untimely death at the beginning of February that year.

The Parisian police were good; the Cardinal had no complaints, good Catholics almost to a man and knew the exact meaning of the word discretion. Father Ubriq was fast approaching 70 years of age and what was the point of upsetting his family at that stage of his life.

The Cardinal spent some time reading the report and then closed it. He clicked open the official police photographers best shot of the unfortunate man.

As the image loaded the Cardinal took a sharp intake of breath. He'd viewed the image over twenty times but it never failed to have that effect. How could a person do something like that to an old man?

Ubriq hung from the high wooden beam, his broken frail body twisted at a grotesque angle.

The Cardinal took another mouthful of cognac. The old priest's wrists had been bound behind his back and he had been hoisted up with a pulley system. The rope had been hoisted over the ceiling beam and the police said he'd been repeatedly dropped towards the tile floor. His old wasted muscles hadn't held on for long and both shoulders had dislocated quite quickly. And then the perpetrator had dropped him time after time allowing his old body to come into contact with the floor. A fractured skull, a broken right fibula and ankle, four broken ribs and then eventually the priest's heart had decided to call it a day.

The Strappado. There was no doubt about it. No mistake.

Cardinal Barberini leafed through the ancient book that had lain on his desk for several days now. He traced a finger over the image.

He wanted to shout coincidence but knew three deaths reflecting the ancient torture methods from centuries ago was more than mere coincidence.

It was time to talk and time for action. He was angry now. Just who did this lunatic think he was taking on the might of the Catholic Church? He would pay with his life there was no doubt about it.

Fortified with a little courage he picked up the phone and pressed the direct line button.

It was time to unleash the dogs.

Seven

Women have slippery tongues, and are unable to conceal from their fellow-women those things which by evil arts they know; and, since they are weak, they find an easy and secret manner of vindicating themselves by witchcraft. MM

It was yet another milestone in Samantha Kerr's life. To most people it would be insignificant but to her it was another brick in the wall, a brick in the wall of life, a wall that needed to be rebuilt, carefully, slowly, and with caution otherwise it would all come crashing down and transport her back in time to the days she described as *the dark side*.

Her story had made the front page of the Liverpool Echo and as she sipped at her mint tea she allowed herself the briefest smile of satisfaction. Her life was on track again... at last. After the disaster of her marriage she'd thrown herself into an on-line study course and persuaded the human resources department of Liverpool's biggest newspaper to give her a chance. They'd agreed. Not bad for someone who couldn't read or write until she was twenty one. She started her career at The Liverpool Echo on the mundane stories found several pages into the broadsheet. She'd interviewed anyone they'd thrown in front of her and helped to write the advertorial features for the companies who wanted something a little less subtle than a plain old advertisement. It was her feature on domestic abuse in Liverpool that got her noticed. The feature had attracted more readers letters than anyone could ever remember. It was concise and hard hitting and she spoke from the heart. Not surprising for someone who'd suffered seven years at the hands of a maniac who'd hospitalized her several times and at one point nearly killed her, punching and kicking her unconscious which left her in a coma for two weeks.

The only good thing that came out of her debacle of a marriage was that she'd survived and came out of it a lot tougher than when it had started.

That was the past she whispered to herself. The future was all that mattered now and although those days could never be erased from her mind she could deal with the memories and draw on her reserves of courage to get her through an occasional bad day.

But today wasn't one of those bad days. No. It was Friday night and Kevin finished his late shift just after ten. She was meeting him in the city centre and they'd have a few drinks and a Chinese meal.

At nine fifteen she logged off her computer and closed it down. She was last in the office as was usually the case. She still found it easier to put the hours in the office than go back to an empty flat. She didn't like the atmosphere of an empty home but neither could she put up with anyone invading her territory either. How crazy was that? Poor Kevin. He was a nice man, caring and gentle and oh so patient. He had to be. They'd been together just over three months and she had to admit that she was very fond of him and looked forward to each date. But that was as far as she'd allowed him to get. They'd kissed and fooled around a little but she still hadn't taken him into her bed. She would... soon. She wanted to... she really did.

They met in Chinatown, on Elliot Street in a pub called JRs. Kevin was propping up the bar as Sam walked in.

"Fancy meeting you here," he said.

They kissed briefly and Kevin ordered her a glass of wine.

"Busy day?" he asked.

She nodded. "Yes, have you—"

He smiled as he interrupted. "- Of course I have, congratulations on making the front page, it was a well written piece."

"I was lucky to get the story. It's not every day four Bishops are killed in a Liverpool street," she said.

Kevin took a drink from his beer and replaced it on the bar counter. "Luck has nothing to do with it Sam, you've worked bloody hard to get where you are and you're a great journalist."

His flattery still embarrassed her as she hid most of her face with the large glass. She knew he was right of course, she had worked her tail off for some years now and when her older and more experienced colleagues looked for ways to cut corners in order that they could spend more time in the pub Sam would remain in the office until lights out.

"The poor bastards," he said. "What a way to go."

"Horrible." She replied.

Kevin had a quick look around the pub as he leaned into her and whispered. "I'm in charge of the investigation."

"You are?" She said.

He nodded. "Yes. There's always an investigation into incidents like this to see if any foul play is involved. We have some specialised mechanics on the car now trying to ascertain what caused the fire."

Sam took a drink from her glass. "And?"

Kevin shrugged his shoulders. "An electrical fault they think but we won't know for sure until we have their report next week."

Kevin checked his watch. "Are you hungry?"

"I am but can you tell me anything else?"

Kevin laughed. "You bloody reporters don't you ever take time off?"

"But Kev' I want ...."

"No Sam, that's enough. I shouldn't have told you anything now come on and let's get something to eat. I'm starving."

Samantha sighed and drained the last of the wine from her glass. Kevin reached for her hand and led her outside into the cold Liverpool night. Sam couldn't help feeling something about the whole incident surrounding the bishops deaths didn't make sense.

Eight

It is in accordance with the Catholic faith to maintain that the Devil must intimately cooperate with the witch. MM

The Papal Nuncio's Office, Mayfair. London

"A terrible business sir."

The Papal Nuncio nodded as he stared at the headlines in the newspaper before folding it and handing it to his secretary. "Cardinal Barberini is on his way?"

"Yes." said the secretary looking at his watch. "The flight from Rome will be leaving in less than an hour and a driver will be collecting them at Heathrow. You have a breakfast rendezvous at 8.30 tomorrow morning. From there a car will drive you to Liverpool."

The Cardinal stood. "Thank you Thomas, once again your efficiency is second to none."

"Thank you sir, would you prefer to walk to the hotel or should I inform your chauffer?"

The Papal Nuncio, Cardinal Cameron Adams walked towards the window as he stared up into the ever darkening late evening London skies. "It depends on the weather of course."

The secretary spoke. "I took the opportunity to check the forecast and it looks rather settled with sunny spells for most of the morning."

Cardinal Adams smiled. "What would I do without you Thomas?"

"Just doing my job sir, that's all."

The secretary reached across the desk and lifted the tray containing the empty coffee cup and caffetaire. "If that's all Cardinal I'd better be going."

With a hand gesture the Cardinal waived his secretary away. He reached for the paper once again. The headlines screamed out to him.

Holy men burned alive in car fire horror.

He read the first paragraph for the umpteenth time.

> *In a tragedy of Biblical proportions four senior bishops of the Catholic Church were killed as the car they were travelling in burst into flames in a busy Liverpool Street. Police have ruled out foul play stating a rare but not altogether unexpected engine fire in the ten year old Mercedes could be the cause of the fire which spread rapidly trapping the occupants inside. It is not yet known why the elderly men did not evacuate the vehicle and investigations are on-going, however a police spokesman suggested that the fire may have damaged the electrics connected to the central locking system of the car.*

Cardinal Adams removed his glasses and squeezed the bridge of his nose with his thumb and forefinger. "Why Lord?" he whispered quietly to himself. "How on earth could you put my Bishops through a death like that?"

Cardinal Angelo Barberini stood as the Papal Nuncio walked into the large dining room of the Mayfair Hotel.

He greeted him warmly. "Cardinal, so nice of you to come and breakfast with us, I hope you don't mind but we've already ordered coffee."

Cardinal Angelo Barberini formally introduced the other men around the table and soon after a waitress arrived to take their breakfast order.

Cardinal Barberini got down to business straightaway. He spoke quietly.

"Our friends here know all about our little investigation, I briefed them on the aeroplane on the way over, you may speak freely and with complete confidence."

Cardinal Adams nodded his head once as he took mouthful of coffee then spoke. "I don't think this has anything to do with our investigation in fact I'm fairly certain. I spoke with one of the detectives from Merseyside Police last night. The Mercedes was Bishop O'Malley's pride and joy and although he kept it highly polished and serviced regularly he was also a little bit tight with his money and his garage had recommended on several occasions that the electrics should undergo a complete overhaul."

Cardinal Barberini listened as the Papal Nuncio continued. "What was recovered of the fuel hose almost disintegrated in the investigators' hands. It was only a matter of time before leakages occurred."

"And the petrol poured out into the engine and onto the electrics and a spark from somewhere caused the catastrophe?" said Cardinal Barberini.

"Exactly," said Cardinal Adams. "Nothing untoward, no car bombs or any evidence of sabotage. Whoever it was who tortured our three priests in Madrid, New York and Paris did not have a hand in this.

Adams sat back in his seat. "It's been some time now since he struck, I can only hope he's gone to ground or prison or something else or better still died an excruciatingly painful death."

Barberini smiled. "My son, remember who it is you are sitting with and please show a little compassion." He smiled. He was joking.

Adams wasn't smiling as he answered. "I shall show no compassion for any man with a personal vendetta against my church. I mean what I say Cardinal, I hope from the bottom of my heart that the killer is now making peace with his maker."

An uncomfortable silence ensued before Cardinal Adams changed the subject and went through the funeral arrangements. He explained that the ceremony would be held at Liverpool Cathedral, the cathedral dedicated to Christ the King.

Everyone around the table agreed that Liverpool Metropolitan Cathedral was a fitting dwelling for the four bishops who had served the church so well.

After breakfast the holy men took mass at the church of the Immaculate Conception nearby in Farm Street then climbed into two chauffer driven cars for the journey north.

Cardinal Adams said they could prepare for the late afternoon funeral service en route. It would surely be a grand affair and he had agreed to television cameras from Sky and the BBC to intrude on the relatives' grief.

The full requiem mass lasted the best part of two hours and afterwards Cardinal Adams and Cardinal Barberini took a car across town to the offices of Merseyside Police.

Adams was more than a little puzzled why Cardinal Barberini had called the meeting with the young detective and had requested to view CCTV footage of the incident. He'd applied the full pressure of Cardinal Adams Papal Nuncio on the police and Detective Kevin Howey had no option but to comply.

They were greeted politely as they walked through the largely unimpressive doorway. A young female sergeant on the desk could not have failed to notice their holy robes and was up on her feet before they even reached the desk.

"Cardinals Adams and Barberini I presume," she said.

The two Cardinals nodded and they obeyed her instructions as she told them to take a seat.

"Can I get you a coffee gentlemen?"

Both Cardinals shook their heads.

"DI Kevin Howey will be here soon, he knows you are coming," she said.

A little while later DI Howey edged nervously into the front office. He approached with an extended hand.

"Kevin Howey, pleased to meet you; I wish the circumstances of our meeting could have been a little more pleasant."

The two Cardinals shook his hand as he continued. "I'm not sure how to address men of the cloth, not being a regular church goer myself."

Cardinal Barberini spoke. "We are both Cardinals detective, this is Cardinal Adams and I am Cardinal Barberini and if you are not a practicing Catholic then Mr Adams and Mr Barberini will suffice."

The detective nodded. "Fine then, please follow me Mr Adams and Mr Barberini."

The detective led them into the heart of the station through several security doors and an inspection desk where both men needed to produce identification. Eventually they entered a room with several TV monitors fixed on a wall at eye level.

"I have everything prepared gentlemen." The detective pointed up at a screen. "It will be coming through on monitor number three. Just give me a minute."

The detective took a remote control from a draw and pointed it at the monitor. He pressed several buttons as the images of a Liverpool street whizzed by in fast motion.

"They were travelling down Blacklock Street just after seven o'clock. It was busy but not congested and you can make the car out quite easily," he said.

He punched at the buttons several times as the footage slowed to a frame by frame speed.

He turned to face the two cardinals pointing at the screen. "There gentlemen, there you have it."

The picture was grainy and in black and white but the image of the old Mercedes was unmistakeable and the four bishops clearly visible. The detective pushed a button and the camera zoomed in on the car. It blurred the image somewhat and as he pressed another button the image sharpened.

"At this point I need to warn you that I can take it through frame by frame but it doesn't make for pleasant viewing. You will need to tell me at what stage you wish to stop it."

Cardinal Adams looked at his colleague from Rome as if to say *do we have to* but his stare was fixed firmly on the screen as if in anticipation of a drama or a movie he was looking forward to.

"That won't be necessary," said Cardinal Barberini. "It's something we have to see."

He looked across at his colleague then back to the policeman. "Frame by frame detective; we need to see it."

The three men sat staring at the screen intently as the drama unfolded before their eyes. The white Mercedes pulled up to the traffic lights and soon after a motorcycle pulled alongside. The policeman clicked the remote control and the action continued frame by frame. It seemed to be an eternity before anything happened. And then, a wisp of smoke escaping from the bonnet of the car and soon after a small flame, another frame and another frame and more fire. Despite the slow motion of the images the flames appeared to take hold quite quickly. Twenty five, thirty frames and the car was gradually engulfed in a huge fireball. Cardinal Adams head fell into his hands as he started weeping gently.

The detective placed a hand on his shoulder. "I'm sorry Mr Adams but you did—"

Cardinal Barberini interrupted. "It's not your fault detective but we had to see it for ourselves."

The policeman shrugged his shoulders as he stood. "I really don't know why."

"We have our reasons," said Cardinal Barberini.

The detective spoke. "If there's anything you think will shed light on the investigation then you must disclose that now sir."

Cardinal Barberini spoke firmly. "Detective Inspector Howey, we do not need to disclose anything we do not wish to."

"But Cardinal, it is essential that we all—"

The Cardinal held up his hand cutting the detective short like a little schoolboy in the headmaster's office. "Detective, I don't need to remind you that Cardinal Adams here is the Papal Nuncio to the Vatican. That carries the full weight of any diplomat in London. In fact I do believe it carries a little more than most. You may check that out with your superiors or I have a number in Whitehall if you would rather call someone in authority. I will repeat again that we have our reasons for viewing this footage but it does not concern any person or any police force in the United Kingdom."

He threw a slight grin in the direction of the detective. "Not that it makes any difference but I'm sure it will put your mind at rest. We have an on-going investigation into similar incidents in New York, Paris and Madrid but I can assure you we do not intend to share that information with you."

He pointed at the screen. "Now if we could move on please, I would like to go over the footage again, we are very busy men."

He tapped Cardinal Adams on the shoulder. "Cardinal if you could compose yourself we need to watch this several times. Would you like a few minutes?"

"No thanks I'm fine, just give me a few seconds." He let out a deep sigh and wiped a few tears from his eyes with a handkerchief. "What a terrible way to go. Dear God what were you thinking of?"

Cardinal Barberini nodded at the detective who picked up the remote control once more and sighed as he repeated the sequence of buttons as the film rewound and started over again.

Each time the footage came to an end, Cardinal Barberini asked the policeman for a rerun. Eventually, after more than an hour he appeared satisfied and asked for a copy of the tape. At first Detective Inspector Howey protested. Again Barberini reminded him of Cardinal Adams diplomatic status and he relented.

"I'll have a copy put onto DVD and sent over to your office within a few days."

"That will be fine detective."

He moved forward and shook his hand. "Twenty four hours is plenty time enough detective. I'm told the postal service in

England is more than reliable. Your efficiency and professionalism complement your position."

Soon after the two cardinals left the offices of Merseyside Police at Canning Place and a rather frustrated policeman made a telephone call to Whitehall.

Nine

Because in these times this perfidy is more often found in women than in men, as we learn by actual experience, if anyone is curious as to the reason, we may add to what has already been said the following: that since they are feebler both in mind and body, it is not surprising that they should come more under the spell of witchcraft. MM

It was business as usual for Samantha Kerr as she hurried quickly into Liverpool Lime Street Station trying to catch up with the victim of a mugging who was waiting in an office beside the left luggage department. Sam had several sources throughout the city, friends and friends of friends, acquaintances and downright nosey parkers who wouldn't hesitate to pick up the phone to a reporter if they felt they could assist with a decent story. The lady in question had been accosted in the toilets of the station by two teenagers who threatened her with a knife and punched her in the face before running off with her handbag and the latest I-phone.

The woman was still in a state of distress when Sam arrived outside the office. Her source, a ticket inspector, was waiting for her.

"You'll need to hang on a little while Sam, the police are still with her but I can fill you in on the details." He pulled out a slip of paper. "Marjorie Hall from Bootle, aged fifty one, on her way to meet her sister for a day's shopping."

Sam was already making notes. "Can I get to speak to her Tom?"

The source was in full flow. "The little bitches cornered her in the bogs and pulled a kitchen knife on her."

"Can you get me an interview Tom? The story's not worth Jack Shit if you can't."

Tom eased himself onto his tiptoes peering through the high window. "Looks like the law are just about finished with her. I'll see if she's up for a little chat."

A minute or two later the office door opened and two uniformed policemen walked out. Tom the source scuttled through the gap. It was a full five minutes before he reappeared.

"I've made her a cup of tea and said it was her civic duty to speak to you, told her that we need to make the public more vigilant about these types of attacks. It's the first time she's experienced anything like it."

Sam placed her hand on his arm. "Thanks Tom, you have a way with words we must have another coffee some time."

Tom the source touched his standard issue British rail cap. "Pleased to be of service Miss Kerr," he said proudly.

Sam made her way into the office and was just about to introduce herself to the victim when she was aware of a familiar voice.

"Fancy meeting you here."

"Kevin," she replied surprised. "What are you doing here?"

Kevin raised his eyebrows. "Is that from the bank of stupid questions? I'm a policeman remember and there's been a crime."

Sam wanted to laugh but thought the timing would be inappropriate. The victim was pale in the face and red around the eyes and she detected a slight trembling. Sam remembered how she felt after the beatings at the hands of her husband. The first one was always the worst.

Kevin looked at his watch. "How long will you be? I can take an hour off for some lunch if you like."

Sam leaned across and introduced herself to Marjorie Hall. She turned back to Kevin. "Give me twenty minutes and I'll meet you at the cafe on the concourse."

Kevin was nursing a coffee as Sam walked through the door and she joined him at the window bar. He pushed a sandwich and a coffee towards her as she sat down. "I took the liberty in choosing a sandwich for you and I've only just bought the coffees so they should be plenty hot enough."

"Thanks."

He reached for her hand and she pulled it slowly away. As always he ignored her rebuke. She so wanted to get closer but something always stopped her. Kevin let out a silent sigh as if to say not again. He was the perfect boyfriend, not too pushy, not too demanding and although he was obviously tough as old boots having learned his policing on the streets of Liverpool he was gentle and as a meek as a lamb.

"This makes a nice change," Sam said.

"Yeah lunch isn't something we normally do together is it?"

Kevin took a mouthful of coffee. "A good story?"

Sam nodded. "I suppose so; the poor woman is terrified though, won't leave the station office until her husband arrives."

"I don't blame her," he said. "It's getting bloody worse."

There was a pregnant pause as Sam caught a strange look in her boyfriend's eyes. Despite the infancy of their relationship she could read him well. He wanted to say something but wondered if he should. She tensed up. He had suggested a weekend break in the Lake District some weeks back. She had refused; he would likely be bringing it up again.

A smile flicked across his face.

"What is it?" she asked.

He grinned. "I shouldn't really tell you?"

"What is it Kevin? Tell me."

His eyes scanned the room and his voice lowered several octaves as he leaned across and spoke. "I want you to promise that this will not make it into your beloved newspaper."

Sam sat with an open mouth as Kevin whispered the details of the high ranking Vatican visit. He explained how they'd sat down together and studied the footage of the four bishops' death frame by frame and he told her how the Cardinal from Rome had hinted at similar incidents like this that had happened before.

"I'm not with you," said Sam. "What are you saying?"

"This Barberini bloke studied the film of the car fire over and over again. I watched him Sam and he was looking for something, he was looking for something that wasn't quite right."

"And?"

Howey stretched back in his seat. "Well, I watched the footage as well, I watched it with them but I'll admit I watched this

Barberini fellow more closely than the film. He had a strange look on his face, he had hate in his eyes and when I questioned him on why he was so interested he blatantly admitted that there had been other similar occurrences around the world, not here in England but in Paris, Madrid and New York."

"You mean he was hinting they had been murdered?" She said.

Kevin Howey was shaking his head. "No he didn't say that ...and yet his eyes..."

"What?"

The policeman opened his mouth slowly as he stared blankly into space. "His eyes told me he knew that something was seriously amiss."

This couldn't be happening she thought to herself. She'd somehow sensed something wasn't quite right with the story even as she typed it out onto her laptop. She asked him what course the investigation would now take.

He shook his head. "It won't Sam, at least not by Merseyside Police."

"What?" she asked incredulously. "What do you mean it won't?"

Kevin leaned back in his seat smiling. "Barberini pulled rank. He told me to back off and gave me a number to call in Whitehall."

"And you called it?" She asked.

"Yes," he nodded. "The office deals with matters of national security, the next rank up would be the bloody Prime Minister himself and they knew all about Barberini and the other cardinal and their little visit. They reminded me about the official secrets act and thanked me for my interest in the case but told me straight that the matter was closed and the Vatican would be picking up the pieces from now on."

"You're not investigating?"

"We can't, they are untouchable; they carry more weight than an international diplomat and if they shout jump it appears the British Government shouts how high. They will be leading the investigations from Rome and we are not to interfere one little bit."

It was a jaw dropping moment. Her memory drifted back to when she was a little child and the respect and admiration the priest was afforded when he dropped by to visit them in Liverpool 8 in the tenement block they called home. The image was crystal clear. The priest took the best seat in the house and when he spoke everybody would sit up straight even her dad. Mum would ply him with tea and biscuits then dad would offer him a drop of the hard stuff, his finest malt whisky, Talisker, made from the water of the shores of the Isle of Skye that he only opened at Christmas and of course for the priest.

"Tis a fine drop of stuff," the priest would say. "Top up the glass now Joseph me boy, there's a good lad!"

The words were etched into her brain and dad would move across the room with the bottle quicker than a racehorse on steroids and even at that young age she knew that dad begrudged the priest every single drop of his favourite whisky and yet it was as if he was almost scared of him.

This couldn't be right she thought. This was 2013 this couldn't be happening; it was like a tale from the middle ages.

"I'll investigate it," she said.

The half mouthful of coffee that remained in the detective's mouth sprayed across the table as he almost choked in shock. "You certainly will not." He exclaimed a little more loudly than he would have liked.

"Why not, I'm an investigative reporter?"

"Sam!" Kevin was shaking his head in disbelief. "I shouldn't have even told you, people will know—"

"No they won't," she interrupted. "I'll tell my boss that some things don't ring true and he will—"

"No, no, no," he said. "What doesn't ring true Sam? How would you have known anything was wrong if I hadn't told you?"

Sam shrugged her shoulders. Kevin was right. She wanted to form a basis for her argument but at this moment in time she couldn't.

"Just tell me you'll bury it," the detective pleaded. "Please Sam it's my job."

"And it's my job too Kevin," she replied. "I'm a reporter and I dig and delve and just occasionally I come across something special and from where I'm sitting what you're telling me is a once in a lifetime opportunity for a journalist."

Kevin slapped his forehead in exasperation. "No Sam, leave it please." He reached across and cupped her hands in his. For once she didn't resist. She knew he was right and she couldn't start an investigation on something he had told her in confidence.

He spoke. "Forget all about it Sam you haven't got the experience anyway and you wouldn't know where to start."

Her hand gripped tightly around the coffee cup and she sighed inwardly. He was right. Just who did she think she was kidding?

Howey continued. "If I can't do anything about it as a policeman what chance have you got?"

He spent the next few minutes explaining what course a normal investigation would take and how many men would be involved. They'd study the film footage that she'd never ever see and conduct door to door enquiries while a dozen men would examine the personal lives of each victim with a fine tooth comb. And then they'd liaise with the other forces across the globe and pool the information.

"You can't do anything like that," he said. "You've got nothing to work with other than what I've told you and you can't use that anyway because if you did I'd get the sack and you won't do that because you're too nice."

She had no option but to agree with him. "You're probably right," she said. His hands relaxed and he leaned over and kissed her.

"All the same," she said with a cheeky grin, "it would be nice if you could get me a copy of that footage."

They didn't mention the four bishops again but Sam couldn't stop thinking about the case. They said their goodbyes on the station concourse and as soon as Kevin was out of sight Sam reached for her mobile phone. She called the office and said she'd send the mugging story from home as she had a meeting with another source. She hailed a taxi in the rank outside and within twenty minutes she walked through the front door of her apartment, almost ran into her bedroom and booted up the PC. It took her only three searches to find a link to the mysterious death of Father Ubriq in Paris. Within a short period of time she'd located a New York Times article relating to the death of Father O'Neil in New York and soon after she had everything she wanted on the apparent suicide (for that's what the newspaper was saying) of a priest in Madrid. She was almost shaking as she printed the information off. She spent the next ten hours online and by the time her eyes cried out for mercy in the early hours of the morning she had accumulated over 120 sheets of A4 paper in a plastic file. She closed down the computer, picked up the file and wandered through to the kitchen placing a couple of slices of bread in the toaster. She poured herself a glass of milk and carried her snack through to her bedroom. After she'd eaten she removed her clothes and walked through to the bathroom.

She lay in bed going through the file. She had pictures of each priest and had filed in another section the official line from the Vatican. It was three thirty in the morning before her body cried enough and she fell asleep still holding the file.

The alarm clock kicked in at 6.30am. She normally groaned and turned over weekdays as the overloud ringer disturbed her slumber. Today was different. Today she jumped out of bed and within a minute was feeling the hot shower cascading over her body.

She reached the offices of the Liverpool Echo just after 7.30 and was ready to greet the chief editor with a cup of coffee as he walked in just before quarter to eight. It was just a hunch she said, something that bothered her when she was writing up her front-page story and she'd taken the opportunity to do a little on line digging where she'd discovered the other deaths in Madrid and Paris and New York.

Her argument was compelling and backed up with documentation. She was asking for time out from the mundane routine reporting she was used to. She begged John Fitzsimons for a chance to get her teeth into some real investigative journalism and explained how she believed the Vatican were more than happy to keep a lid on the deaths.

"It's too big for you Sam."

"What do you mean it's too big John?"

Fitzsimons didn't really have an answer and yet Sam knew where he was coming from. Just what was it she was investigating? Murder? Mass murder? A cover up on a huge scale by the most attended and influential church in the world?

But still she fought her corner. She didn't know what it was she would be investigating but something wasn't right and if she came up with anything the Liverpool Echo would take the credit.

Fitzsimons wasn't so sure but he was certainly thinking about it.

"How long has it taken you to pull this little lot together?" He said pointing at the file that lay on his desk.

Sam smiled. "Twelve hours."

Fitzsimons jaw nearly hit the desk. "Fucking hell Sam are you kidding me?"

"No. I met with..." She hesitated. No one knew about her relationship with the policeman. Best to keep it like that she thought.

"It's amazing what the internet can yield."

Fitzsimons picked up the file and spent the best part of a minute flicking through several pages.

"Leave it to the Merseyside Police Sam. If there's any truth in what you are saying it will come out sooner or later and we can get you onto the story then."

She stood up and leaned across the desk her voice an octave or two higher. "But it won't come out John."

"What do you mean it won't come out?"

She paused again. She wanted to tell her boss that Merseyside Police weren't investigating it, that the Church had pulled some sort of diplomatic privilege and insisted that the police back off but of course she couldn't.

She changed the subject.

"Most of the victims were involved in child abuse."

Fitzsimons mouth fell open. "No."

"Here, look at page 33, the names of the bishops and the accusations against them." She pulled out a newspaper cutting from the Irish Times detailing an accusation against a priest in 1978. The priest was Robert Erskine; one of the bishops who had died in the fire was Robert Erskine.

"And here," she said pointing half way down another piece of A4 paper. "Bishops Powers and O'Malley all accused or tried for offences in their parish some years before." She paused for breath. "O'Malley was also in charge of one of those Magdalene Laundries for over twenty years before his establishment near Dublin closed in 1996."

"The Magdalene Laundries?"

"Yes, surely you've heard of them? It was a business ran by the Church in Ireland. The so called fallen women of the country were locked up and forced to work in these laundries who in turn supplied a service to hospitals, major industries and even the Irish Army. The poor girls were never paid a penny. Some were locked away for years in these laundries and mentally, physically and sexually abused by the priests and nuns."

Fitzsimons buried his head in his hands. "You're fucking joking, 1996 you say the last one was closed down?"

"That's right. The church wanted to hide the girls deemed not to be conforming to the ways of the pure church but of course made millions from the slave labour conditions. The girls were treated worse than common criminals and those that did manage to escape and were caught were brought back to the laundries by Irish Police and severely punished."

Fitzsimmons couldn't quite take in what he was being told.

"It was a cover up on a monumental scale," she said.

"The Bishop was one of four male priests in charge of the establishment in Limerick. There is a blog which originates from the United States for girls who worked there and let's just say he was mentioned several times."

"In what context?" said the editor.

"No less than twenty three young girls as they were back then said he coerced and forced them into his bed."

"Piss off," said Fitzsimmons. "You're winding me up."

Sam Kerr was shaking her head. "I wish I was. There's the link to the blog," she said, pointing at the blue highlighted line of words half way down the page. "Take a look when you get a spare half hour."

"How on earth did he manage that?" he asked.

"Think about it John. He was a priest, isn't it obvious?"

Fitzsimmons looked up. "No... not the confessional box?"

Sam was nodding her head. "Exactly right. A blow job was his chosen punishment for something as innocuous as a young girl forgetting to read her bible."

"The bastard." he said, as he removed his glasses and fell back into his leather chair.

Fitzsimons studied the papers again. "And none of these priests were ever convicted."

She shook her head. "Most were simply moved on to another parish hundreds of miles away, the families of the victims either paid off or convinced by some high ranking church official that the offender would be dealt with internally."

Fitzsimons was shaking his head. "This shit still goes on doesn't it?"

"It's there in black and white."

There was a long pause and Sam thought better of interrupting her editor who was clearly considering her request.

Fitzsimmons stood and paced the room for some minutes. Eventually he turned to her and spoke.

"So let me get this straight Sam. You want to take time off to investigate a serial killer who is bumping off members of the clergy throughout the world and it just so happens that four of them have been murdered right here on our doorstep and yet our boys in blue are powerless to act."

"Yes," she replied.

He continued. "Members of the clergy, rapists and perverts who have somehow managed to evade justice. This... this serial killer is torturing them and the most powerful church in the world is covering the whole thing up?"

"Yes."

"And you – Samantha Kerr, a 29 year old reporter with a limited amount of journalism experience and zilch by way of Police training want to take time out from your day job to take on this serial killer and at the same time hang the Vatican out to dry?"

As soon as the words had left Fitzsimmons lips she realised how preposterous and utterly unbelievable it all sounded, and it did. As Fitzsimmons dismissed her from the office saying he'd never heard anything so ridiculous in his entire life she had taken an almighty step backwards. She was questioning her own sanity again.

It *was* ridiculous. Just who on earth did she think she was and why had she just made such a fool of herself?

Ten

But the natural reason is that she is more carnal than a man, as is clear from her many carnal abominations. And it should be noted that there was a defect in the formation of the first woman, since she was formed from a bent rib, that is, a rib of the breast, which is bent as it were in a contrary direction to a man. And since through this defect she is an imperfect animal, she always deceives. MM

The Papal Nuncio's Office, Mayfair London.

Cardinal Barberini stopped the DVD at the precise moment prior to the first sign of smoke coming from the bonnet. He zoomed in on the motorcyclist.

"Look."

Cardinal Adams leaned forward straining his eyes.

"Watch very carefully. The motorcyclist has something in her mouth."

"*Her* mouth? Cardinal Adams questioned.

"Yes. The motorcyclist is a female, it's quite clear from her build... and look." He pointed at the screen. "She is wearing dark goggles but her feminine features are clearly visible. She's quite pretty."

"I'll take your word for it Cardinal I hadn't really noticed."

Cardinal Barberini continued. "She has something in her mouth that looks like a cigarette." He pressed pause on the computer. "And right at this point if you watch carefully she throws it under the wheels of the car."

"Then we have our answer," said Cardinal Adams. "It may indeed be the cause of the fire but then again there's no law against smoking in a Liverpool street on a motorbike."

Cardinal Barberini stood and ruffled his fingers through his hair. "You're right of course, but then again what if she threw the cigarette under the car deliberately?"

Cardinal Adams looked at his colleague in amazement. "Cardinal Barberini, I must tell you I am growing rather weary of watching this DVD and seeing four good men burned to a cinder as they struggle to get out of their car. It is like something from a horror movie and I fear I will not sleep much in the next few months and yet you watch it over and over again and I look at your face and it's almost as if you are enjoying it."

"You misunderstand Cardinal Adams," said Barberini. "It is my duty to protect my church and it's employees, it is my job and yes I freely admit I enjoy my job immensely and you'll forgive me a moment of satisfaction when I feel I am a small step closer to solving a crime against our church."

"I don't understand what it is you are saying Cardinal Barberini," said Adams. "Your job appears to be complete, it was an unfortunate accident or at the very worst a careless action by a young girl but where is the crime against our church?"

Cardinal Barberini was already shaking his head. "This girl knew exactly what she was doing. Watch."

Barberini pressed *play*. Cardinal Adams looked on yet again as the fire in the Mercedes took hold.

"Look," said Cardinal Barberini. "We have flames coming from the radiator grille and all around the bonnet. The bishops are clearly in distress." He pointed at the screen. "Bishop Mackenzie here is banging on the window and the girl simply looks on. We can't see her face from this angle but her reaction is almost calm as if she knew what was going to happen."

Several frames elapsed and the flames licked around the sides of the car. "And see, still she looks on until this point."

The screen froze.

"Until she eventually puts the machine into gear and speeds off."

He reactivated the footage and they watched as the motorcycle disappeared from the screen.

Adams frowned. "I see what you mean but who knows what a person's reaction is when faced with a situation like that. She probably couldn't believe what was happening and just wanted to get out of there as soon as she realised the danger she was in. Don't forget a motorcyclist sits on a tank of petrol."

Cardinal Barberini stood and paced slowly around the office. "Perhaps you are right cardinal; perhaps I am jumping to unnecessary conclusions. Will you do one thing for me?"

"Certainly what is it?"

"Can you get back on the phone to Detective Inspector Howey and ask him if this girl has been questioned as a witness? We can be back in Liverpool first thing tomorrow morning if necessary."

Cardinal Adams walked across to his desk on the far side of the room and picked up the telephone. "If it makes you happy sir I'll do that right away."

Cardinal Adams was placed on hold for around three minutes before Howey came to the phone. Adams put the conversation on loudspeaker and explained to the detective that they had good reason to believe the bike rider was a girl and they would like to speak to her if she had been located. It could well be that she was indirectly responsible for the fire.

"The bike was stolen." Howey answered. "We found it burned out in Stanley Park in Liverpool two days ago, it had been hidden by branches for some time. "

Cardinal Barberini had his answer as a smile pulled across his face.

"Of course that doesn't mean the girl was up to no good Cardinal. Car and motorbike theft is quite common in Liverpool." He said. "We've traced the owner of the bike, a man in his 40s who wasn't even aware that his bike had been stolen. He's what we call a fair weather biker and only took the machine out of his garage when the sun shone."

"And you haven't been able to trace the rider Mr Howey?"

"No Cardinal and to be quite honest we don't hold out too much hope. There were no finger prints able to be taken from the bike at all. It could well be that the fire was caused by the motorcyclist's cigarette but even if we found the rider what could we charge her with, a litter offence?"

"I understand Detective. Don't worry about it. It's probably better for the families concerned that we say nothing and just put it down to an unfortunate accident."

"That's what it looks like from the evidence I've collated," said Howey.

Cardinal Adams ended the conversation pleasantly, thanking the Merseyside Police and Detective Howey for all their help. He replaced the receiver and turned to Barberini who sat silently in the corner of the room giving nothing away.

"I need a drink," said Adams. "Do you want to join me?"

Barberini gave a wave with his hand. "In a moment, you go on ahead."

Adams stood, stretched and walked from the room.

Something had come to him as he'd listened to the conversation between the detective and Adams. They had always watched the CCTV footage on mute. Was it possible that the CCTV contained sound?

Barberini stood and walked over to the computer desk yet again. He moved the mouse and the computer screen reacted. And yet again he clicked on the video icon. He moved the cursor to the bottom of the screen and located the sound icon and clicked on the x at the right of the screen. As the video began to play the dull drone of Liverpool traffic filled the room and Cardinal Barberini smiled.

There was no need for any slow motion this time, all he was interested in was the sound.

It was unmistakable. Faint, barely audible above the noise of the street but it was there and it was real. He rewound the film and watched again and as the motorcyclist dropped what looked like a cigarette and as it hit the ground he eased his ear nearer to the computer speaker.

A crack, a tiny detonation. She had used a firework that exploded on impact with a hard surface. One spark would be all it took to ignite any surplus fuel.

Cardinal Barberini was certain. He'd be out of Heathrow on the next flight and would set his department to work as soon as he reached Rome. But this wasn't any department it was a department that the Vatican knew about but never publicised. There was no record of any employees, no evidence of any payments to anyone connected with the organisation. It was the best kept secret in the Catholic Church. The finest policemen money could buy was how one Monsignor described them. And they were. Even to this day.

The Vatican Secret Police had been in existence since 896 set up by the then Pope Stephen VI.

Cardinal Barberini smiled to himself. How ironic that the very police force Stephen VI commissioned conspired to eventually kill him. That wasn't always the case of course, normally a death squad dealt with people who threatened the Vatican and yet occasionally for reasons only known to the privileged few even the most Holy Father had to be taken care of. It happened again in 974 with Benedict VI and in 1012 when Sergius IV stepped out of line.

As recently as 1978 the huge conspiracy theory arose after the death of John Paul I who died after only 33 days in office.

The Vatican survived. They always did. They always would.

Cardinal Barberini recalled David Yallop's book, In God's Name. He proposed the theory that the Pope was murdered because of corruption in the Vatican's most powerful financial institution, the Vatican Bank. At the time they'd invested in another bank which collapsed and the Vatican Bank lost a quarter of a billion dollars.

The interfering fuck.

Barberini laughed. Six million book sales and not one of Yallop's theories disproved and yet the Vatican remained as powerful as ever. The Vatican; the oldest and most successful business in the world; a fifth of the globe being regular contributors to an already obscene amount of wealth.

Barberini opened the door to Cardinal Adam's office and walked down the long corridor to the small bar at the end. Adams sat with two other men and a young attractive nun Barberini recognised as one of the secretaries. They all looked up as Barberini gave a little cough to announce his presence.

"Cardinal Adams," he said. "I wonder if I could trouble you to give the chauffeur a call? I will be heading to the airport to catch the next flight to Rome."

Within four hours, Barberini had landed at Aeroporto Leonardo da Vinci Fiumicino and took a taxi to the Hilton Hotel barely 5 minutes away. He'd stay three or four days and hold his meetings there, away from prying eyes.

He called them agents and they had to be addressed only by their first names. They arrived at 9am prompt the following morning and blended in with the tourists and businessmen en route to other destinations around the globe.

"Gianfranco, David, Antonio." He greeted them. "I'm glad you could make it at such short notice." Barberini had enormous respect for these men, and yes a little fear too. He knew exactly what they were capable of and how much they enjoyed their more than unusual occupation.

"When the Papa calls we always come running, you know that Cardinal Barberini," said the eldest of the men.

"It is very much appreciated," said Cardinal Barberini. "I have booked a room on the second floor. It was arranged less than an hour ago so it is quite safe."

They took the lift to the second floor. The four men remained silent. The lift doors opened and they walked the short distance along the corridor. It was set out like a boardroom with two jugs of iced water in the centre of the table. Cardinal Barberini as host invited the men to sit before opening his briefcase in front of them and pulled out a laptop computer.

"I'm going to show you the film footage of what the police are still calling an accident," said Cardinal Barberini. "Of course we now know differently."

As he loaded up the computer he spoke again. "Your task won't be easy, the killer is clever."

Barberini booted up the laptop. It was state of the art, the latest Apple Mac and the film footage appeared on screen within seconds.

"The motorcycle was stolen and then found burned-out a few days later. There were no fingerprints and the goggles she wore rule out any form of iris recognition. I'm not really sure where we go from here gentleman but I suppose that's your job."

He pressed a few buttons on the laptop as the film sped up before looking up and making eye contact with the three of them.

"You will be well taken care of as usual." He paused before questioning them. "Same bank accounts as usual?"

The three men nodded in turn.

They sat for some time as Cardinal Barberini took them through the CCTV footage several times.

"I think we've seen enough," said Antonio. He looked at his companions and they nodded their approval. "This footage tells us very little and we need more."

"What exactly do you need," said Cardinal Barberini.

I need the entire day's footage from within five square miles of where the incident happened."

The cardinal let out a long whistle. "That will be difficult, I'm not too sure the Merseyside police are eager to cooperate."

"Make them. We have diplomatic power and make them aware of that and offer to cover all expenses. That should do the trick. Even the Merseyside police will bend for twenty or thirty thousand pounds to help with their annual budget."

The Cardinal smiled. "That much is true; I will make contact with them tomorrow."

Gianfranco spoke, he was a thin but strong, muscular made man, saliva building in the corner of his mouth as he formed his words. "Make contact with them today, we don't have any time to lose. This bitch must be caught and she must be caught sooner rather than later. She is on some sort of mission and I've no doubt she will kill again and kill quickly. "

The meeting came to a close and they retired to the bar on the top floor with a spectacular view of approaching aircraft.

Merseyside police and Cardinal Adams came to an arrangement that £45,000 would cover all expenses associated with obtaining the film footage from the 2,500 local authority and private CCTV cameras operating within a five mile radius of the fire that killed the four bishops. The film was downloaded onto three separate hard drives and delivered by courier to Cardinal Adams just over a week later and dispatched in a package to Rome within the hour.

When the package arrived Antonio picked up his mobile phone. "They have arrived. Contact David and arrange for a team of around 20 men. They can come here and I'll set everything up for them. It may take a week or even a little longer but I'm convinced this girl has made a mistake somewhere along the line."

Antonio's calculations were slightly out. It only took 48 hours before one of the men picked up the motorcycle driving down a Liverpool street three miles from Blacklock Street. At the junction of Anfield Grove she stopped. She was either hot or her goggles had misted up. Whatever the reason she lifted them up and breathed into them before wiping them with the fingers of her glove. It was all they needed. The iris recognition expert was already in place and was set to work immediately. It took him only 43 minutes before he was satisfied with the images and loaded them into his software programme. Within thirty seconds the computer displayed a small window that said *satisfactory iris capture.*

Antonio smiled. "Excellent news." He looked at David. "And now my friend where do we go from here?"

"Back to the police," David said. "We have a contact at the very highest level in UK police special operations. The photographs taken over the last five years of anyone arrested are good enough for iris retina matching." He smiled. "And as you know no two irises are the same. In many respects they are more conclusive than fingerprints."

"Excellent," Antonio repeated. "So if our young lady has stepped out of line in the last few years then we have our killer."

"We do. We just have to hope that she has been a naughty girl within the last five years."

Antonio stood and paced the room. "She has to. You don't just become a killer overnight. My guess is that she has a record as long as her arm, a juvenile delinquent, theft, criminal damage and violence, the usual stuff."

He reached into his briefcase and pulled out the photograph of Father O'Neil trussed up in his Judas Cradle. He threw it across the desk and it landed face up in front of Gianfranco.

"I mean what sort of sick individual can do something like this?"

Gianfranco picked it up. He nodded. "You're right. This is one crazy mother fucker we're up against."

Eleven

The devil can inflame a man towards one woman and render him impotent with another. This can secretly be caused by the application of certain herbs which he well knows that virtue of this purpose. He can suppress the vigour of that member which is necessary for procreation just as he can deprive any organ of the power of local motion he can also prevent the flow of the semen to the member by closing the seminal duct so that it does not descend to the genital vessels. MM

It was a row of epic proportions. Sam had taken to carrying her ever growing files wherever she went; she was bordering on the point of obsession and realised it was more than just a little unhealthy. She couldn't help it, everything was as clear to her as daylight; she just wished someone would listen to her and give her the green light to devote more time and effort to a story that most big London journalists would kill for. She'd had more meetings with her boss than hot dinners and bent his ear on more than one occasion during a coffee break. For some reason he just wouldn't have it. No wonder the paper was going nowhere, he was too set in his old ways and as long as the advertisers were happy and plentiful he was quite happy to stay away from too much controversy.

And yet she understood; half the readers and advertisers were probably Catholics anyway and why upset the applecart?

She looked at her watch. Kevin was a little late. She just about managed to squeeze all the papers from the file into her old lap top case but this time it wouldn't close; it was an impossibility. She squeezed a little harder. The zip was sticking that's all. She groaned and strained as the zip made a few millimetres progress. As the door to the café opened and Kevin walked in the teeth in the zip cried *no more* and quickly parted like the Red Sea. Sam's reaction was to snatch at a photograph that had taken on a life of its own as it floated towards the floor and her elbow hit the side of the case and catapulted it into the air. She let out a shriek as Kevin walked over to help her.

"No, no, it's okay," she exclaimed, realising that it was her boyfriend who was now helping her to pick up the oh so sensitive material. At first he didn't look, didn't realise exactly what he was collecting but then his eyes focussed on the photograph that lay on the floor. He picked it up and studied it. He read the inscription underneath. *Father O'Neil from the diocese of New York.* In an instant the policeman's soft blue eyes had turned to stone and his face looked like thunder.

Their eyes met as Sam squatted on the floor and felt like a schoolgirl banished to the naughty corner as she realised the cat was well and truly out of the bag.

"Everything's in the public domain Kevin, keep your shirt on," she said, immediately on the defensive.

"You promised—"

"I promised Jack Shit Kevin, I'm a journalist and this is what I do."

"But if it hadn't been for me you—"

She cut him off again, her anger rising by the second. "Don't give me that bollocks, I'd already told you I suspected something wasn't quite right, you just confirmed what I was already thinking."

He stood, shaking his head. "I told you about the visit to the police station and the high flying delegation."

He stared at a piece of paper he had been holding; it detailed the murder of a priest in Paris. He paused for a second then spoke.

"If any of this sees the inside of a newspaper I'm telling you that's me and you finished."

What was at first a slightly heated discussion spiralled into an irretrievable breakdown at the point Kevin Howey issued the thinly veiled threat. Sam Kerr had endured threats throughout the sham that was her marriage and once out, had sworn never to suffer the same way again. The argument was finished as she gathered up her papers threw them into her case and stormed from the café.

He had no right to talk to her like that, she thought, just who the fuck did he think he was. Her anger hadn't dissipated as she climbed into her car, drove the short distance to her apartment and stormed through the front door. The hot sweet cup of tea started working after about five minutes. As she got to the bottom of the cup she told herself she'd regained her composure. Only a slight trembling of her fingers holding the bottom of the cup gave the game away.

As the clock passed eight o'clock she uncorked the half empty bottle of white Rioja that had sat in the fridge for some weeks. As she drained the last of the bottle she'd made up her mind and whatever happened she promised she wouldn't go back on her word.

She was waiting for John Fitzsimons as he walked into his office just after 8.15. She was a little nervous of Fitzsimmons; there was something about him that she didn't like, though couldn't quite put her finger on it. He was a real man's man or so he liked to profess, always ready to share a smutty joke with the boys in the office and more than prepared with a sexual innuendo or two in front of the girls. But he was harmless, everyone seemed to take it in their stride, he was the boss after all and maybe the problem lay with her? Deep down in her psyche she knew that things were not yet back to one hundred per cent... far from it.

Her speech had been well rehearsed and she told herself she had to appear more confident than she was feeling.

She laid it on the line, presented him with what would run to a four page story complete with photographs. She told him to print it or she would be handing in her notice with immediate effect, a threat she hoped with all her heart she wouldn't have to carry out.

Fitzsimons took his time and read with interest.

"I have to hand it to you Sam this is very good," he said.

"So you'll print it then?"

Fitzsimons held up his hand and appeared to waiver. "I didn't say that, I'm sitting on the fence at the moment." He replied.

Sam breathed a sigh of relief as she realised he was truly considering it. She might still have a job at the end of the day after all.

"There's just one thing wrong," he said

"What's that?"

He stood up and walked around to Sam's side of the desk, sat down and steepled his hands.

"There's one thing you need to do."

"And what's that."

"We need to say who the source is or at least where he's from."

He'd caught Sam by surprise as she stuttered her next sentence.

"How do you know there's a source?" she said.

"There has to be, some of this stuff won't be on the Internet."

He held up page three and pointed. "Here; you say there has been a delegation from the Vatican visiting Merseyside Police?"

Sam shrugged her shoulders unsure of what to say.

"The Vatican would not announce something like that. How did you find out?"

Sam was thinking on her feet. "Someone I knew saw them go into Canning Place."

Fitzsimons was shaking his head. "I don't believe you Sam. I think you've got a man inside, and if you have I need to know. I don't need his name I just need to know."

Shit... Fitzsimons was a lot shrewder than she had given him credit for.

"Tell me you have a copper on the inside and we'll include that in the report, you know what I mean. If you can't give me that assurance then I won't run the story because you could be making any old bollocks up. An insider from the police gives it credibility."

This wasn't the way she'd planned the conversation and yet she was tantalisingly close to getting the story printed. But what of Kevin Howey? What if he'd told one of his mates or worse, his supervisor that he was dating a reporter from the Liverpool Echo?

It would be a simple matter of putting two and two together and he'd be in the shit.

She couldn't do that to him.

Sam stood up slowly. So near and yet so far she thought but she'd committed this far and if this newspaper wouldn't print a story like this then what was the point in working for them?"

She stood up and reached for her handbag. "I'm sorry John I can't do it. You can't put that condition in there so I guess the story doesn't run."

Fitzsimmons stroked at his chin as a smile, almost a grin pulled across his face.

"I'm the boss here Sam remember? I have to make the decisions around here no matter how hard they are."

Sam nodded, picked up her bag and left the office.

Twelve

For Cato says: When a woman weeps she weaves snares. And again:
When a woman weeps, she labours to deceive a man. And this is
shown by Samson's wife, who coaxed him to tell her the riddle he
had propounded to the Philistines, and told them the answer, and
so deceived him. MM.

"Fuck, Fuck, Fuck, I don't believe it."

Barberini threw the letter to the floor. "This can't be right."

Antonio nodded sheepishly. "I'm afraid it is Cardinal Barberini. No iris match at all, everything has been thoroughly checked, the girl is clean, no police record whatsoever."

Cardinal Barberini gasped. "It's not possible."

"Hard to believe I know."

Barberini eased back in his seat as he removed his glasses and placed them on the table. He pinched with his thumb and forefinger at the bridge of his nose before removing them and looking up. "Tell me Antonio you are the expert. Where do we go from here?"

"We haven't given up Cardinal."

"I'm glad to hear it."

"We haven't given up on iris recognition."

"Tell me more."

Antonio stood. "There are over five million Catholics in the United Kingdom and as you know most of them attend church on a fairly regular basis."

Cardinal Barberini gave a wry smile. "We are doing something right then."

"What you may not know is that every Catholic Church in England, Scotland and Wales was fitted with CCTV cameras in the last ten years."

"What?"

"Yes. We were experiencing a large volume of break-ins and vandalism particularly in Northern Ireland and the West Coast of Scotland. It was deployed purely as a security measure and for evidence we can hand across to the local police.

There are over 3000 churches that have CCTV both inside and outside of the premises and they are of very high quality. The data is stored on a central computer in Liverpool."

The Cardinal smiled. "I'm beginning to like the sound of this Antonio. Tell me what I want to hear."

Antonio let out a sigh. "I'm not sure if I can do that Cardinal, they aren't wonderful statistics. Only one in six of the population of the UK visit a Catholic Church. For weddings and funerals the odds increase in our favour a little but even then it's a bit of a long shot and a lot of work once again. I'll need to call the team in and repeat the exercise we carried out a couple of weeks ago."

Cardinal Barberini felt somewhat deflated. At first he thought they were onto something. He stayed silent as Antonio continued.

"If we do get a match then it's a case of hoping the local priest knows his congregation intimately."

"But it's worth a try?"

"Of course Cardinal, of course it's worth a try." He picked a mobile phone from the desk and slipped it into his jacket pocket. "I'll check out the Liverpool flights and get my men over there as soon as possible. That's the easiest way to do it."

"Okay," the Cardinal said, "just do it and let's keep our fingers crossed. Failing that we can always pray."

"If you could clear everything with London and inform them to notify Liverpool that we'll be there within the next couple of days."

Cardinal Barberini had already picked up the phone. "I'll do that now, right away. If the whore has been anywhere near a Catholic Church in the last ten years we'll string her up and torture her until her heart calls it a day."

He grinned. "That's what happens, Antonio. When they can take no more pain, when every muscle cries out for mercy nature has its own little safety valve and the heart shuts down."

Antonio held out his hand and the Cardinal took it and shook it warmly. They embraced and then parted. "I know Cardinal," he said. "I know only too well."

~

Gianfranco Desiro would never give up hope. It was the way he had been trained. Sixteen years with the Italian special forces and then another two years training with the Vatican before he was ever assigned to his first mission. He had to hand it to them, the training had been first class and he'd learned more about himself in those two years than he had in the preceding years with the Italian military. Even at 47 years of age he was in peak condition undergoing a regimented physical training routine on a daily basis. He seldom drank, didn't smoke nor did he do drugs of any kind. That's why even now, after 8 hours meticulously staring into a computer screen attempting to match up the irises of strangers he was still ready to go on. Unfortunately others were not so dedicated to their profession.

"Let's call it a day Franco," the man said. "I'm tired and I am hungry and I am thirsty."

Gianfranco reluctantly nodded. I've only about another 20 parishioners to check out from this one in Scotland and then I'll be done."

"Okay but make it quick."

Typical thought Gianfranco. *Make it quick?* Make it quick was what made mistakes and he wasn't about to do that. The transparent white oval icon was no bigger than half a fingernail. First the subject was brought into focus, zoomed in on until the full head almost filled the screen. Then the icon was strategically positioned on the eye and needed to be held still for a fraction of a second. The iris recognition software was then able to lock on to the individuals eyeball scanning the iris almost immediately. Gianfranco gave it two to three seconds before he cancelled the action and started afresh.

An attractive girl he thought as he moved the camera into position. He had been too long without a woman and he fantasised how this tall and elegant girl in her twenties would fit the bill just perfectly. His actions were automatic as he dragged the icon towards her pretty face. He hovered the icon over her mouth lusting over what it was he would like to be doing with her delicious looking lips. As he lifted the icon slightly higher there was an unmistakable high-pitched shrill that blasted out from the computers speaker system filling the small room.

"Jesus fucking Christ," he said. "We've got her. I don't believe it we've fucking got her."

A small crowd had already assembled behind Gianfranco and his machine. For three weeks the twenty seven men had painstakingly worked on over 500 subjects every day and the noise was music to their ears.

"You're sure?" Antonio asked leaning over his left shoulder.

"You heard it as well, there's no mistake, this equipment is second to none. The Israeli intelligence service, Mossad use it in their hunt for old Nazis. It's flawless sir I'm telling you."

"Take it off," Antonio said. "Take it off and try it again just to make sure."

It was exactly what Gianfranco was about to do. He moved the icon down to the left-hand section of the computer monitor. The sound stopped. He waited a few seconds and then began dragging the cursor towards the girls face. It settled over her left eye and the system locked on once again. Cheers and howls of delight coincided with the sound that told the assembled members of the Vatican special operations team, housed in a back office of Christ the King Metropolitan Catholic Cathedral in Liverpool that they had located the person who was wreaking havoc within their ancient organisation.

The three men were on the next available evening flight to Aberdeen. Although just a short flight David Perini took the opportunity to order a bottle of Don Perignon by way of a celebration. Naturally Gianfranco ordered his normal nonalcoholic favourite – water and warned his two colleagues that the bird wasn't quite within their grasp.

"She will be," said David. "She is as good as ours. Monsignor Campbell is in charge of the Cathedral in Aberdeen and it's a tight knit community that he knows intimately."

"Not too intimately I hope," joked Antonio, "we don't want another scandal. These priests are like fucking rabbits on Viagra."

The three men laughed. They'd hardly time to finish the bottle of champagne when a cabin announcement asked the passengers to prepare for landing.

"Such a small place the United Kingdom," said Antonio to no one in particular. "We haven't even been in the air for forty minutes."

Monsignor Campbell met the men at the airport and looked more than a little excited to be collecting the special envoy from the Vatican. During the short journey into Aberdeen city centre he attempted to make conversation and asked many questions but most were met with polite refusal. Antonio explained that they were trying to discover the identification of a wedding guest who had attended a service at his Cathedral some weeks ago. They were not obliged to tell him the reason why but suffice to say he would be assisting the Vatican at the very highest level.

"That would be young Stephen's wedding," the Monsignor said. "I've known him since he was a little boy; he married a girl from London. A beautiful day, a beautiful service and a tremendous reception at Slains Castle in Cruden Bay. That's the only wedding we've had in the last six weeks."

"And you know your congregation well?" asked Antonio.

"I do, but I confess there were quite a few strangers there too. Nearly five hundred people if my memory serves me right."

Antonio reached for his briefcase. He took a quick look around at the countryside outside. The road was quiet and traffic sparse. He asked the priest to pull the car over into a layby and he obliged. The car came to a stop.

"I don't need to tell you Monsignor that whatever we say to you today and whatever answers you give us must remain a secret."

Campbell looked more than a little nervous but nonetheless nodded his head.

Antonio took out the envelope, pulled out the A4 black-and-white photograph and handed it to the priest. "There was good reason why we couldn't fax this to you or send it as an attachment over the Internet. Our entire organisation is being targeted and we need to locate this girl sooner rather than later."

He handed the photograph to the priest. "Do you know her?"

The priest nodded. "Yes... yes I do. Indeed I do. I had an interesting conversation with her at the wedding. She's called Celine, Celine MacArthur, an English girl, came up to Scotland for her sister's wedding."

Antonio nodded at his two colleagues in the back of the car. "Excellent," he said. "Do you have an address for us?"

The Monsignor nodded. "Indeed I do, she lives in a pleasant part of London, if I remember correctly. I have all the names and addresses of the guests. I send them all a thank you message a week or two afterwards."

Antonio was more than a little content as the final piece of the puzzle fell into place. He smiled as he took the Monsignor's hand and shook it warmly. "You have done well Monsignor, can we all partake in a little supper? You can tell us everything you know about this girl. Take us to your favourite restaurant and don't worry about the cost, the bill is on us."

Monsignor Campbell drove them to the airport early the next day. Antonio thanked him for his help and promised they would keep in touch. But of course they never would, Monsignor Campbell was just another employee in the oldest commercial business in the world.

∼

"That's first class news Antonio. Where are you now?"

"Aberdeen Airport, in Scotland."

"Okay let me think for a second."

"We can take her within 24 hours Cardinal Barberini."

"No don't do that. Take the next flight to Rome, you've been out in the field too long and I don't want any questions asked when this girl disappears." Cardinal Barberini was thinking on his feet.

"And what of Monsignor Campbell? Can he keep his mouth shut?"

"He knows nothing your Eminence."

"You're sure?"

"Positive."

"If you suspect he'll talk I want you to take care of him."

"He's fine I promise."

"You have a name and an address?"

"Yes, she lives in London, quite the successful business woman and just so happens to have been in New York, Paris and Madrid at exactly the time our colleagues lives were so cruelly snuffed out."

"And the bishops?"

"In Liverpool on the exact date. We have a credit card receipt dated the same day at a chemist in the city centre."

"So there's no doubt."

"None whatsoever. Iris recognition is fool proof."

"How old?"

"She's twenty nine, a pretty, elegant girl."

"Good. Good." Cardinal Barberini hesitated for a few seconds before giving his final instructions. "Come to Rome Antonio. Come quickly and I'll send a team to London immediately. We can have her watched for a few days and then strike before she knows what's hit her." Cardinal Barberini slid a hand down the front of his holy robes and rubbed at his groin. "We'll take her to a safe house and have some fun I promise you. It will be just like the old days Antonio."

"I hope so Cardinal Barberini; it's been a long time."

Cardinal Barberini replaced what was affectionately known as the Bat Phone, a secure connection to his office very seldom used.

Only a handful of people in the entire world had direct access to it.

Cardinal Barberini smiled. It *had* been a long time. The nun had been sweet and frisky, stubborn and yet a fighter and she had held out for some time. That was the way he liked them. No family, no ties, no questions asked, no answers necessary.

Thirteen

Concerning the enormity of crimes it is asked whether the crimes of witches exceed both in guilt and in pain and in loss all the evils which God allows and has permitted from the beginning of the world up until now. MM

The team had been in place for 24 hours but had not yet been given the exact address in London where Celine MacArthur lived.

Cardinal Barberini and Antonio had double checked everything and had despatched a small portable iris recognition system to London, pre-programmed with the retina image of the girl. A further match had been secured from the CCTV camera in New York that had been taken in the entranceway of the apartment block where Father Murphy had been killed. All three matched perfectly.

At 8 AM on a Sunday morning when most of London still lay in slumber the team were instructed to move in and make the pickup.

It was a swift, well executed exercise involving only two powerfully built men and a third, a driver who waited in a stolen vehicle at the rear of the property. The break in was silent and the victim still fast asleep when the chloroform soaked handkerchief was forced over her face. As soon as she was helpless they deployed the iris recognition device. It was a match.

They changed cars another two times before they eventually arrived at their location in the middle of Dartmoor. A remote holiday cottage, left to the church in a pensioners last will and testament some years back.

The perfect setting.

Cardinal Barberini would see that it was never sold on.

The girl was slowly coming round as she was lifted from the boot of the car and they picked up the pace and secured her in the basement.

Finally they made the all-important phone call.

"Cardinal Barberini?"

"Si."

"We have her secured as you instructed."

"No trouble?"

"We are professionals your Eminence, it was like taking a baby from its cradle."

"And you're sure it's her?"

"The retina match is exact."

Cardinal Barberini felt a warm glow envelop him. They had her. At last her murderous exploits were at an end. And she would pay, Dear Lord above she would be punished, he would see to that.

"Leave her. We will be there in a few days."

"Leave her?" he questioned.

"Yes leave her. I trust you've chained her securely?

"Yes your Eminence, but it will be—"

"Leave her I said, she won't die. Let her think about what she has done for a few days. It won't do her any harm."

"Yes your Eminence."

"I will make your bank transfer tomorrow, American dollars to the Cayman's as requested."

"Thank you your Eminence, it was a pleasure doing business."

"As always."

As soon as Cardinal Barberini had ended the call he reached for his mobile and located Antonio's number.

"You'd better be packing a case."

"We have her?"

"We have. I'll have a couple of flights arranged and a car. Prepare to leave in a day or two."

Fourteen

He would have passed a pleasant life of it despite of the Devil and all his works, if his path had not been crossed by a being that causes more perplexity to mortal man than ghosts, goblins, and the whole race of witches put together, and that was a woman. – Washington Irving

Cardinal Barberini and Antonio Montserrat pulled up outside the cottage that was more than a little familiar to them.

"Here again," whispered Montserrat as he opened the boot and pulled out three large cases.

Barberini smiled. "It seems like only yesterday."

"Eighteen months," Montserrat said. "I hope this little lady gives us as much pleasure as Sister Jocelyn."

"I'm sure she will Antonio, I'm sure she will."

Sister Jocelyn had been specifically chosen from the convent in Napoli. In the eyes of the Catholic Church she had committed the worst thing possible in that she had renounced her faith. Thirty three years of age, she claimed to have been wavering for some years and during a meeting with the Mother Superior she not only requested release from her duties to the church and her marriage to Jesus but she had the barefaced affront to claim she was an atheist. She didn't believe any more, couldn't accept that an invisible man ruled and oversaw the entire world.

There was worse to come. The Mother Superior had persuaded her to stay on for a further three months and placed her in charge of teaching at a local orphanage. Almost immediately she dispensed with morning assemblies and mass. The children were encouraged to think and she gave lessons on evolution and read from books that were forbidden by the Catholic Church.

She was caught just in time, she was the perfect victim. She had no family to speak of other than a distant relation in England. She readily jumped at the chance to spend a few weeks at a cottage in

Dartmoor, all-expenses-paid by the church. Mother Superior told her it was a little thank you for her years of devoted service.

Barberini and Montserrat allowed her a couple of days to settle in to her new surroundings and then arrived unannounced.

They tried her for witchcraft and crimes against the church. She'd lasted four days before she eventually confessed.

Her remains were buried out on the moors where they would never be found. There were a couple of enquiries several months later as to her whereabouts. The Mother Superior in Napoli showed the police the release papers and said that she'd flown on a one way ticket to Heathrow in London. The police checked with the airline authorities who confirmed the story. From there the trail went dead.

She would be filed as just another missing person and no real effort would ever be made to find her.

Montserrat opened the boot of the car taking out three large suitcases. Barberini took a key from his pocket and walked towards the cottage door.

Once inside Barberini opened the shutters of the window allowing the fresh air to permeate the stale smell. Almost immediately they heard the weak screams carry through the room. Both men looked at each other and smiled simultaneously. The girl had heard them. She had hope. All of a sudden she would believe that her rescuers, her knights in shining armour had arrived and she was not going to starve to death after all.

Barberini and Montserrat picked up their individual suitcases and walked to their respective rooms where they changed. They took their time savouring the moment and it was a good thirty minutes before both men returned to the lounge resplendent in their ancient uniforms.

Barberini carried his head high. He would play the part of the inquisitor. On his head was perched a squat cloth cap trimmed with a gold band and finished off with the large tail feather of a falcon. He wore an oversized golden medallion that hung loosely over a flowing cloak that scraped the floor as he walked. It was silver grey in colour with intricately patterned gold stitching. It was an impressive costume and the Cardinal knew it.

Antonio Montserrat's attire was somewhat more conservative. He'd take the part of the priest. He wore a white hooded cassock tied at the waist with rosary beads and a heavy wooden cross. He wore another wooden cross around his neck and of course carried a copy of the Holy Bible for realistic effect.

"You look splendid as always Cardinal," Montserrat said.

"Likewise," said Barberini. "Come, it's time to make an appearance."

The prisoner lay in the darkened basement shackled to a large marble plinth. Her hair was tangled and matted and dirt and mascara blackened her pale, drawn face.

As soon as Barberini and Montserrat walked into the room she begged them for help.

"Please help me," she cried. "I need water, give me some water."

The cardinal stepped forward, lifted the plastic bottle he was carrying and poured a little water into her open mouth. As soon as the liquid touched the back of her dry throat she gagged and spat it out involuntarily into the air. The Cardinal persevered. He placed his hand under her head and tilted her head forward a little. Eventually she began gulping the water greedily.

"Food," she gasped. "I need something to eat."

"Patience woman," said the cardinal. "First we have work to do."

He nodded at Antonio who lifted the side of his cassock and pulled out a scroll of paper which he read from.

"I conjure you by the bitter tears shed on the cross by the Lord Jesus Christ the salvation of the world and by burning tears poured in the evening hour over his wounds by the most glorious Virgin Mary, his mother and by all the tears which are being shed here in this world by the Saints and Elect and let God from whose eyes he has now wiped away those tears. If you be innocent you do now shed tears but if you are guilty you shall no means do so. In the name of the Father and of the Son and of the Holy Ghost, Amen."

He took a deep breath. "It will be found by experience that the more you are able to conjure tears the more innocent you shalt be."

The gravity of the words was just beginning to sink in as Cardinal Barberini leaned forward.

"Look at me girl," he said pulling back her head. "You are charged as follows with witchcraft. These are the words from the Malleus Maleficarum. You seduced the priests with your devil ways and caused them death. How do you plead?"

She was confused, hungry and thirsty. Her eyes rolled into the back of her head as she closed her eyelids. This was a dream, a nightmare; it had to be.

The cardinal shook her violently by the hair. "How you plead, I said."

"Please stop," she said. "Let me go, give me more water please I don't know what the fuck you're talking about."

Barberini shook his head, looked at Antonio. "Her hair please."

Antonio walked over to the workbench by the door in the basement. There were many instruments and devices laid out but he reached for a pair of scissors. As he approached the accused Barberini gave a command.

"Strip her."

Antonio cut away her clothing as she thrashed and protested and cursed and swore. She lay naked and exhausted and he reached for a handful of her hair.

"Now your hair shalt be shaved off and abraded."

Cardinal Barberini held her head firmly as Montserrat proceeded to cut her hair and let it fall to the ground. She wept and wailed but the two men showed now mercy.

"Please... no," she cried in desperation. "I beg you, no."

Montserrat walked over the table and picked up the cut throat razor.

As he approached her she struggled even more pulling at her shackles thrashing about squealing for mercy.

He stood over and waited until sheer exhaustion took over. He smiled as he applied a little water to her scalp and shaved until her head bled in places.

Barberini spoke. "And the secret parts too, priest."

Montserrat tried hard to suppress a look of satisfaction as he positioned himself between her legs.

"You wanted to kill in the ways of medieval times so we shalt treat you likewise." Barberini said.

He walked slowly over to the ceramic sink and turned on the tap waiting for the water to run warm. At the same time he took out a small Bunsen burner, lit it and placed a steel container on top. He applied a liberal amount of soap to his hands and began to lather up. He turned, walked back towards her.

"I must look for the Devils marks. I must look everywhere."

He examined her head for several seconds as he continued to work the soap between his fingers. He turned his attention to the area between her legs.

"Perhaps we will find one here." He thrust a hand between her legs and began to massage the soap around the area of her pubic hair and her vagina. He lingered on his task clearly taking pleasure from his work. The cardinal was already beginning to feel himself getting erect.

He took a step back and turned to the priest. "Do it."

Montserrat grinned as he held up the razor once more so that the victim could see it. Barberini returned to the sink and dried his hands off.

He waited until the inquisitor returned then despite the cries from the girl systematically shaved her pubic hair while she shouted out all manner of insults and curses. Slightly to the left of her prepuce Montserrat spotted something. He edged a little close as his mouth fell open.

"Look inquisitor," he said. "The mark of the devil."

The girl was dazed now, as still she struggled against her shackles and abused her tormentors in the only way she could... with words.

"You fucking perverted cranks, let me go."

Barberini looked at the mark, a small mole. "You have it priest, tis the mark of the devil. It is proven beyond doubt."

Barberini returned to the Bunsen burner to check on the progress of the now molten lead. He walked over to the open suitcase and reached inside for what looked like a holy water sprinkler. He opened it lifted the container from the burner and poured the molten lead inside.

He stood over her naked body.

Her screams filled the basement and beyond as he cast the first spray of molten lead around the area of her vagina.

"This is to cleanse you, for thou shalt not suffer a witch to live. I will cast out the devil inside you and you will confess your crimes and sins against humanity and the Catholic Church. Confess... confess I tell you."

"Fuck off you warped cunts, fuck you and fuck your stupid church."

She had reached the point of no return. She knew she would have to die, they had gone too far and death was the only escape.

"You and your heretic ways thought you could kill our own and not be punished. The law punishes those who have done evil, the devil will face by means of a witch but he is merely employing an instrument."

He threw more molten metal over her breasts and she arched up in agony, squealing like a trussed up animal awaiting the slaughter man's knife.

"You are that instrument you are not acting of your own free will. We understand. We will cleanse you."

He did not let up.

Her skin had blistered and split in places and still he continued until the sprinkler was empty. She wondered if there was a point in time when the pain would not register. It took approximately seven minutes before the supply of red hot lead was totally exhausted.

The Inquisitor returned to his suitcase and placed the sprinkler alongside before reaching inside for something else.

He returned to her.

"You are a blasphemer and you have fornicated with the devil and seduced our priests."

He placed his new instrument only inches from her face.

He leaned over and whispered in her ear. "Confess and it will all be over, confess and I will put you out of your misery.

"Fuck you, you prick."

The Inquisitor turned to his priest. "A witch of the vilest kind."

He picked up the strange shaped object.

"Do you know what this is?"

There was no reaction.

"We call it the pear of anguish. We use it on women who perform abortions and on liars, blasphemers and homosexuals. We insert it strategically into one of the orifices of the body. The anus for homosexuals and the mouth for liars and blasphemers." He smiled as he held it up to her face.

"We haven't quite made our mind up about you but we will."

He pointed to the bottom of the device. "Look here, it consists of four leaves that slowly separate from each other as I turn this screw at the top." He looked to his priest who was also grinning. "The device will tear you apart, mutilate whatever opening we decide to push it into and eventually dislocate and break your bones."

He replaced the pear of anguish on the bench beside her. "But not yet. The time isn't quite right."

Cardinal Barberini removed his hat and reached down for the hem of his frock. In one swift movement he had pulled it over his head and stood naked before her. He massaged his already swollen penis for two or three minutes as he pushed his fingers roughly into her vagina.

"Do you find pleasure in this you whore? Look at me. You bring your devils thoughts to me. I have no choice, I will cast your devil back to you."

He stepped forward and forced his penis inside her vagina. He found his rhythm as his hips began to push back and forth. He started slowly taking care to study the pain and anguish in the victims face and as he felt the familiar sensation welling up deep inside he bucked and thrashed hard and violently, his body arched and he grunted as he jerked faster and faster until he climaxed. Breathing hard he lowered his sweating body onto her as their faces came together.

"That is as good as it gets," he whispered panting hard. "The priest here has far more warped tastes than me. I swear his family is descended from the Arabs."

He cackled as he climbed from her.

Her cries had stopped now as she lay barely able to move.

"Now rest girl and gather your thoughts for we will be back," he said. "And know this. We will get this confession out of you if it's the last thing we do. The pear is a very powerful tool."

As they gathered their things they walked towards the open door. The girl summoned all of her energy and shouted out.

"Wait."

The Inquisitor and his priest turned back to face her.

"Please no more...I confess," she whimpered. "...I confess."

They woke her with a bucket of ice cold water. It took her breath away but shook her from her slumber. She didn't know how long she had been unconscious.

"Wake up," Montserrat shouted, "You have been sleeping in the pits of hell where you came from. I will ask you again do you denounce the devil."

"I do," she said. Her voice was barely audible.

The priest turned to his colleague. "Inquisitor, listen to her. I suspect she may be broken."

"Praise the Lord," said Barberini. "For he gives us strength to carry out his work."

He raised his eyebrows in the direction of his colleagues. "But you forget she is the whore of the devil and she tricks us. There is no sincerity in her voice and we have much work left to do."

Montserrat loosened her shackles one by one and the two men turned her onto her stomach. She didn't have the strength or the fight in her to resist. Once they had her in position they relocked the bindings to her wrists and ankles.

Barberini looked at his anxious priest. "Do it."

Montserrat disrobed. He was already erect as he climbed on top and spread the cheeks of her buttocks. As he penetrated her the ear piercing scream was so loud Barberini covered his ears. He watched with a smile on his face as Montserrat satisfied his urges.

Montserrat dressed and knelt on the floor. "Holy Father who delivered your people from the bondage of the adversary and through Your Son cast down Satan like lightning, deliver me also from every influence of unclean spirits. Command Satan to depart from this witch by the power of your only begotten Son. Rescue her from demonic imaginings and darkness. Fill her with the light of the Holy Spirit that she may be guarded against all snares of crafty demons. Grant that an angel will always go before me and lead me to the path of righteousness all the days of my life, to the honour of your glorious name, Father, Son and Holy Spirit, now and forever."

Barberini stood in the corner nodding his approval. "You learn your lines well Montserrat; I hope your words comfort her."

He stepped forward and leaned over so that his lips were only inches from her ear. "Do his words comfort you witch?"

Slowly she turned her head to face him. She had not eaten a morsel for five days. It took every ounce of effort she had.

"Fuck off you crazy cunt." she spat.

Barberini wiped the saliva from his face. "Get the pear father," he commanded. Dislocate every damned joint in her body."

They worked on her for another four hours, but by now it was impossible to wake her. The priest picked up her head by the neck and let it drop onto the table.

"Is she dead?" he asked.

Barberini gazed at her bloody, blistered chest. He detected a slight movement.

"Not yet Montserrat, not quite but she will be soon. "Get the wood, let's do it. I am afraid she will give us no more satisfaction."

They unshackled her and carried her from the basement up the flight of stairs that led to the ground floor of the cottage and out into the garden. She regained semi consciousness as the cold still air came into contact with her broken naked body. She moaned loudly as her feet scraped the ground causing shooting pains to rip through her hips. Blood ran from her anus and her vagina streaking her thighs red. Soon death would come. She knew it.

Soon it would all be over.

They carried her into the ancient kiln two hundred meters from the house. In days gone by the previous owners had been potters and used the kiln to fire their vases and pots and jugs that they would sell in the local markets. Nowadays the kiln was used for a far more sinister purpose

They tied her to the stake and loaded the hunks of wood around her feet. Montserrat placed twigs in between each log and poured on a little accelerant to help the fire on its way. And then Barberini lit a large cigar with a match before dropping it onto the base.

"Green wood burns very slowly," he said.

As the flames took hold and lapped around her ankles they watched her die in agony.

Fifteen

In Aquitaine a woman had been for six years molested by a devil with incredible carnal abuse and lechery and she heard the Devil threaten her that she must not go near the holy man. It will avail you nothing he said and when he is gone I will laugh because up till now I have been your lover but now will become the cruelest of tyrants to you. MM

Cardinal Barberini and Antonio Montserrat were sitting in the departure lounge of Gatwick airport awaiting notice of their flight to Rome. An announcement advised them there would be a delay of two hours.

Cardinal Barberini sighed. "That's all we need, we won't be back into Rome until the early hours of the morning now."

Montserrat looked at peace with the world. Satisfied with the recent work he had carried out. "What about a little drink in the bar over there? God knows we deserve it after all our hard work."

Barberini grinned. "I wouldn't call that hard work. It was a real pleasure to do business with her. A really enjoyable experience."

"I'll drink to that," said Montserrat, as he stood. "Will a bottle of Chianti Classico be in order Cardinal?"

"That would do nicely Antonio; you took the words right from my mouth."

The only available table was almost directly under a large television screening the latest Sky News. The TV was silent with subtitles flashed along the bottom of the screen at regular intervals.

The two men settled down to enjoy their wine and passed pleasantries as the news stories continued to roll. Cardinal Barberini had one eye on the screen when the unmistakable picture of the girl they had tortured and murdered filled the LCD screen. It was a little dated, perhaps taken twelve to eighteen months ago but the features were more than familiar. He aimed a swift under the table kick at Antonio Montserrat's shin and as he jumped Barberini pointed at the television.

The two men watched in silence as the picture disappeared and a live broadcast team stood in place outside Queens Gate Mews, Kensington in London.

A middle aged man was interviewing a high-ranking policeman. They read the subtitles as they were typed onto the screen. The policeman explained that they could find no reason why the woman had disappeared. She was young and pretty with everything to live for. Her mother had commented that she was every parents dream with a smile that would brighten the dullest of rooms.

Barberini surpressed a grin. They would be in Rome within hours with full diplomatic protection of the Vatican to hide behind and the police were clueless.

He glanced at his colleague. "We shouldn't be drinking wine Antonio."

"No?"

The Cardinal shook his head, "No, you should have bought champagne."

Antonio grinned. "Drink up Cardinal, we have plenty time."

As Cardinal Barberini relaxed back into his seat he took another mouthful of Chianti. The next news information that scrolled across the bottom of the screen forced him to take an unwanted intake of air. The temporary air pocket in the middle of his throat forced the wine from his mouth as he spat it involuntarily onto the table in front of him.

"Look," he managed to gasp, "look at the screen," he said as he pulled a handkerchief from his pocket and began wiping his mouth and the table. Montserrat caught what it was that had caused the Cardinal such consternation. The missing, possibly kidnapped woman's name had appeared along with the previous photograph again.

Miss Marnie Wishart, aged 29 .

"Holy Mother of God what have we done?" whispered Cardinal Barberini. "In Jesus name we've killed the wrong girl."

Montserrat was shaking his head. "No, it's not possible. It was her. The same girl on the photograph in Aberdeen, their eyes were an identical match, iris recognition, the machine is infallible.

Cardinal Barberini cast a glance towards the ceiling before turning to Montserrat. "Incapable of making mistakes, infallible, A word we Roman Catholics are more than familiar with."

"The machine has never failed us," said Montserrat. "There must be some other logical explanation. Perhaps it's a trick by the police; I know we had the right girl."

Cardinal Barberini pushed his glass away from him. He had suddenly lost his desire for wine.

The two men sat in near silence for the next hour until their flight was called. On the aircraft they flew business class and were offered a selection of fine wines champagnes and spirits. Cardinal Barberini refused it all while Montserrat drank just about everything it was possible to drink during the three hours the aircraft was in the air.

Sixteen

As to the method in which witches copulate with Incubus devils, six points are to be noted. First, as to the devil and the body which he assumes, of what element it is formed. Second, as to the act, whether it is always accompanied with the injection of semen received from some other man. Third, as to the time and place, whether one time is more favourable than another for this practice. Fourth, whether the act is visible to the women, and whether only those who were begotten in this way are so visited by devils. Fifth, whether it applies only to those who were offered to the devil at birth by midwives. Sixth, whether the actual venereal pleasure is greater or less in this act. MM

They had spent more than three hours checking the iris recognition system against at least 100 different sets of eyes. They'd tested it on themselves too and conducted a series of tests on different sized photographs of the girl on the motorcycle, the girl in Aberdeen Cathedral and of course the girl who they'd tortured in the basement of the cottage in the south of England. The irises were identical.

Montserrat was struggling to concentrate, his hangover getting worse by the minute. He could no longer look at a computer screen and sweated profusely in a soft armchair in the corner of the room. An expert on iris recognition had been flown in from Florence that very morning and towards lunchtime he too delivered his conclusion that the three pictures were the same person despite the fact that the girl lying on the bench in the cellar had had her features rearranged somewhat. And whilst her eyes were slightly swollen and blackened the eye lids remained open and the photographs of sufficient quality to take a reading.

He reached for his coat that was hanging on the back of the chair. "My work here is done Cardinal I am in no doubt."

Barberini didn't move a muscle and continued to sit in the same position he had sat for most of the morning. His head lay slightly tilted to the left leaning on his hand with a vacant expression on his face. He gave a slight nod in the direction of the man who was now making his way to the door.

"The money will be in your bank account within the hour Senor. I thank you for your help."

Senor Grimaldi was more than happy to assist his friends at the Vatican. He was a practising, committed Roman Catholic and took great pleasure in being able to assist the department who answered directly to the Holy Father. They had asked him for cooperation and secrecy and he would not dream of betraying their confidence. The little matter of a €10,000 payment for a morning's work helped to seal the deal.

Cardinal Barberini stood up and walked over to his computer desk. The machine was on standby and the screen was black. He moved the mouse no more than a millimetre and the screen lit up. He browsed through a few old e-mails and internal memos.

One of them, from the diocese of Aberdeen caught his eye.

"Well, well." he said. "It appears that our Scottish Monsignor was not able to keep his mouth shut after all."

Antonio Montserrat looked up.

"He was found hanging from the upper balcony of his cathedral yesterday morning. A cleaner found him."

Cardinal Barberini read on. "The police are not looking for anyone in connection with the incident, an apparent suicide."

Barberini looked at his hung-over partner in office, his *collega*. "David and Gianfranco have been a little naughty have they not?"

Montserrat looked confused. "They did not tell me about the Cardinal. They should have advised me."

"But they were in Scotland keeping a careful watch."

"Why yes, but even so a simple phone call would have—"

Barberini interrupted. "-Why Antonio, the Pope himself with the entire Orchestra Sinfonica di Roma in attendance could not have woken you last night. You were on a mission to drink the aeroplane dry." Barberini frowned, wagged a finger in front of his colleague's face. "Most unprofessional."

Montserrat hung his head. "I do apologise," he mumbled. "It was a bad end to the day."

Barberini looked at his watch. "Anyway, David and Franco will be here before too long. Do yourself a favour and pull yourself together." Barberini opened a desk drawer and reached for a key. He threw it over the room and miraculously Antonio caught it in mid-air.

"Take yourself down to the spa. Take a long sauna and drink plenty water, your system is poisoned with alcohol. Take a shower and clean yourself up."

He glared at Montserrat. "You positively fucking stink."

Cardinal Barberini and his select delegation took lunch in a small expensive, exclusive restaurant in Borgo Angelico. Barberini had felt the need to leave the confines of the walls of the Vatican, walk a little and not be surrounded by men in cassocks and flowing robes. The Monte San Giuliano served traditional Sicilian food and the owner Luigi kept a tight ship. He made sure that only genuine tourists were allowed in the restaurant or people he had personally vetted himself. If he had any doubt they were told that the restaurant was fully booked. He did not allow journalists in or anyone from the media and he was particularly sensitive about Americans, interfering Americans.

Barberini was among friends and he knew there would be no prying eyes or oversensitive ears. He could talk with confidence.

He ordered two bottles of water and asked for the menu. Luigi made a point of attending to the table himself. It was a nice gesture, one of respect and the little matter that the Vatican paid a monthly retainer to Luigi for his services.

The men exchanged pleasantries before Barberini got down to business. He took some time going over everything, running through the iris recognition system and the photographs taken in Liverpool of the motorcyclist and in the Cathedral in Aberdeen. Montserrat gave his theory that the two girls could in fact be the same person. The girl known as Celine MacArthur could have had an alias. It was possible and it would explain iris recognition that nobody doubted at the present time. Gianfranco explained that they had used iris recognition for more than 25 years and it had never failed or let them down. Montserrat backed him up saying that the system they'd used in the cottage in Dartmoor had been tested since.

"It has to be the same person," he said, stating the obvious.

Barberini turned to Gianfranco. "It is possible Franco?"

Franco turned his lip up as he spoke. "It's possible." He shrugged his huge shoulders. "Marnie Wishart existed of that there's no doubt, she had a British National Insurance number and a passport as did Celine Macarthur. We need to investigate a little, see if Wishart had a different address and what she did for a living. We know everything there is to know about Macarthur but I'll need a few days and I'll be able to tell you."

"Tell me they're the same person?" Barberini asked with a hopeful but not over confident look on his face.

"We have Macarthur placed at several locations on different dates," Gianfranco said. "We tracked her movements for some time. We are trying to track Wishart's whereabouts as we speak via credit card transactions and if we have her and Macarthur at different places on the same day at the opposite end of the country then we have a serious problem."

Barberini sighed. "I hope not, I sincerely hope not."

Gianfranco dangled a little carrot of hope. "It's not difficult to hold down two identities, not difficult at all."

Luigi placed a large plate of cured ham and a dish of caponata in the centre of the table.

"My friends," he said producing a bottle of wine, "may I recommend this to start with? It will satisfy your pallet I am sure."

Barberini acknowledged the owner with a wave of his hand. Luigi uncorked the wine and poured a finger's depth into Cardinal Barberini's glass.

"No need," said Barberini bluntly. "Just pour and leave us. I am sure you have made a fine choice as you always do."

Luigi did as he was told and disappeared quickly.

"You're sure she was the only person in the apartment?" questioned Barberini.

"One hundred per cent."

And you've watched the apartment since as instructed," said Barberini.

"We have," said Gianfranco. "We've had a team there 24/7."

"And?"

"Nothing. Celine MacArthur has not been anywhere near the place."

Montserrat leaned back into his seat forking an oversized forkful of ham into his mouth. He chewed for a few seconds. "I'm sure it's the same girl."

Barberini wasn't so sure and yet it all appeared to make sense.

Barberini sat back and contemplated his next move.

"Okay. Get your men on the case and bring me some good news as quick as you can."

He turned to David. "Keep the team on the apartment for the next two weeks just in case and if she does show up take her out as soon as possible. They don't need clearance; tell them they have that as from today."

David nodded, made a note on the memo section of his phone.

"Let's assume until we hear otherwise that Macarthur is still out there and she knows we are on to her. She needs to spend money to survive, on food and travel, hotels, that sort of thing."

Montserrat drained the last of his wine and reached across the table for a refill as he spoke. "Sir, no two irises in the world are the same. David and Franco checked her eyes in the apartment and we did the same at the cottage, there's no mistake."

Antonio hadn't spoken for some time as he sat deep in thought. Was it possible there were two girls? The Monsignor in Aberdeen had mentioned something about a wedding and a sister but of course they were so excited at finding Celine Macarthur that not one of them thought to ask the name of the bride. Was it possible Macarthur was attending her sister's wedding and that her sister had been staying over at her apartment when the kidnap took place and the sister is none other than Marnie Wishart? No, surely that wasn't possible, no irises are the same... except very occasionally in identical twins.

Barberini reached for his glass too. He took a long deliberate mouthful as he swirled the pleasant tasting liquid around his mouth before swallowing it in one. It had the desired effect. It calmed him somewhat. Suddenly his appetite was returning again. He picked up the menu and traced his finger over several of the dishes. Meat he thought to himself, a rare Sicilian steak. He found exactly what he was looking for and snapped his fingers in the direction of the owner. Luigi was in attendance in an instant.

"Would you recommend the steak?" he said to Luigi pointing at the menu.

"I would your Eminence, with a little of my spicy tomato and basil sauce and baked Sicilian potatoes in cream and cheese."

Cardinal Barberini was already salivating. "Then my mind is made up Luigi. Take my friends orders and be as quick as you can. We have much work to do."

Halfway through the main course Cardinal Barberini brought up the subject of the dead Monsignor in Aberdeen.

"It's a shame you killed him Franco, I suspect he may have been able to help us again. He knew his congregation well."

Gianfranco laid down his knife and fork as he leaned forward. He took a quick look around the restaurant before whispering across the table.

"Not us your Eminence. We didn't kill him."

A sick tight feeling welled up in the pit of the Cardinal's stomach as the meat in his mouth lost its flavour. Suddenly his appetite had disappeared and he was more than a little worried because that was a second member of the Vatican Bank Finance Committee whose life had been snuffed out. Who would be next?

Seventeen

Therefore a wicked woman is by her nature quicker to waver in her faith, and consequently quicker to abjure the faith, which is the root of witchcraft. MM

There was further bad news for Cardinal Barberini the following morning as the world newspaper reports filtered through to his PC. There were generally half a dozen each day, six or seven articles that had appeared in the previous days press that the various Catholic Church employees around the world felt should be drawn to the attention of the Vatican. It was Barberini's job to decide what action if any needed to be taken. Sometimes it would come in the form of a denial or sometimes a damage limitation exercise, normally a priest who had been accused or even tried and convicted.

He read over the four page feature that had appeared in England, in the Liverpool Echo and he cursed and wondered if it weren't so early in the morning, the female reporter's words might warrant a large brandy.

The reporter's headline screamed out at him.

The Great Vatican Cover Up.

And as he read on he grew ever angrier. The reporter, Samantha Kerr, had done her job; he couldn't fault her on that. Everything she had written was accurate and well researched and her guesswork was almost perfect, suggesting a serial killer at work with revenge as the motive behind the killings. And there was more. Just at the point where he was wondering where the story had originated it was there in black and white. The report had mentioned a high-ranking visit from the Vatican to Merseyside Police Headquarters. The information had come from a Merseyside Police insider.

Barberini was livid. Who was the leak, the desk sergeant, a civilian pen pusher or the detective who ran through the CCTV with them?

Barberini shook his head. The detective wouldn't be as stupid as that; it was obviously someone with a far lower rank, not someone that obvious.

~

Sam Kerr almost took the door from the hinges as she barged into John Fitzsimmons' glass bubble office. She threw the newspaper onto the desk.

"What the fuck's the meaning of this?" she shouted. "You had no right."

Fitzsimmons leaned back in his seat and a slight grin crept across his face as he spoke. "I had every right Sam, you left the article on my desk and so I was entitled to use it. You were after all still my employee at the time; I didn't get your resignation letter until 48 hours afterwards remember? And anyway your contract states we can use your work up to six months after your contract terminates."

Sam was dumbfounded, she expected him to backtrack and apologise, come up with a major excuse of how the story accidently made it into the newspaper but he didn't.

"You mentioned a police source, you bastard; I didn't say there was a police source."

Fitzsimmons shrugged his shoulders. "I guessed Sam, a well educated guess wouldn't you say?"

"You fucking bastard you don't know what you've done."

Fitzsimmons stood up and raised his voice a decibel or two. "Just a minute Sam. I don't like your attitude and you shouldn't even be in the building. Anymore of this and I'll have to call security. I can see you're angry but there's no need for this."

"There's every need my boyfriend—"

It was a slip of the tongue but there was nothing she could do to retrieve the mistake.

Fitzsimmons was grinning broadly. "I knew it. That's how you knew. What better place than to share a few secrets with a copper than between the sheets."

It's not like that she wanted to say. Suddenly it was all looking rather sleazy and Fitzsimmons had reduced her worth to that of a common streetwalker. He had no right to do that; she didn't want to go back there. But he was in full flow; he had her exactly where he wanted her. She had resigned from his newspaper but she wanted this job badly. She'd been bluffing and well he knew it. He held all of the aces in the pack.

He leaned over the desk his face just inches from hers. "I guess he won't be too happy eh?"

Tears welled up in Sam Kerr's eyes; she could find no words to answer her former boss. Kevin didn't deserve this, if only she'd shown a little more commitment, opened up to him a little more, allowed her natural feelings to rise to the surface. He was a good guy and as honest and trusting as the day was long. She'd let him down, let him down badly and she'd been stupid with some of the details she'd left in the article. Fitzsimmons' words were alien to her, he might as well have been speaking in another language. She stood up and walked towards the door.

"That's a top lead and you're a good reporter, I think you should retract that resignation letter and get back to work," he said.

She turned to face him and although still angry she wanted her job back. She was ready and willing but feeling more than a little vulnerable.

He continued. "He'll be a little pissed off for a few weeks but..."

Fitzsimmons eyes scanned her body and his gaze settled on her backside. "I'm sure with a little gentle persuasion you can bring him round to your way of thinking."

Sam walked back towards the desk. "Print a retraction; say that it was an error and that we don't have an insider in the police," she said.

Fitzsimmons was shaking his head.

"Why not John?"

"Because I'm the boss Sam that's why. Now why don't you reconsider your position? I love your writing and I'm prepared to tear that resignation letter up, pretend I never even saw it and further more I'll give you an extra four grand a year."

Sam's jaw fell open. "You mean that?" she said.

"I do," he said with a broad smile.

Suddenly the article didn't seem so bad, there was a new light at the end of the tunnel and she wanted to run towards it.

"There are a few preconditions but nothing we can't sort out."

"Preconditions?"

Fitzsimons was growing more confident by the minute. He leaned forward and placed his elbows on the desk. "I've always liked you Sam, you must know that, I've always found you attractive."

Fitzsimons had a different look on his face now, a look that told her that he didn't just want her for her writing skills. Fitzsimons was moving in for the kill.

"My wife's away this weekend. She's away until next Tuesday and I'm sure we can work something out over dinner. I'm quite a decent cook."

Sam was speechless.

"Nothing permanent, you understand, no commitment, just a little dinner and see what happens from there."

Sam remained composed as it slowly sank in.

"Do you have a pen John, give me your address?" she said.

Fitzsimmons looked a little surprised but nodded and opened the drawer to his desk. "You'll come for dinner Sam?"

She nodded and grinned as she walked around the desk. Fitzsimmons hand was desperately trying to locate a pen in his draw. She leaned in towards him as her hand brushed softly against his thigh and she watched as he eventually found a cheap biro. She timed it well; she used the knee strike quite often in her Muay Thai fighting classes and she waited until his hand was neither in nor out of the draw as she applied as much force as she could to the strike.

It was executed perfectly; she connected in exactly the right place. She hit the draw so hard and as it slammed against Fitzsimmons knuckles it broke into several pieces as did Fitzsimmons metacarpals, five of his proximal phalanges and three intermediate phalanges. The pain was instant but so excruciating that he couldn't even raise a squeak.

He fell back into his seat as the colour drained from his face.

Sam leaned in and kissed him gently on the cheek.

"Dearie, dearie me Mr Fitzsimmons it looks like you've hurt your little handie."

As she walked towards the office door for the final time she turned and spoke. "Mrs Fitzsimmons away all weekend and you won't even be able to satisfy yourself with a decent wank."

As she walked out into the bright sunshine she took out her mobile from her handbag, located Kevin's number and pressed call. At the very least she owed him an explanation. The phone rang out three times and disconnected. "Damn," she whispered to herself.

Eighteen

And as to her other mental quality, that is, her natural will; when she hates someone whom she formerly loved, then she seethes with anger and impatience in her whole soul, just as the tides of the sea are always heaving and boiling. MM

I have been doing a lot of reading lately. I have moments of doubt about what I am doing and sometimes I feel I must stop and yet at the same time I know that will never happen as she will keep on coming.

I am reading the bible? Not all of it just selected passages.

You see I was more than a little puzzled at the sheer hatred those witch hunters seemed to have for the female form. Where did it come from and why were they so without mercy, so vengeful? Slowly but surely as I began leafing through the pages it became clear.

In the mind-set of the scribes of the good book it was sex that perpetuated evil and the fall of man which of course was the fault of a woman, namely Eve. It was Eve and not Adam who had been tempted and succumbed and they were damn sure no one was ever going to be allowed to forget it.

Eve's so called sin was disobedience and because of this one misdemeanour those fucking scribes and frauds and charlatans were going to make sure that generation upon generation upon generation of future women were going to suffer. The bible told us we would suffer the pain of childbirth because of Eve's actions. He seems like a vengeful evil spiteful bastard this god of theirs but that's just my perception of their good book I suppose. How can I still doubt you Maven? Our bond is stronger than ever.

Like Eve with Adam, women were ultimately responsible for temptation and the moral corruption of all men we were the weaker vessels, easily given over to lasciviousness. We needed to be kept in our places and kept away from men of piety.

Is it any wonder then that they (they being the charlatans and tricksters and frauds) gave over that the mother of Jesus Christ needed to be a virgin? Fuck, we can't have her even thinking about sex let alone doing it!

In time the Virgin Mary, the sacred feminine was eventually accepted into Catholicism, albeit a sexless meek "queen of heaven" forever at the hierarchy's beck and call. All other females described in the Bible were harlots and whores or females ready to be offered up for gang rape or child abuse. I had to laugh as I read from Joshua that the prostitute, Rahab, saved her own skin by betraying the city of Jericho. She hid Joshua's spies, lied about it, and then aided their escape. Rahab's reward was to be given to a Jew and to bear the line of David which of course would lead to Jesus Christ himself.

The hypocritical naïve bastards.

"Let the women keep silence in the churches," it states quite clearly "for it is not permitted unto them to speak; but let them be in subjection and if they would learn anything, let them ask their own husbands at home: for it is shameful for a woman to speak in the church."

My dear sisters, it appears the sins of our past is stronger than we ever realised and even now the Catholic Church is not in the mood for acceptance, something which they preach in almost every other sphere. In modern days our sisters dared to ask if times had changed enough to allow women to be ordained into the priesthood. Pope John Paul II put the females firmly in place when he said it was not even possible to discuss the issue because the Church had no authority to do so.

Judeao-Christian tradition will never change, they are the same men in power now as they were in the 15th and 16th century, the men who approved the Malleus Malefaction and used it as a manual to abuse women right across Europe.

I feel the urge to stall my quest for revenge. Whenever I do Maven tells me to pick up the good book. I need no further motivation.

I wonder if they've discovered the truth about the four bishops in Liverpool? Ha ha!

That was so easy. They now know I mean business. Don't doubt me. I'm getting more cunning and better with each job. Burning the bastards to a frazzle was simply so satisfying. Once again I have been clever, so very clever. I'd watched Bishop McKenzie only for a few weeks and pinpointed his weekly meeting with the other three bishops as an ideal time to take them. The night before, I managed to get to their car and tamper with the electrics. I downloaded an electronic device from the internet and synchronised it to the central locking system. I placed six capsules of highly flammable lighter fluid around the engine. As I pulled up alongside them on the motorbike I activated the device and they were locked within their prison cell. I'd locked the bastards in on death row and the power I held was almost orgasmic.

The tiny firecracker was all I needed to complete the job and it exploded on impact with the ground emitting a shower of tiny sparks.

The next thirty seconds were poetry in motion and I wish I could have stayed around a little longer to watch as the flesh melted from their holier than thou bones and they welded together in perfect harmony with their vehicle.

They would know just how it felt to be powerless in the heat of the flames and I heard them cry out for their so called God as he listened but did not act.

My dreams still come and go but they are becoming more three dimensional now. I could now almost smell, taste and feel everything as if I were actually there. When you go to sleep where is it you exactly go to? Am I experiencing astral projection? It's all very complicated and for the first time tiny doubts are beginning to creep in. I'm sleeping for nine and ten hour's right through without a single disturbance and yet awake tired, my body occasionally marked. Am I thrashing about in my near comatose state or is there something else there, something else the mind cannot comprehend.

Two nights ago I was there with those priests in the car as one by one their bodies combusted. I sat there with them as I watched them singe and burn, their hair catch fire as the flames slowly engulfed them. I sat in the back with them as I taunted and laughed and yet I was immune from the flames. I told them to repent their sins and they did. They confessed all as if somehow it would make the fire stop. And they begged their God for divine intervention and then mercy as he failed to help them. What is it that goes through a holy man's mind when he knows he is going to die before his time? What about the young priests and cardinals and Fathers, the nuns who dedicate their lives to the church and develop terminal diseases way too early? What becomes of the choirboy who is struck down with

114

cancer as a teenager? What do they all think, what goes through their disease ridden heads? Is their faith tested as the last rites are read to them?

I wonder. I wonder indeed.

Nineteen

*No might of the flames or of the swollen winds, no deadly weapon
is so much to be feared as the lust and hatred of a woman who has
been divorced from the marriage bed. MM*

Marnie and Celine MacArthur had been separated just before
their first birthday and not reunited until Marnie had decided
to try and relocate her twin sister in her early twenties. She had
discovered a photograph which had fallen from her mother's
purse one day, an old fashioned Kodak snap, creased and dog
eared at the edges and by the look on her mother's face when
Marnie picked it up and handed it back she knew it was something
of immense significance.

At first her mother tried to deny the obvious, and it was
obvious. Marnie looked into her own eyes when she looked at
that photograph and the eyes of the baby girl sat next to her in a
battered old pushchair were not the eyes of a stranger, she knew
that. It took no more than fifteen minutes before her mother
reluctantly disclosed she had a twin sister and that as far as she
was aware the girl was alive and well although contact with her
had been lost.

It was the bitterest most complicated divorce ever and her
estranged husband held all the aces she explained through the
tears. He had the money and the power and he had made her make
the impossible choice, he wanted to hurt her as much as he could.
He wasn't even a good father and showed no affection towards
his two beautiful daughters, yet had insisted that the question
of paternity was a simple and obvious one. They would divorce
and one child would live with her and the other move south with
him. If she disagreed he would fight her in the courts of the land
and claimed he had no end of witnesses to back up his claim that
she was an unfit mother. The local GP would testify that she was
an alcoholic with self-destructive tendencies and he would claim
both girls for himself, the doting father, a fine upstanding pillar of

society, well respected with the financial means to give both girls the kind of life they could only dream of.

Marnie's mother cried as she relayed the next part of the story and explained how she had no choice but to take the agonising deal. Their father had promised to send money and allow bi-monthly visits.

She would see her other daughter on a regular basis. And yet, as the car had pulled out of the driveway with one tiny, lost soul belted into an oversized car seat in the back of his Daimler Sovereign she sensed it would be many years before she set eyes on her gorgeous daughter again. She had tried her hardest she explained to Marnie, but their father had severed all links with the family and disappeared from the face of the earth.

John Wishart didn't even want a child, just revenge, nothing more, nothing less and what better course of revenge to take out on a mother than to deprive her of the very thing she held dear to her heart.

He'd put Celine up for adoption shortly before her second birthday and made a point of informing her birth mother via an untraceable telegram several years later. He said Celine's name had been changed and that she would never find her. Sweet revenge indeed.

It had taken Marnie the best part of two years before she'd found her sister who had been living no more than ten miles from where she'd set up her own home. It was a tense, first initial meeting and Marnie could sense a troubled defensive soul but gradually her twin sister had opened up to her and they'd become quite close, as close as it was possible to become after such a long time apart.

It was more than three years before Celine even allowed her to visit what was the private and very personal domain of her own home and another year after that before she allowed her to stay over after an occasional night out in the West End. The grand wedding in the Cathedral in Aberdeen had been the twins' finest hour and they'd bonded like never before as their mother looked on and absorbed every delicious second.

Celine MacArthur blamed herself.

Why had she agreed to let her sister back into her life and why had she allowed her the key to her apartment? She'd screwed up, she knew that but the Church had screwed up too and they'd know about it soon enough. They'd crossed the line and she'd make the men at the very top pay with their lives. For now it was time to box clever, time to flee, and time to adopt a new identity.

Identical twins. An easy mistake to make but one they'd pay for tenfold.

Twenty

And indeed, just as through the first defect in their intelligence they are more prone to abjure the faith; so through their second defect of inordinate affections and passions they search for, brood over, and inflict various vengeances, either by witchcraft, or by some other means. Wherefore it is no wonder that so great a number of witches exist in this sex. MM

The girl had to hand it to the reporter; Sam Kerr had done her homework. The article was articulate, informative, yes sensational but above all else incredibly accurate. On page seven of the Liverpool Echo, Kerr had gone into detail about the various methods of ancient torture the 'deranged serial killer' had deployed on similar killings outside of the UK, they were, she wrote, inextricably linked.

The girl sat back in her chair and opened the other screen on her computer. It was amazing what one could find out on the internet. Facebook, Twitter, LinkedIn and My Space all held details about the rookie reporter from Liverpool.

The girl worked for several hours finding out more details about the reporter and then created a false profile, with the IP location protected by a sophisticated firewall and befriended Kerr on Facebook.

Within 24 hours her request was accepted and she had a direct line in. It would be fun the girl thought and at that precise moment had an overwhelming urge to type the first of many messages to her new acquaintance.

Twenty One

Women also have weak memories; and it is a natural vice in them not to be disciplined, but to follow their own impulses without any sense of what is due; this is her whole study, and all that she keeps in her memory. MM

It was a hoax. Surely it was hoax? Some crank had read her article in the newspaper and sent her a message through Facebook. She continued to read right through to the end, at times it took her breath away but... yes, it was a hoax, and what did they call it, trolling? She had been trolled, someone was dangling a little bait on a hook and she would sure as hell not bite.

An interesting article Miss Journalist, well written and an interesting theory. Have the charlatans from the Vatican really been to Liverpool, are they on to me, do they know about my other jobs further afield?

Well I suppose it had to happen sooner or later because the Vatican police are no mugs. Veteran special forces, ex policemen, more often than not disgraced and booted out of the force for sexual indiscretions or a bribe or two. But the Vatican don't care who they bring on board as long as they possess the necessary qualities they are looking for because the Vatican has the power and money to manipulate or snuff out those rumours and stories, they can easily silence a journalist or an author who knows too much and if not they don't care anyway because they are untouchable.

Oh you'd better believe that your article has found its way to Rome and already they'll have a file on Samantha Kerr from Liverpool, England and they'll know all about you, where you went to school, university, whether you dabbled in drugs and who you fucked last night and they'll have downloaded and analysed every article you've ever written too, and perhaps, who knows even hacked into this very computer you are looking at right now. Ha ha.

That's what Rome do and they do it well.

You'd better take care Samantha, better be careful what you write about from now on. Me? I loved it, spot on the truth as it happens and the fact you warned me about the Vatican has put me on my guard and I believe it's time to move on.

Many thanks, pretty one.

She eased back in her seat wondering who this crank could be. It had to be her ex-boss, Fitzsimons. This would be right up his street and revenge for breaking his wrist. She didn't want to take the hook but nevertheless needed to find out who it was and if it was him, she'd march right into his office and smash his other hand up.

Sam clicked on the Facebook profile of her mystery friend, *Lucrecia Mathren.*

Shit, *Lucrecia* had no friends, not one. She'd listed her relationship as complicated and in work and education it had been left blank. This was pointing to Fitzsimons; this account had been set up for no other reason than to taunt her. The basic information was also left blank and although the gender did read female you didn't need any ID to join Facebook so Fitzsimons could have entered anything he wanted.

Sam stretched back on her seat lifting her hands high into the air. She'd been on the damn Mac too long, she was stiffening up. She clicked the minimize sign in the top left hand corner, closed the lid, stood up and wandered through to the kitchen. She didn't feel much like eating but was conscious she hadn't eaten anything all day. She turned on the grill, opened the fridge and cut a little cheese. She placed it on some bread and pushed it under. She leaned on the bench top waiting until the cheese bubbled, reached back into the fridge, took out a bottle of milk and poured herself a glass.

She read on for an hour or more until her Mac gave out a little noise indicating she had a new Facebook message. She opened the page. It was from her new friend Lucrecia

Oh well, she thought, in for a penny.... She clicked open.

I will make them pay. I may not be able to change the world but I will make them pay and they will beg me for forgiveness for the rape and torture and mass murder they have committed in the name of their Lord.

It is late and I must bring my writing to a close for now. I need peace but I confess I am happy with what I am doing. I need my needle. I need my needle and my medicine and I need to talk to her. Oh what pleasure it gives me when I feel that tiny prick of pain knowing where it will take me, perhaps back to Aberdeen?

This was not Fitzsimons style; it was just some nut who read newspapers with a warped perspective on life. Why was she wasting valuable time on this drivel? She knew she needed to *unfriend* this unhinged twisted idiot. She stood up and stretched and let out an over exaggerated yawn. She would, first thing in the morning she'd get rid of Lucrecia just as quick as she'd come in and she would make a point of not accepting people she knew nothing about even though it got her an occasional decent story. As she peeled back the sheets to her bed and climbed in she wondered what sort of crazy she'd disturbed.

Twenty Two

If we inquire, we find that nearly all the kingdoms of the world have been overthrown by women. Troy, which was a prosperous kingdom, was, for the rape of one woman, Helen, destroyed, and many thousands of Greeks slain. The kingdom of the Jews suffered much misfortune and destruction through the accursed Jezebel, and her daughter Athaliah, Queen of Judah, who caused her son's sons to be killed, that on their death she might reign herself; yet each of them was slain. The kingdom of the Romans endured much evil through Cleopatra, Queen of Egypt, that worst of women. Therefore it is no wonder if the world now suffers through the malice of women. MM

Gianfranco Desiro was perfectly happy with his wife of nearly seventeen years. In fact he looked more than forward to his wedding anniversary in just a few weeks time. He'd booked a surprise trip to Paris in a hotel just off the Champs Elysees. Three days. They'd wander the Boulevards she loved so much frequenting the street cafés and watching Parisian life passing by. They'd do the usual tourist trail venturing up the Eiffel Tower, a bateaux-mouche river cruise, the museums and of course like all good Catholics take in mass at Notre Dame.

She'd been a good wife and a wonderful mother to their four children and of course he'd provided for his family well. She knew exactly what was expected of her, when to look nice and could read her husband like a book. She knew it was not right to ask questions of his new position since his days in the military had ended. All she knew was that he worked in Rome in security.

There were some things a wife couldn't provide, things the mother of your children wouldn't be expected to do. That's why he used prostitutes and why he'd had numerous affairs over the years. He suspected she probably knew but he'd trained her well and she had never confronted him. Gianfranco always thought that wives were like little puppy dogs and it was important to instil a little discipline in the early days of the relationship. Start as you mean to go on his old grandfather had told him. And he had and it had worked out more than satisfactory. He'd never leave Carmen, she knew that and she knew that he'd always provide well for her and their family. It was what a good Italian father should do. The last year's income had been handsome, the Vatican paid well there was no doubt about it and now he was closing in on the big stakes bonus.

It had been slow, painstaking work but when the phone call came through from one of his old associates that the girl had flown into America, Gianfranco approached Cardinal Barberini and claimed the job for himself. He'd traced the girl as she'd flown in from London to New York. She then took a flight to Chicago; he'd spotted her through CCTV footage at banks, car hire firms, filling stations and the malls. His contacts had traced her to the area of Bridgeport where she had set up home but then the trail had gone cold. The bitch had changed her identity, that was fairly obvious and what he'd expected anyway. She'd also moved apartments and changed her car. She was clever.

His employers had been patient... probably more so because she hadn't killed during the period Gianfranco was tracking her. She was lying low he told them as she had realised that they were on to her and dared not make a move.

That was all very well they had said but there was a limit to the time they were prepared to wait.

Gianfranco's flight left Rome airport early afternoon. With the seven hour time difference he should be settled in the city centre hotel in Chicago by late evening with a meeting scheduled first thing the following day.

He was placing an awful lot of trust in the man but then again he had no option. The Hispanic known only by the name of Jose had contacted him out of the blue with a simple, "I hear you are looking for a girl."

Jose knew an awful lot about Celine MacArthur and there was no doubt in his mind that the man was genuine. So genuine in fact that Gianfranco had wired $25,000 to an unnamed bank account with the promise of the same again on delivery of the goods. A small part of him thought that he may never hear from Jose again and that he had possibly been conned but it was a chance he had to take.

It was an anxious seven days before the stranger called again and said that Gianfranco's presence was required in Chicago. The Hispanic knew where she was and could lead him straight to her.

Gianfranco was like a big kid at Christmas time. The presents were assembled neatly under the tree; he simply had to remove the wrapping paper to get to her.

He didn't sleep well that night, tossing and turning, restlessly dozing more than sleeping. At 5.30am he showered, dressed and took the lift to the ground floor walking past the reception area and into the street. He picked at his breakfast in a café on West Maddison Street, constantly checking his watch. The Hispanic had said he'd find him some time around ten, nothing more specific than that. Gianfranco had to admit he felt a little uncomfortable that the man appeared to know all about him and in return he knew no more than a name.

He'd wired a ridiculous amount of money to an account of a person he'd never met, didn't know what he looked like or where he lived. He looked at his watch again as he signalled to the waitress for yet another black coffee.

9.47am.

How long would he wait before accepting he'd been stitched up? No, that didn't make sense. The man had his money and he could have ran but he hadn't. Gianfranco had worked on instinct and gut reaction all his life. He was seldom wrong. He tried hard to push the feelings of doubt from his head.

It was just after eleven when a young couple approached the table.

"May we sit here?" the girl asked.

Gianfranco sighed, checked his watch again. "I'm waiting for someone," he said. "Find somewhere else to sit."

The girl smiled as she pulled the chair away from the table. Very attractive. Dark almost jet black close cropped hair with perfect olive coloured unblemished skin, Mediterranean looking

125

with a figure that screamed gym. He liked that in a girl, someone who worked out and took care of themself.

"We'll sit here," she said confidently. She leaned forward and whispered. "Relax Gianfranco; sorry we're a little late."

Gianfranco's initial surge of relief was quickly replaced by an uncomfortable feeling that he was outnumbered and had been taken by surprise. He turned to the man. "You said nothing about an associate. She has to go."

Jose was already shaking his head. "We're partners' hombre, she stays, she's the brains behind the operation and she's the only person who can lead you to the girl."

Gianfranco's objections were quickly met with reasoned argument and within a few minutes it was clear that the girl held sway in the relationship. The Hispanic was a mere pawn, a go between, the face prepared look over the parapet for a fee.

The girl was all together more professional and he was already warming to her as she sat back smiling allowing her partner in crime to take centre stage, for the time being at least.

Jose pointed to the girl. "Paula will take you to her. It may take a couple of days as she's out of town at the moment but we have it on good authority that she's due back soon." He looked down at the bag between Gianfranco's feet. "You have the money Senor?"

Gianfranco nodded slowly, disliking the Hispanic with ever growing intensity. He was the bagman, nothing more.

"What guarantee do I have that you won't disappear with the money and Paula here rides off into the sunset?" Gianfranco asked.

"You don't," said the girl.

The big Italian looked at the Hispanic who looked more than a little nervous. He read the look, so close to the big payday. This was his money, the sweat on his top lip told him so. Whoever it was who received the initial payment is wasn't this man.

"The money stays with me," said Gianfranco, "until I get the girl."

"No Senor that is not what we agreed. I would—"

The nervous Hispanic was cut short in mid-sentence as the girl interrupted him. She spoke fluently with an air of supreme confidence. "Celine MacArthur, date of birth 12-6-87 arrived in New York on a flight from London on 16th September last year. She took a hire car from Jake's Rental the following day and drove non-stop to Chicago. Seven weeks after her arrival in Chicago she took on an alias by the name of Kate Horden and resided at three different addresses in the Lower West Side, Prairie District and Bridgeport area of the city. Blonde hair, blue eyes, pretty, an interior designer by profession though currently we think working as a freelance secretary."

The girl smiled briefly and continued. "Wanted by the Vatican and possibly several police forces around the world for the systematic torture and murder of several Vatican employees." She paused before continuing.

"Gianfranco Desiro, born in Bologna 17th August 1962, ex Italian special forces with an almost unblemished service record apart from a slight indiscretion in 1999. Married to Senora Carmen Desiro for almost 17 years, two little boys and two girls who attend private school in Rome. Girlfriends..."

She looked up and glared at the astonished Italian. "Many of them. 2001 Loredana Busconi. 2003 two more Signorina da Corte and Pacelli, Signorina Pacelli the daughter of a prominent politician and—"

"Enough," said Desiro, a little too loudly as he glanced nervously around the cafeteria. He didn't know whether to be impressed or more than a little worried that the girl who he'd only just met knew more about his business than his wife, his mother and the Vatican combined.

He pawed anxiously at his stone cold empty coffee cup but he was close to his prey, oh so close and he could feel the excitement building by the minute. He looked up and caught the attention of the waitress. "It's a little early for a drink but I think I need one." He ordered a beer and Jose followed suit. "And Paula what will you have?"

"A black coffee will be fine Mr Desiro."

The waitress nodded her approval and left the table.

"So are you going to tell me where you got all of this information from?" he asked.

"Most of it can be obtained via Internet search engines on sites that are legal or otherwise," she said. "The rest comes from the street." She glanced at the Hispanic. "From sources we have built up over the years."

Gianfranco was still in shock as he took a long drink from his glass. "So what happens next?"

He had directed the question to the girl almost ignoring her colleague completely.

She pointed with a lazy thumb. "Jose here gets to leave with the money. He'll take it away and make sure it's all there. When everything is kosher he'll call me and then I'll take you to her."

Gianfranco already had his hands up in the air before she'd even finished the sentence. "Whoa, hold on a second, all I want is an address; I'll take it from there."

Paula was laughing as she cradled her cup in two hands. "Suit yourself but I'm telling you she won't be there. She'll know you are on to her and she'll disappear again. You need to take her somewhere neutral, somewhere where she will never expect it. She's good, about the best person I've ever followed and she's hard to track down. You work on your own if you want Mr Desiro, but I'm telling you she'll see you coming from a country mile."

"I'll have to take that chance."

Paula fumbled in her pocket. She handed across a piece of paper. "That's her address, now give Jose the bag. If there's as much as one dollar missing she'll get a phone call from me telling her you're on your way and you'll never see her again."

"It's all there don't you worry about that." Gianfranco said.

He kicked the bag under the table and it rested against Jose's shins. He reached down picked it up and stood. Paula stood with him. She held out her hand. "Be lucky Senor you'll need it."

As she turned to walk away he stopped her. "Wait, Signorina." She stopped and looked round.

"Let Jose go. Tell him to make the phone call when everything is in order. I'd like you to stay a little longer if that's okay?"

She checked her watch. "I think I'm free for most of the day," she said.

It was two hours later when Paula received a phone call. It was almost like a signal to her that she could talk freely and she did. She revealed even more information about MacArthur, some of which took his breath away. As the morning turned into early afternoon they left the cafeteria wandered a few blocks and had lunch. Before he knew it Gianfranco was agreeing to everything the girl said allowing her to plan the kidnap of Celine MacArthur and even be a part of it.

"There is a small church on West 32nd Street," she said. "St Mary of Perpetual Help, she started visiting the church some weeks back, it's small and the congregation sparse."

"That's not possible," said Gianfranco. "This cannot be the same girl; she hates the church and everything it stands for."

Paula grinned. "It's the same girl don't you worry about that and she's not going to church for mass and confession."

Gianfranco shrugged his shoulders and frowned. "I'm not with you, what do you mean?"

"The priest is only 29 years old, tall dark and handsome. Celine Macarthur is fucking him."

"What? I don't believe it, how can you possibly know that?"

"I've started attending the same church myself and planted a small remote-controlled listening device on the back of one of the pews. Believe me I'm a woman and I know the sort of sounds a girl makes when she's getting screwed good and hard."

Gianfranco was shaking his head. "Holy Mother of God I don't believe it."

She was planning to kill again. The bitch. The poor priest had risen to the temptation of the flesh and was getting tangled ever tighter into the web of death in the confines of his own church. It was the perfect set up.

"When is she next due there?" he asked.

"Wednesday morning at 10.30." She replied coldly. "She attends one to one bible reading with the priest or so the parishioners are made to believe."

Gianfranco raised his arm and stroked gently at the girls face. She made no attempt to resist.

"You operate like a true professional Paula. When this is all over we could work well together."

Paula tilted her head into the palm of his hand and kissed it. "I think I would like that very much. I'm tired of this city and I could do with a change of scenery."

"That can easily be arranged." He leaned forward to kiss her but at the last moment her hand came up to his lips and she stopped him. "Not now," she said. "Not here. We have much work to do."

Gianfranco sat alone in his hotel suite brooding. Never had such a character made such an instant impression. He chewed on an unappetising vending machine sandwich and sipped at an overwarm tin of Budweiser. She wouldn't even come to dinner with him, said she had an immense amount of preparation to do before Wednesday morning. He was ashamed to admit he was like putty in her hands and he'd been only too pleased to let her take the lead in the operation to kidnap Celine MacArthur.

He'd telephoned Cardinal Barberini as soon as he'd returned to the hotel, said the girl was as good as his and that he'd found a great new recruit for the cause. Barberini wanted her alive. There was a safe house on the outskirts of the city. She could be taken there and held.

Barberini tried not to count his chickens but nor could he control his elation. He was planning another trip, this time to Chicago and he'd deal with the girl personally. As he placed the receiver he picked it up again. He located a number in New York, he hadn't spoken to the man for some time but he answered and Barberini gave him his instructions. The man replied that Chicago wasn't that far away and whatever the Cardinal wanted he would have. The call lasted no more than five minutes and as it drew to a close Barberini jotted down the man's bank details. Barberini would need receipts for the purchases but of course his fee would be handsome as always.

It had been a big call Desiro made to Barberini but he was more than confident in Paula's ability. He'd recalled some of the brightest, bravest and strongest men he'd served with over the years and the girl was up there with the best of them. They'd team up together for the duration and yes he would take her into his bed. Of that there was no doubt. He'd talked long and hard with her and even disclosed details about the team she would one day be working with.

The call came just before midnight. They'd rendezvous in a café close to the church at seven o'clock on Wednesday morning and she'd run through everything. MacArthur was on her way back to the Windy City. Paula had had confirmation less than an hour ago. She gave him one instruction and one instruction only and that was that he'd need to secure a side loading van that they could drive to the alley entrance to the church. She'd said Chicago was a busy place and they couldn't take the chance to be seen bundling a body into the boot of a car. She also wanted the address of the safe house in the city; she needed to complete a 'dry run' just like a good bank robber. She would plan their escape route meticulously. Desiro gave it to her without hesitation and if it were remotely possible his admiration for her professionalism jumped up another notch. Desiro asked her again if she would reconsider a late night drink and a little supper. Without answering the line went dead.

The safe house was no more than thirty five minutes from the church of St Mary of Perpetual Help. The girl spent fifteen minutes in the house, no more. What she saw in the large cellar of the detached house took her breath away.

The café was quiet as Paula ran through the plan. It was simplicity itself.

"I disabled the priests' car overnight and also his cell-phone. When he realises the car won't start he'll try and call her to say he'll be late but of course it won't connect." She took an overlong drink on a bottle of sparkling water. "MacArthur will think it is business as usual and head for her weekly sex session with the priest but of course he won't be there. Getting a key to the church was easy, the priest gives them out to the cleaners and church elders like confetti. We'll let ourselves in and wait for her. She always uses the side entrance and of course she'll wonder what the van is doing there but will wander in regardless to find out what's happening."

"And we'll overpower her and get her into the van?" said Desiro.

Paula was shaking her head. "Not necessary, no need for any physical violence or noise I have something in my handbag that will do that for us."

Gianfranco smiled. "You think of everything."

"That's what you've paid me for. When I tell you I'll come up with the goods you can be sure I'll deliver. I want to work with the church again and meet your colleagues; this is my one and only chance to prove myself."

Gianfranco wanted to tell her that she'd done more than enough but why tell her now.

The girl appeared to be willing to do anything to please him. Anything at all. It was good to know and might come in useful should she decide to reject his advances at a later date. There was something immensely satisfying in getting a girl into bed against her will.

~

Father Todd Powell could not shake the feeling of guilt as he walked towards his car. It was the same every week as he made the forty minute drive to his parish church. He knew it was wrong, against everything he had been taught from an early age and yet deep down he knew he was only satisfying the natural urges that the good Lord had instilled within his body.

He had been a virgin when she first came to him and instinctively knew that the request for individual tuition of the Bible would lead to something far more dangerous. And he had fought it... initially... he convinced himself that God would give him the strength to resist her. The musky aroma of the natural body odour and expensive perfume had awakened something in him that he had never felt before. And as she edged ever closer during the class their thighs touched. They instinctively looked at each other at that precise moment and a surge of something he couldn't quite describe flowed through him. He read somewhere that it was a chemical reaction; a mixture of lust and love that try as he might was unable to control.

She made the first real move. He convinced himself that it wasn't all his fault and what normal man could have possibly backed away from what happened next. She kissed him hard and her tongue probed and pushed forcefully between his lips. At that point he was positively useless, a shaking, nervous, inexperienced, quivering wreck. She had felt for him and as she squeezed hard he convinced himself that it was the most exquisite feeling he had ever experienced. That first session hadn't lasted overlong. She'd unzipped his jeans lowered herself onto her knees and taken him in her mouth. She brought him expertly to climax within a minute or two as he exploded into the back of her throat and she'd kept her mouth there as she drank down every last drop.

And then he had cried. The tears had flowed as she held him tight and he knew that his life would never be the same again. Everything he had worked for, everything he believed in lay in ruins.

But the individual Bible classes continued and he realised how hard it was to say no. He longed for his weekly trysts with the mysterious girl. He told himself it was wrong but there was nothing he could do about it and yes, he had to admit it he was falling hopelessly in love. He would tell her exactly that today.

Light rain fell from the grey Chicago sky as he opened the car door and climbed into the driver's seat. He closed the door and took a deep breath.

Decisions decisions.

He had contemplated leaving the church but then again was that the coward's way out? Why shouldn't he serve the church as he always had and continue with God's work? Nobody need ever know.

He needed to find out exactly what her feelings were too. That was the first step. If she truly loved him as much as he loved her then they could work anything out.

"Damn. What was wrong with this bloody car?"

Twenty Three

For truly, without the wickedness of women, to say nothing of witchcraft, the world would still remain proof against innumerable dangers. Hear what Valerius said to Rufinus ... he means that a woman is beautiful to look upon, contaminating to the touch, and deadly to keep. MM

Paula had laid the small syringe on a table by the side of the doorway. Gianfranco paced nervously around the church.

"Where is she damn it?" He looked at his watch yet again. "Twenty minutes late."

"Relax," she said. "She'll be here soon."

There was a slight pause before Paula spoke again. "She's closer than you think."

Desiro turned to face her. At that moment it came to him. She had said *boot of the car*. When she'd been discussing the kidnap she'd said boot not trunk. An American wouldn't say boot an American would say trunk.

His mouth dropped and the words he wanted to say just wouldn't form.

"I changed my appearance," she said calmly. "It's amazing what a little plastic surgery can do."

She reached into her handbag. "Everything has worked out just fine Gianfranco, just perfectly."

"You – MacArthur?" he said.

The girl nodded. "That's right Celine MacArthur." She raised the weapon and pulled the trigger.

∼

It was just after 11.30 when Todd Powell ran into the church all flustered. She was sitting patiently on a pew.

"Paula I'm so sorry, my car wouldn't start and then the phone ... I couldn't contact you I'm sorry."

She stood. "Don't worry Todd, better late than never."

"And that dirty great van out there. Who's parked that there? I could hardly get through the door."

She looked towards the open doorway and she walked towards him. "That's your vehicle Todd... your hearse."

She opened her handbag and reached inside.

Twenty Four

Let us consider another property of hers, the voice. For as she is a liar by nature, so in her speech she stings while she delights us. Wherefore her voice is like the song of the Sirens, who with their sweet melody entice the passers-by and kill them. For they kill them by emptying their purses, consuming their strength, and causing them to forsake God. MM

Samantha Kerr hadn't slept well. It was over a month since her last message from Lucrecia Mathren, she'd gone to ground or got bored.

She made a quick cup of tea and made her way through to the computer where she quickly logged on. Something was gnawing away at her about what Lucrecia had mentioned in her last message about Aberdeen and she had every intention of spending an hour trawling through the archive newspapers from the north of Scotland, she'd put it off far too long, had had a half-hearted attempt a couple of weeks ago but needed to really get her teeth into it, there was something about Aberdeen that was significant. It was then that she noticed the Facebook icon was displaying a message.

She clicked open.

Oh such joy such pleasure. Two birds with one stone or should I say two birds with one gun. What an incredible weapon the tazer is and freely available on the streets of Chicago for around fifty dollars. The joy to see the fear on the Italian's face knowing there was nothing he could do. Not that I gave him a chance, I squeezed the trigger and before he knew it he was thrashing about on the floor like a floundering fish as one hundred thousand volts interrupted his superficial muscle functions. Oh how I enjoyed that beautiful moment. His face was contorted in agony and his eyes begged for mercy but of course I had none to give.

Sam almost choked on her tea and a wry smile crept across her face. This girl truly was mentally unbalanced, now she'd jumped across the pond and killed a couple more in Chicago. As much as she wanted to delete Lucrecia Mathren and log out, she couldn't help but read on.

Eventually he lapsed into unconsciousness and I administered the drug that would keep him that way for several hours. Lover boy wandered in fifteen minutes later. By that time I had managed to bundle the first of my bodies into the van and my priest was unaware that he was next in line. I told him to sit down as I took out the tazer. I asked him if he had seen one before. Before he could answer the two stun probes had embedded themselves in his chest.

It was the priest who came round first. I watched from a darkened corner of the basement, as his eyes grew accustomed to his surroundings. His eyes fell on the interrogation chair and the Strappado and the other various pieces of apparatus. His look changed from one of bewilderment to that of sheer horror. I raised myself from my seat and walked towards him.

"See what games the Vatican has supplied for us priest."

He shook his head.

"Your wonderful, peace loving, goodwill to all mankind, hypocritical fucking church."

I stroked at the interrogation chair. It was as clear as bottled water that the chair had been meant for me.

I ran my hands over the sharp spikes that protruded from the backrest, the armrests and the seat. Normally reserved for the poor bitches accused of practising witchcraft. The poor unfortunate was forced into the chair and the straps were gradually tightened until her body was a mass of holes. Sometimes the inquisitor would place weights on her too. I walked over and knelt in front of him. My priest, my lover was on the verge of tears, he was sweating and mucous ran freely from his nose as he thrashed and pulled at his bindings. He was in denial I could see it in his eyes. Surely he'd been given a little tuition on the inquisition and the witch hunts? Surely he'd been given a history book somewhere down the line?

The priest looked me in the eyes and told me he loved me. I confess he took me by surprise. He asked me what game

I was playing and repeated that he loved me with all his heart and he would forgive whatever I had done. I froze. I do not like these words they do not sound sincere. Words. Mere fucking insincere shit and drivel, words and letters fucking words and letters. My thoughts were interrupted by a muffled groan that came from the other side of the room. Senor Desiro was coming round too.

He was in a swivel chair and I spun him round. He focussed in on the machinery that would ultimately kill him, the Strappado, a very simple method of torture that harnesses the use of gravity to exploit a weakness in the human body, the shoulder joints. I told him his hands would be tied behind his back and I'd hoist him up by a pulley.

Oh how I laughed at him as I described what would happen

"Your muscles will kick in of course but they can only do so much. It takes about 140 pounds of force to dislocate both shoulders." I walked over to where he sat and squeezed at his biceps. They were solid, a testimony to good clean living and thousands of hours in the gym. I'd need to tie some weights to his feet to dislocate those strong well defined shoulders.

Desiro spat at me. "You crazed fucking bitch you won't get away with this."

I was enjoying the moment. Of course I'd get away with it.

"You might kill me," he spat, "but we're on to you, the whole might of the Vatican are on to you and even now our men are on their way here."

A bluff.

I pulled the rope of the Strappado over towards him and secured the rope tightly around his wrists that were tied behind the back of his chair. Once I was certain they were secure I untied him from the chair. He made a lunge for me but I was expecting it. His head was at the perfect height as he propelled himself from the chair. My foot caught him square on the chin as his jaw bone shattered and he collapsed onto the floor. Blood ran from his mouth as I knelt down beside him and told him he'd need to be a little quicker than that. He was groaning. "You're not so fucking big and clever and powerful now are you?" I said

It took him some time before he spoke again.

Was I imagining things or was he forcing a smile?

He grimaced in pain as he spoke. "Montserrat and Barberini are on their way bitch."

Sam froze as the teacup fell from her grasp and smashed onto the floor. *Barberini!* She'd said Barberini, the Cardinal who had been to Liverpool Police HQ. How could Lucrecia Mathren possibly have known about him?

Sam picked up the broken pieces from the floor and dropped them into the bin and then walked through to the kitchen for a cloth. She was shaking her head, muttering to herself. "She's telling the truth, that's the only explanation; she's in Chicago, killing again."

She walked back through and knelt down to wipe at the small pool of tea. She almost didn't want to read on but she forced herself.

"They are coming for you and they will fuck you up good," the dying man told me.

Hah! Montserrat and Barberini. I doubted they were on their way but I would catch up with them soon enough.

"They will torture and abuse and fuck you up and kill you like they did with your whore of a sister."

Even though I suspected what had become of Marnie, his words ripped into my sole like a red hot poker. I wanted to kill him there and then but composed myself knowing that that was exactly what his strategy was. And therefore I took my time.

I stripped him naked. I shattered six of his fingers with thumbscrews before I deployed the Strappado and it took nearly thirty minutes to finally dislocate his shoulders. It would be a slow lingering death I explained. It may take all night. Then I would start on the priest the following morning. At the moment his right shoulder 'popped' I turned to the priest. "Do you forgive me now Father?" I asked.

He nodded. The bastard nodded — he fucking nodded and I saw the sincerity in his eyes and it hurt me... it pained me so much.

I forced my gaze away from him and tried desperately hard to concentrate on Desiro but it felt as if my mind had slammed into a brick wall. My arms were sluggish and my body a dead lead weight. I could feel the perspiration enveloping my entire body droplets falling from my face and my brow onto the Strappado and the room started to spin and I forced myself to focus, focus, focus.

Sam was trembling as she closed down the MAC. Her head was pounding and she rubbed her hands together. They were wet with perspiration. She had to think, work this through. *Barberini*, she'd said. And another name too. Marnie. She wondered where she had heard the name Marnie before. An unusual name, a déjà vu moment, she'd seen that name somewhere else recently... on a TV screen perhaps.

Twenty Five

Woman is a wheedling and secret enemy. And that she is more perilous than a snare does not speak of the snare of hunters, but of devils. For men are caught not only through their carnal desires, when they see and hear women: for S. Bernard says: Their face is a burning wind, and their voice the hissing of serpents. MM

Montserrat and Barberini landed at Chicago's O'Hare Airport in the early hours of the morning. They were both exhausted and in need of rest and thought it a good idea to check into their hotel before making their way over to the safe house. As usual Montserrat was second in command and took Barberini's suggestions as orders.

"We'll catch a few hours sleep then call the car." Barberini checked his watch. "It's just after six in the morning Chicago time so if we agree to meet in the hotel bar at noon, take a drink and something light to eat then call Desiro to see how he's getting on."

"Have you heard from him?" asked Montserrat.

Barberini was already on his mobile phone scrolling through the messages and voicemails. He shook his head. "No. I spoke with him last night and he said the trap was all set. He seemed supremely confident and said he would only call if there was a problem. The girl is due at a church this morning and Desiro will be waiting for her. He'll incapacitate her and take her to the safe house."

Montserrat smiled. "He's good, Desiro?"

"One of our best brother and I have every confidence in him."

Montserrat begged the question. "So no news is good news."

"Precisely brother. Precisely."

Barberini slept surprisingly well and the alarm woke him with a start just after eleven o'clock. He checked for any messages. Nothing of any significance; a missed call from his sister in

Florence and a text message from his bank clarifying a large transfer to an account in New York.

He lifted his feet over the edge of the bed and stroked at his throbbing erection. How he wanted to pleasure himself. He resisted. Not long to wait and then the girl would do it for him. It had been far too long since he'd satisfied himself with the female form. The prostitutes of Rome were not to be trusted and his profile was too well known. It would not stand right if the whores of Rome kissed and told the world's media just what it was that the right hand man to the Holy Father, Cardinal Angelo Barberini, liked to do in a private tryst with the young female form.

Once bitten twice shy. It had been over fifteen years now. Fifteen years almost to the day that the two prostitutes came to him with their demands. He'd been stupid, allowing their games to go further and further until he'd seriously injured the younger of the two. He liked to dominate, beat and torture his whores but he'd paid them well to endure their suffering. Hell, they were the best two paid whores in Italy. What the fuck did they have to complain about? He'd went too far that day and when the whore had begged him to stop he hadn't, he'd pressed further until eventually she'd lapsed into unconsciousness with a seizure. They couldn't wake her and her accomplice had begged for an ambulance for her friend. He wouldn't allow the phone call until the equipment had been removed and he had left. Only then did he allow the call to be made.

She recovered well enough. Her brain had been starved of a little oxygen that affected her speech for a month or two but other than that she made a full recovery. But the stupid little sluts hatched a plan and came back for more with a concealed camera and a demand for a ludicrous amount of lira. The bitches thought they'd been so clever.

He'd called Antonio. Antonio would know what to do and he did. And when two headless bodies of young females were found in the River Tiber three weeks later he knew the exact identity of the two unknowns unlike the police.

He laughed to himself. Antonio's fee had been a fraction of what the whores were demanding. Antonio had understood too. He said a man had to do what a man had to do but he also had to be clever. Antonio advised that Barberini needed to indulge his pleasure away from Vatican City and from Rome, preferably outside the country.

Two or three times a year Barberini requested leave of absence from the Holy Father and he always granted his wishes, he was a good man the Holy Father. Barberini blamed the pressures of the job. He needed a few days away... no more.

He'd taken an incognito trip to Paris earlier in the year and feasted himself considerably but that vacation seemed oh so long ago. Alas there were times he wondered about his career choice and if he'd made the right decision all those years ago. He reminded himself that he was put on this earth to serve the Lord and the Church in that order and he must count himself lucky for those occasional moments when his lust was fully satisfied. He was strong willed and he would cope. Not long now he thought to himself.

He'd make up for lost time.

The cold shower quickly stemmed the blood flow to his penis and as he shivered under the water he recited the Lord's Prayer. As he finished he turned the water up to an almost unbearable level and allowed himself thirty seconds of unadulterated luxury. As he stepped from the glass cubicle his body tingled and he looked forward to the day ahead.

He dressed slowly checking himself meticulously in the mirror and then reached for his mobile phone. No missed calls while he was in the bathroom. Strange. Desiro knew what time he was landing, he should have called by now. Barberini located Desiro's number and pressed *call*. It connected... and then went straight to the provider. *The cell phone you have called is not currently available please try again later.*

Barberini frowned. And then smiled. Of course... no reception. Desiro had her and he had her in the basement of the safe house five metres below ground. That was why there was no reception and phone wouldn't connect. He made a call to the Vatican, asked them for a location on Desiro's mobile phone. The device fitted in his phone gave an accuracy of just a few metres. Precisely three minutes and 17 seconds later they returned the call. The phone was static, Desiro or the phone was in a fixed location in an area ten kilometres north of the city centre known as Lake View. The Vatican secret agent gave him the address, 41 West Roscoe Street. Barberini could not help breaking out into a wide grin. The safe house. He had her; Desiro had come up trumps once again.

The two men dined on a cold pasta salad with a side dish of selected shellfish. Barberini allowed one glass of white Chianti Reserva and informed the waiter to cork the rest of the bottle for later in the evening.

They wouldn't kill her today. They'd return tomorrow and the day after perhaps. Today was about rape and abuse, nothing more nothing less, let her know she was well and truly impaled on the hook and there would be no escape. Today they'd degrade and humiliate her in a way that she could never have imagined.

After lunch Barberini summoned the car and gave the driver the address which he punched into the sat nav. The speaker in the front of the car barked out *destination found* and Barberini settled back in his seat to enjoy the scenery en route to Lake View.

There was no need for suitcases or luggage on this particular cleansing mission. Everything they would need had been ordered in advance and yet Barberini couldn't help feeling he'd forgotten something.

Montserrat was quiet studying the route as they travelled along at a fairly sedate pace. The Chicago rush hour traffic was building and progress was slow. Barberini reached for his phone in his inside pocket and tried Desiro again. Connection. One ring. *The cell phone you have called is not currently unavailable please try again later.*

Barberini could think of only one thing, that Desiro was taking his pleasure with the girl. The bastard. If he'd spoiled her in any way this would be his last job.

The car drove along the Fulton River District and became snarled up in traffic. To the east Barberini caught glimpses of Lake Michigan. It was pretty. After they'd disposed of the girl perhaps they could stay on for a few days and make a real vacation of it. No perhaps not; it wouldn't be right. If something went wrong then they'd need to get back to the Vatican as soon as possible, they'd need to get back to the place where they'd be untouchable. He laughed inwardly. What could go wrong? He thought back to the girl's sister and the blood began to flow again. There was something incredibly satisfying about taking two sisters, and he'd make sure this bitch knew all about what they'd done to her sibling, every fucking detail. It would be the first thing they'd do. He had the lap top and he'd make sure she watched every damned frame, even the burning. Yes, especially the burning. What wonderful devices the modern day mobile phones were. Who'd have thought the quality would be so good.

"Your phone is fully charged Montserrat? He asked.

"Of course Cardinal Barberini. As always."

They passed a Bank of America on the right and as he leaned towards the dividing window that separated them from the driver, the satellite navigation screen indicated they were nearing their destination. *Turn left into West Roscoe Street one hundred yards* it announced. Barberini tapped on the window. The driver pressed a button and the window lowered several inches.

"Yes Cardinal?" He asked.

"Could you pull over as we turn into West Roscoe Street please? I feel like stretching my legs."

"Certainly Cardinal. And where would you like me to wait?"

Barberini was quick with his reply. "There's no need to wait we may be some time. I'll call you when we're ready to leave."

The driver touched his cap by way of understanding and thirty seconds later indicated as he turned into the street. He pulled over fifty metres up the road and the two men got out.

The street was well kept, the lawns at the front of each detached house well-manicured. White picket fences separated each garden and the cars in the driveway were upmarket, 4x4s, Audis and BMWs. They walked across a railway crossing and passed a fenced off baseball park on the right, children were playing in the street on bicycles and skateboards. Mid to upper class America. Once again the church's house had been chosen well, a valuable piece of real estate that would continue to grow in value and when the time was right and a sale made, a handsome profit for the Vatican. It had been that way for centuries. In the back of his mind a little voice whispered...the best bankers in the world.

As they approached the house Barberini made the sign of the cross on his chest and whispered under his breath. "Thou shalt not suffer a witch to live, whoever lieth with a beast shall surely be put to death, he that sacrificeth unto any god, save to the Lord only, he shall be utterly destroyed."

"Exodus 22 if I'm not mistaken cardinal?" Said Montserrat

"Versus 18-20 Senor Montserrat. Well done, excellent memory."

Twenty Six

All witchcraft comes from carnal lust, which is in women insatiable. See Proverbs xxx: There are three things that are never satisfied, yea, a fourth thing which says not, It is enough; that is, the mouth of the womb. Wherefore for the sake of fulfilling their lusts they consort even with devils. MM.

Ed Flynn had requested a further meeting with New York's Bishop De Genelli. It had been some months since the death of one of his priests and he had a few more questions to ask. It's not right he thought as the cab pulled up outside the apartment block in Lexington Avenue, one of the most prestigious addresses in New York. Surely the bishop would be better placed living and working in one of the less salubrious areas of the city helping where it really mattered, hands on so to speak.

He took the lift up to the 21st floor and the bishop greeted him at the open door of the apartment.

"I saw the cab pull up detective," he said. "You are as punctual as ever."

Flynn shook his hand. "I try my best Bishop I really do."

The Bishop beckoned him through the open door; the smell of freshly brewed coffee filled the spacious entrance lobby.

"I like that in a man detective, we all have busy lives these days."

Flynn couldn't shake the feeling that the Bishop was already throwing hints for him to leave even though he'd barely been in the apartment ten seconds. The Bishop took a deliberate look at his wristwatch. Flynn's suspicions were confirmed.

"Coffee?"

"Please Bishop, that would be just what the doctor ordered.

"Maria," the Bishop called out.

A Philippino girl appeared holding a garish feather duster. She wore a black and white matching maid's uniform and asked Flynn how he took his coffee.

"Black with one sugar thanks."

Bishop De Genelli led them through to the lounge.

"It's always nice to see you again Mr Flynn but I'm assuming this little rendezvous is about business and not pleasure?"

Flynn stood by the large dining table by the window. It had to be one of the finest views in New York.

"Yes Bishop you've guessed correctly. If I may I want to ask a few more questions relating to the death of Father O'Neil. I've been going through some unsolved cases further afield, in Europe, Spain and France to be exact and there are one or two similarities with the death of your priest."

The maid placed two coffees on the table and the bishop sat at the table. Flynn pulled out a seat and joined him. It wasn't in Flynn's nature to dwell on small talk. He got straight to the point.

"Are you familiar with the torture methods of the mediaeval inquisitions Bishop?"

The Bishop took a small sip from his coffee cup. Ed Flynn caught the look. He was composing himself, thinking before engaging his brain. He gave a carefully thought out answer, one he'd given a hundred times before.

"I am familiar with my church's history detective. I consider myself well read and I have indeed indulged in many books relating to that black period. You have to remember that mankind was still evolving, the great scientists had not yet discovered the secrets of how the planets moved and behaved, many believed that if a sailing ship travelled too long in the wrong direction it would fall off the edge of the earth. My predecessors were no different and strange legends and superstitions were believed by most men, no matter how far-fetched they appear to us now. Witchcraft was considered common place."

Flynn was nodding. "I agree Bishop, don't forget I am a practising Catholic too and I'm not proud of what our church did to those poor women."

"It's better that we bury the past and move on," the Bishop said. "They were dark times, the world was a wicked place back in those days."

"It still is." Said Flynn.

The bishop took another deliberate look at his watch. "Detective I'm a very busy man can we cut to the chase?"

"Certainly," said Flynn. "I might be a million miles from the mark here Bishop but over the last few years there have been a series of deaths across the world that appear to have been stage managed to simulate some of the tortures deployed by the church from those err... as you call it, dark times." He paused for a second. "In France and in Spain, in England and Scotland too."

The Bishop shrugged his shoulders. "I'll take your word for it detective but what has this got to do with me?"

Flynn reached for his briefcase. "And here in New York too."

He carefully pulled the photograph from an envelope and slid it across the table. The bishop winced as he focussed in on it.

"Detective, I thought I had managed to erase that image from my mind. Thank you for bringing it back to me again, I fear I will endure many more sleepless nights."

Flynn thought about apologising to the Bishop but decided to leave it for the time being.

"This is the photograph of Father O'Neil and what I believe was a crude attempt to replicate the Judas Cradle."

The Bishop appeared to study the picture closely. "Yes I agree, I am familiar with the Judas Cradle and I take your point. The Judas Cradle was so named because it's purpose was that of betrayal. Many a victim gave the name of a heretic or a witch after a short period of time on the cradle."

The Bishop stood and walked towards the large window. Sunlight streamed in and for a moment he was almost silhouetted as Flynn's eyes grew accustomed to the light change.

The Bishop turned. "So NYPD now believe Father O'Neil was murdered?"

Flynn shook his head. "No Bishop they do not."

The Bishop frowned. Deep furrows rippled across his brow. "You speak in riddles detective. Suicide then? An accident perhaps?"

Flynn pulled the photograph across the large table glancing at it before pushing it back in the envelope. He stood and walked over to the window gazing out across Long Island.

He spoke. "NYPD have an open mind at this stage. I'm in no doubt however that he was murdered."

Flynn let out a deep sigh as he turned to face the Bishop. "I only have a short period of time left Bishop and I am overworked. There are ten murders in this City every week and I swear they have me and my partner on most of them." He took out a handkerchief and wiped at his brow. "If something looks like an accident or a suicide then the NYPD take on it is that it probably was and therefore why spend valuable resources trying to find the murderer of what could turn out not to be a murder after all."

"I see..." said the bishop. "It makes sense I suppose."

"Yes," said Flynn. "Unless the death is beyond all doubt the cases are generally pushed into a slush pile until something new comes to light."

"So something has come to light?"

Flynn was already shaking his head. "Not really."

The Bishop frowned, a puzzled look pulled across his face.

"Then why are you here detective?" He asked. "We are no further forward regarding the unfortunate death of Father O'Neil and I don't know anything about the deaths of priests and bishops in France or Spain and England."

Flynn's heart skipped a beat. He'd never mentioned that the victims were priests and bishops. Had the Bishop just assumed that they were or did he know more?

He paused for a second or two and then spoke. "I'm here to ask you an honest question
Bishop De Genelli."

"Go on."

"Have the Vatican connected these murders, have they contacted you for further information."

The Bishop laughed. "Ha detective, do you think I have a direct line to the Pope?"

"You're a Bishop and a murder has been committed in your diocese," Flynn said. "One of your own priests, I would think that someone in the Vatican would have at least picked up the phone to offer their condolences."

The Bishop appeared a little taken a back. Of course someone would have phoned that was fairly obvious. Flynn watched as once again he took a little longer than was normal to answer the question.

"I remember now. One of the Cardinals in the Vatican, Cardinal Barberini did call me." The Bishop said. "He offered his and the Holy Father's prayers a week or so after Father O'Neil's death."

Flynn had been a policeman on the streets of New York for too long. He'd lived on his wits and his intuition and his hunches and he knew when a man was lying. He laughed at the television talk shows that interacted with the public and used lie detector machines to catch out the cheating husband or the son who'd stolen from his mother for the price of a fix. There was no need for machines when Flynn was around and as he bore into the soul of the holier than though Bishop who watched over his flock from New York his eyes cried out LIAR! He'd had a lot more than a polite phone call and he knew about the other murders in France and further afield, he'd stake his reputation on it.

"Bishop De Genelli," Flynn pleaded. "Please tell me if the Vatican are involved in these investigations, I want to catch this killer as much as you do."

The Bishop offered no response.

He again denied any Vatican involvement and started checking his watch every few minutes to the point of rudeness. The deaths were a mere coincidence he claimed and wasn't so sure they were even murders especially the four bishops in Liverpool.

Eddie Flynn produced more photographs, the Monsignor hanging in his Cathedral in Aberdeen and a Priest trussed up stone dead hanging from a rope in an apartment in Paris.

"These are not coincidences Bishop," said Flynn, "and they are not suicides or accidents." He pushed them across the table. "Look at them for Christ's sake!"

The Bishop turned to face him anger etched on his face. "I'll ask you to leave now detective, I won't have anyone take the Lords name in vain under my roof."

"But Bishop I need—"

The Bishop had raised his voice several decibels. "Maria."

The maid appeared in the lounge almost immediately.

"Please show the policeman out."

Ed Flynn protested and begged as the Bishop walked rapidly from the room but his remonstrations fell on deaf ears and he found himself alone with a clearly embarrassed cleaning lady. Flynn picked up his file and his case notes as the maid led him from the room.

The Bishop walked into his study and sat down at the desk. He reached for a glass and the decanter of Cognac and poured himself a generous measure. The large mouthful calmed him somewhat and within a few minutes he held out his hand and steadied it then picked up the phone. The phone rang out for two minutes before he eventually replaced the receiver. Baberini was not in his office. He located his desk diary and flicked through the address section. Barberini had a mobile. For emergencies he said. This was most certainly an emergency.

"Cardinal it is me De Genelli."

"De Genelli. How are you? How is the Big Apple?"

"The New York Police know sir," he said. "I have just had a visit from them and they know all about the murders."

"Tell me Bishop," said the man from the Vatican. "Tell me all about your chat with the NYPD."

The phone call lasted seven and a half minutes. There were no niceties or small talk. Afterwards Barberini made a phone call, to the Mayor's office on Broadway.

Ed Flynn was building his case notes by the day. He was concentrating on the deaths of the four Bishops in the United Kingdom and was now in no doubt that the church was well aware that a serial killer with a vendetta against their organisation was on the loose.

But his hands were tied. What could he possibly do about it when NYPD were still burying their head in the sand? He'd request a meeting with his superiors at the earliest possible opportunity and he'd make them change their mind.

Flynn worked non-stop for six days building his case and felt his argument was more than compelling. He discussed each individual murder with his partner Ken Nugent and as he walked into the meeting at nine thirty on a wet Wednesday morning he was more than confident that NYPD would make the killings their highest priority and give the case international recognition. That would allow him to liaise with Interpol and who knows even the Vatican.

The meeting lasted the rest of the morning and at the end Flynn was physically and mentally drained. He walked back through to his office. Nugent sat with his size nine shoes on the desk, nursing a hot coffee. "How goes it partner?"

Flynn nodded and gave a half smile. "Couldn't have done anymore buddy. They know as much as me now. Go and get your good friend a coffee 'cause I could do with one."

Exactly one week later Flynn was called in to a noon meeting. As soon as he walked in he knew the decision had been made and judging by the faces of the assembled panel it was not good news. They didn't beat about the bush. They were clinical and concise. Their spokesperson explained that Interpol was a politically neutral organisation and their constitution forbade it to undertake any interventions or activities of a political, military, racial and yes, religious nature. They would relook at the New York case of Father O'Neil but the rest of the suspicious deaths were strictly off limits for NYPD.

Flynn felt frustrated and a little angry too. He'd presented a clear cut case he felt, the evidence was overwhelming. What was it with this hierarchy? He appreciated the department was under pressure and understaffed but this was a serial killer targeting a church. He looked at the panel. Good Catholics almost to a man. Commissioner Daly, an elder in his own church and Captain Helton an assistant treasurer to the Diocese of the city.

This didn't make any sense and for once Flynn was speechless. Captain Helton explained that the Vatican were more than capable of cleaning up their own mess and indeed had their own investigators in every country. What was he saying? They were one of the finest police departments in the world. Were they really about to step back and let a church take over?

Commissioner Daly coughed through a closed fist. He was clearing his throat, commanding attention.

He spoke. "There is one other thing detective Flynn."

"Sir?"

"You've been with the department twenty nine years, thirty years come October then you retire."

"Yes sir."

The commissioner caught a frog in his throat, cleared it quickly. "We're bringing that date forward a little. Giving you an extra few months holiday on full pay."

Helton chipped in. "Not many cops make it this far unscathed Flynn, we'd hate anything to happen to you in the next few months."

Flynn was open mouthed, shaking his head. "No – no Sir, I don't want to—"

"Take Mrs Flynn up to the White Mountains," said Helton. "Reflect on your tremendous service to the city and catch a few fish while you're at it."

The commissioner grinned as he said the department had also agreed two months advance holiday pay too. The commissioner said he was one of the best police officers the NYPD had ever had.

"Today," the commissioner replied. "We'd like your desk cleared today."

Edward Flynn was in a state of shock as he walked out of the office down the long corridor and took the lift down to the first floor. As he walked into his office Nugent was shouting and cursing at two plain clothed FBI men who were already clearing Flynn's desk and dismantling his desk top computer.

Nugent turned to his former partner. "Ed, what the fucks going on here? What have you been up to?"

Flynn shrugged his shoulders as he picked up the photo of his wife from the desk and slipped it into his pocket.

A stony faced agent informed him that there was a car waiting outside. They'd travel over to Ed's apartment and remove any documentation relating to an investigation he had been unauthorised to carry out.

Nugent scowled and bellowed at the agent. "You have a fucking warrant for that Mr Feebie?"

The agent reached into his pocket and placed the necessary paperwork on the desk.

Flynn felt like a criminal. There was no other way to describe it. The agents were only doing their job and of course they were full of apologies. Nevertheless they went through his apartment with a fine tooth comb, even though Flynn had handed over a pile of paperwork relating to the investigation, immediately they entered his home. After four hours they appeared satisfied and left.

This wasn't the way he'd envisaged his last day at the office. He checked his watch. Corinne would be home soon. Thank God she hadn't been here to witness it.

Fuck it he thought to himself. Fuck the department, fuck the Commissioner and the Captain and fuck the Church. The bastards, the utter fucking bastards.

Eddie Flynn grinned a beaming smile as Corinne walked through the door. He opened his arms inviting a hug. "It's over," he shouted. "I'm a free man, retired as of today."

Corinne smiled too and rushed into his arms and then Ed Flynn broke down and cried.

Twenty Seven

More such reasons could be brought forward, but to the understanding it is sufficiently clear that it is no matter for wonder that there are more women than men found infected with the heresy of witchcraft. Ed Flynn sat tying some new fishing flies for the trip to Newfound Lake. This was something he'd have time to do now. Usually it was a trip down town to pick up the ridiculously priced fly hooks, the Green Highlanders, Mayfly Cripples and the Ultra Damsel. Not anymore. Now he'd make his own and he'd experiment with different feather colours and bindings and a strip or two of silver paper and save an enormous amount of money at the same time.

Fuck the department. He was still bitter, of course he was and yet determined he wouldn't let them get to him and spoil his retirement.

Corrine sat at the computer desk completing an online grocery delivery to coincide with their arrival.

"Some beer Ed?" She asked.

Ed pushed his right thumb in the air. "Two or three hundred cases." He replied with a grin.

Corinne re-jigged the order onto the screen. "Don't think I'm gonna let you turn into an alcoholic up there now that you've nothing to do. I'm keeping my eye on you Ed Flynn, you bet your life I am."

Ed lowered the glasses further onto the end of his nose trying hard to locate the end of the thread he'd just lost.

"Whatever you say darling. Whatever you say."

A few minutes passed before Corinne spoke again. "Have you been playing around with this PC Ed?"

Alarm bells sounded. "Not for a week or so."

"And what were you working on exactly?"

Ed knew exactly what he'd been working on. He'd been scanning everything to do with that case. "A file called 101." He replied.

"You filed it in your 'Eddie' folder?"

"Yes."

"On the desktop?"

"Yes."

He heard the keypad being tapped again.

"It's not here," Corinne stated. "Your folder is missing."

Eddie stood and walked over to the computer leaning over his wife's shoulder. "That's impossible," he said.

"It's not here," she repeated, "your folder has gone and so is the document file. I have the details of the grocery store in there and an up to date stock list and it's gone too and the copies of our passports and everything else, it's all damn well gone."

Ed massaged his wife's right shoulder. "Calm down honey, files don't just disappear they'll be there somewhere."

But they weren't. Ed stood over his wife while she checked again and again. They then checked the trash icon. That was empty too. They reset and rebooted the computer – twice and still they couldn't retrieve the missing files.

"My documents weren't so important," she said. "It just means I'll have to do the important ones again. What about you Ed, was that file important?"

Flynn was cursing inside but on the surface he remained calm. "I'll take it down to the computer store first thing tomorrow. I'm not sure how these things work but surely the experts can help us out."

"You didn't answer me," she said. "Was that file important to you?"

He let out a sigh and then kissed his wife on the cheek. "Old work stuff honey, I can live without it."

Twenty Eight

That Witches who are midwives in various ways kill the child conceived in the womb, and procure an abortion; or if they do not do this offer New-born Children to Devils. MM

Barberini paused just before the front door. He held out a hand across Montserrat's chest.

"Stop." He said. "Something's wrong. There's no car, no van."

Montserrat looked around. "I'm not with you Cardinal. Should there be?"

Barberini took a step forward as he noticed the door was slightly ajar. How else would he get her in the house without anybody seeing? He'd need a vehicle. He planned to drug her in order to get her here quietly."

Montserrat thought for a moment before speaking. "A stolen vehicle?"

"Probably."

"Then he's probably brought her here then drove the car somewhere else, after all he wouldn't want it parked here.

Barberini still didn't look entirely convinced. He located his mobile phone in his breast pocket and made a call.

"I'm calling Desiro," he said.

The phone rang out and eventually Baberini pressed end. He pressed several more buttons and put the phone to his ear. "It's me. Can you get me a location on Desiro's phone again? I'll wait."

The operating agent came back, quicker this time. "Exactly same location as last time Cardinal."

"The phone goes straight to answer machine, can you tell me whether it's switched off or is out of signal."

"I'm sorry sir I can't."

Barberini pressed end. Desiro should have called by now. He didn't like it one little bit.

Montserrat was encouraging him. "Come Cardinal she is waiting for us. I can almost smell her. You are getting paranoid in your old age."

Barberini took a step closer. "You are probably right Senor Montserrat, please, after you."

The two men walked over the threshold of 41 West Roscoe Street. The entrance hallway was dimly lit but Barberini's eyes grew slowly accustomed to the surroundings. He crossed his chest at the site of the crucifix suspended on the wall opposite. He couldn't believe how normal it all looked and the furniture and the décor made the house almost lived in. But no one lived here nor was it up for rent. This was one of the church's special houses for special occasions. They walked through to the kitchen area. Barberini half expected a freshly brewed pot of coffee standing on the hob but it wasn't to be. Through into the lounge a large plasma television played to itself the sound on mute. The rest of the house was quiet.

Montserrat spoke. "They must be in the basement, how do we get down there?"

Barberini pulled out a map from his jacket pocket. "From the garage," he said. "There's a door that leads from the garage." He looked at the map and turned it 180°.

"Back into the entrance hall, there is a door we missed as we walked in."

The two men walked slowly back into the hallway. Barberini was breathing a little harder than he would have liked despite not exerting himself. He was annoyed with himself, just what was wrong with him today?

Montserrat reached for the handle, turned it and pushed the door open as they peered into the darkness below. Montserrat was grinning but Barberini was unable to raise a smile. Montserrat had already located the light switch and was making his way down the stairs.

"Be careful." It was all Barberini could think to say.

Barberini was still half way down the stairs when he heard the scream that sent a shiver the length of his spine and made the hairs on the back of his neck stand on end. It was Montserrat and now he could hear him sobbing uncontrollably.

"What is it?" He called out. "God dammit what is it?"

Montserrat didn't answer him at first but he could hear him crying. Barberini hesitated and yet knew he had little option but to descend the stairs.

A cry this time, a cry for help between the tears. "Cardinal Barberini, please, please come quickly you need to see this for yourself."

Barberini was a little relieved that Montserrat seemed to be in one piece and he forced himself to descend into the basement one slow step at a time.

His relief didn't last long as his eyes fixed on the scene that had greeted Montserrat causing him so much anguish and distress.

A body hung from the ceiling beam, its arms bent and broken, tied behind its back. As he stood rooted to the spot the naked body swung slowly round so that he could clearly see that it was a man. The torso was covered in blood which appeared to have come from the open mouth of the victim. Barberini crossed his chest and reached into his pocket for a small bible which he carried with him everywhere. It was only right that he should say some sort of prayer for his good friend and colleague Gianfranco Desiro.

Without even touching the body Barberini knew he was dead. His features were cold and his skin bone white. Montserrat kneeled in front of him begging the questions why and who could do such a thing. Barberini walked over to him and ordered him to compose himself. Montserrat stood, tears running down his cheeks.

Montserrat was in no mood to listen. "What sort of monster have we unleashed Cardinal?"

It was a question Barberini was asking himself. All of a sudden Monteserrat's eyes opened wide, his eyeballs bulging, a picture of fear. He was looking over Barberini's shoulder, his gaze locked onto something else.

"An – other – another one."

He raised his hand slowly and pointed into the darkened far corner of the cellar. Barberini swung round. He recognised the inquisitors chair immediately. The man was bound tight by the arms with several leather straps as were his thighs. Around his chest and his waist were two thick buckled belts which bit into his skin. His body and the chair were streaked with blood and a red crimson lake pooled under the seat. The man was naked from the waist up save for one thing. His head hung heavy, his chin lay on his chest but Barberini could still make out the unmistakable shape which hung loosely around his throat. A bloodstained, priest's collar.

Twenty Nine

It is witchcraft, not only when anyone is unable to perform the carnal act, of which we have spoken above; but also when a woman is prevented from conceiving, or is made to miscarry after she has conceived. A third and fourth method of witchcraft is when they have failed to procure an abortion, and then either devour the child or offer it to a devil. MM.

Eddie Flynn had fished for seventeen days in a row. The lake was well stocked and the fishing had been good and because of the limited space in the small chest freezer in the garage he'd taken to throwing his catch back. It was something he'd never done before and prided himself that everything he'd ever caught had been eaten by him and his wife or at least given to family or friends. He couldn't do that living on Newfound Lake because all of his near neighbours were fishermen too.

On day eighteen he decided not to fish and to rig up the new PC and printer that had been delivered several days before. It was just after three o'clock when he had everything how he wanted it and punched the internet codes into the keypad. He hovered the curser over the signal icon in the bottom right hand corner. *You are now connected to the internet* it announced in tiny white writing that had Eddie reaching for his glasses.

He eased back in his chair wondering what site he should browse first. That article by the reporter in Liverpool, he thought. What was it that she wrote that interested him so much?

Flynn cursed to himself as he trawled over and copied all of the old stuff he'd found and stored in file 101. Why was he doing this? He was retired for Christ sake.

The following day he was back in the chair at a ridiculous early hour trying to find and locate the reporter from Liverpool. Everything he'd read on the deaths of the four Bishops pointed to a tragic accident except this one article written by Samantha Kerr. It wouldn't do any harm to speak to her just to clear a few things up and then he could get back to his fishing. She'd probably admit she'd used a little poetic licence, as all good reporters do and that perhaps the Vatican delegation hadn't ever existed in the first place.

Marnie Wishart. It had taken Sam Kerr no more than ten minutes to locate the press article she'd remembered reading in the Sunday Times. It was strange; she'd never known anyone called Marnie in her entire life, not many Marnie's in Liverpool 8 after all, but here, in the space of just a few weeks she'd come across two.

She was speed reading the article when her finger drifted over a sentence that made her catch her breath. It had mentioned that the missing girl had recently visited Aberdeen Cathedral to attend a family wedding; the police were following up local leads. The Cathedral in Aberdeen was where a member of the clergy had been found hanged. A coincidence?

She opened up another Google search window and typed in *suicide, Aberdeen Cathedral* and opened up the third search down. It was the front page of the Aberdeen Evening Express, Monsignor Campbell had been found hanged it stated, a suspected suicide, the funeral held towards the end of the week.

Sam reached for her cup of coffee. She took a mouthful and swirled the almost cold liquid around her mouth before swallowing. Lucrecia Mathren had mentioned a sister they had killed, *Even though I suspected what had become of Marnie, his words ripped into my sole like a red hot poker.*

Sam opened up another window and typed Marnie Wishart into the search engine. Another article this time, The Times, *Marnie Wishart had not been found, no kidnap or ransom demands had ever been received and she was now officially a missing person.*

She was shaking her head. No, this isn't possible she whispered to herself. Marnie Wishart, the sister of the killer, married in Aberdeen, the Monsignor killed several few weeks later and then the bride herself is kidnapped? No, surely it was coincidence, nothing more, the Monsignor hadn't even been murdered, he'd hanged himself.

Her entire being cried out leave it alone, do something more practical like find a job, send those CVs away that she'd been hanging onto for some weeks. She'd do that just as soon as she'd made herself a fresh coffee. She was about to stand up when the g-mail icon flagged up – she had a new email. She pressed open. It was from someone she'd never corresponded with before, *edflynn101@gmail.com*

It was the subject matter that caught her eye, *The Four Bishops* it said, so despite a few reservations she had no option but to open it.

It was short and to the point. The sender claimed he was a retired police officer and wanted to talk to her about the article she'd written in the newspaper.

"That bloody article," she muttered to herself, "the article that should never have been printed."

She hadn't forgiven her boss for printing and manipulating the piece but was more than curious about what this ex-policeman wanted to discuss. He said he had been involved in a similar case in New York and wanted to tie up a few loose ends. He left a phone number of his home in New Hampshire and warned her about the time difference on the other side of the pond.

She searched world time zones and found New Hampshire was five hours behind GMT. She looked at her watch, she'd give him a few hours to wake up and give him a call. Her message to Lucrecia was a simple one. '*Who is Marnie?*'

Twenty seven minutes later Lucrecia replied. '*Ask Monsignor Campbell.*'

She knew thirty seconds into the conversation with Ed Flynn that he was no crank and she was pleased she'd made the call. Ed opened up immediately and she was so relieved that someone else in the world shared her theory about the murders and the cover up by the Church. She told him about another suspicious death, the Monsignor in Aberdeen. Ed knew nothing about it as it hadn't come to light during his investigations. She didn't tell him about

Lucrecia Mathren at that point in time, she'd need to do a little more research.

The conversation lasted over an hour. Towards the end Ed mentioned how he'd been forced out of his job and something told him it was as a direct result of being overenthusiastic in his investigations into the murder of the Priest in New York.

"I'm unemployed too Ed," Sam disclosed, "but I can't blame the church this time as I was the one who resigned."

They spoke a little longer like long lost friends and just before Ed hung up he said she should consider having a little holiday on Newfound Lake. They lived on the lakeshore he explained and the climate was pleasant at this time of year and they both had more than a little time on their hands. They would compare investigation files and do a little more research. Who knows what they would come up with? The picture Ed painted sounded idyllic and she had more than enough money pushed to one side with no ties, not even a bloody cat, but no, she politely declined. It would be sheer madness to jet off to the other side of the Atlantic to spend time with a man she'd known as long as a telephone conversation.

After the phone call finished Sam logged into Facebook and pushed another message across to Lucrecia. It was a simple one. *Who are you?*

Ten minutes passed. There was no reply.

She decided to take a quick look at which airport serviced New Hampshire. The wonders of the Internet. Not that she was going to fly over, she was just a little curious. The nearest airport was Portsmouth and there was another airport called Manchester. She laughed inwardly, Manchester to Manchester, there's a novelty. After twenty minutes browsing she just happened to find a one way ticket for under five hundred pounds and a one slightly cheaper from London Heathrow. I could live with that she thought as she daydreamed, a couple of nights in London and a week or two in New Hampshire. And even though she knew she wouldn't be going she saved the site in her *favourites* file and reopened the Facebook tab. Strange, Lucrecia was showing as on line, she would have received that message over thirty minutes ago but hadn't replied.

The message from Lucrecia came in fifty minutes later and Sam knew why she had taken so long to reply. Her response to the simple question took Sam's breath away. All of a sudden the drama had notched up to a new level and something deep inside told Sam that she was in no doubt that she was in communication with the person responsible for the deaths of Catholic Church employees around the globe.

I'm not your stereotypical type of serial killer if there is such a thing. The experts, the police psychologists and profile builders will tell you on the websites of the world that there is a fairly accurate assessment of the average psychopath who kills more than three people and therefore qualifies the tag 'serial'.

A serial killer is normally a white male in their twenties or thirties, who targets strangers. The average age when serial killers claim their first victim is around 29 years of age and 100% of all serial killers that we know of have had a criminal record prior to embarking on their killing spree. I'm almost laughing as I tell you I have never been in trouble with the police before, not as much as a parking ticket.

I first heard about the mediaeval inquisitions and witch-hunts when I was around twenty years of age and watched a documentary on independent television. I sat gripped, almost trembling with respect and admiration for the poor women who the church massacred en masse for three hundred years. I'll repeat that in case you think you've misread it. The church tortured and killed women for more than three hundred years.

Something in me changed that night. I found the programme on Youtube and watched it over and over again. I immersed myself in the books written around this remarkable period. I knew it was only a matter of time before she would come calling.

Most serial killers are loners... unable to form an adult relationship and generally with a history of physical or sexual abuse.

Again, that's where I differ. I'm not a loner; in fact I'm a well-respected pillar of society, very successful in a business that takes me all over the world.

I am far from religious but I was born into Catholicism. You could say it was an accident of birth much in the same way a Muslim or Hindu child is born and propelled into their religion. That's the really stupid part about religion. Very few are given the choice to even think about the options. They take a child and say "That's your faith." No choice, no discussion. Stupid, stupid, stupid.

You believed your guardians and peers didn't you? If at three years of age they told you that two and two was five then you would have believed them.

Religion is set in stone, an accident of birth and if you are born a Muslim you will always be a Muslim or an Irish Catholic you will always be an Irish Catholic and if the Priest at mass each Sunday told you the poor Church needed a few more pounds because they were a little short of money then the chances are you would reach into your pocket.

The Priests and the Bishops. Respected pillars of society.

I think not. They have killed, maimed, tortured, raped and abused since time and memorial and their organization has at the very least covered up for them and at the worst approved of their actions.

I feel betrayed and sickened to the core and yet it doesn't surprise me in the slightest because it's been happening for centuries.

I am trying to quell my anger. The Bible. The world's best-selling book. The good book indeed, full of references to abuse and torture, sacrifice and yes... child rape.

Numbers 31. No less a man than Moses has orchestrated the massacre of the Midianites. After they'd put every grown man to the sword his soldiers came to him and asked what should be done with the women and children. Moses replied, "Now therefore kill every male among the little ones and kill every woman that hath known a man by lying with him. But all the women children that have not known a man by lying with him keep alive for yourselves."

Read that again, read it two or three times and then go and look the passage up in the bible because I know you have one somewhere in your house because every fucking house in England has one.

Sam reclined back into her seat and drew breath. She could almost feel the venom spewing from the screen and she felt her legs wobble as she stood. She steadied herself against the desk. What had she let herself in for? She was in deep now, there was no doubt about it and she wondered if it was remotely possible to bail out or even jump ship altogether. She became aware of a sickly feeling in the pit of her stomach. The old feelings were coming back again and she was frightened.

Sam was in a state of disbelief as she walked through to the kitchen. She felt vulnerable. This unstable killer had sought her out, perhaps just as a sounding board for the time being but nevertheless she had been targeted. It was Lucrecia who had come looking for her and she'd risen to the bait. She lasted no more than ten minutes before curiosity got the better of her and she walked through to the hallway to the bookcase and located a copy of an old Bible than some distant relative had given her when she was around eleven years old. She wasn't religious by any stretch of the imagination but it wouldn't have been right to throw it out.

Numbers 31, the message had said. Surely not; it wasn't possible that Moses would say something like that was it?

It was there. It was there in black and white and it took her breath away. She remembered her own bible study classes at Sunday school at her Mothers church. The lovely old ladies who took the classes had never mentioned that passage and no wonder!

Sam returned to the Mac and opened the lid. She located the Google search engine and typed in 'controversial passages from the bible.'

There were hundreds of sites listed. She clicked on the third site down. The site had listed the top ten 'worst' or 'most troubling' verses based on a viewer's poll.

Number one was more than a little offensive and touched a raw nerve with her.

"I do not permit a woman to teach or to have authority over a man, she must be silent."

She read on, another was a worrying verse apparently endorsing genocide, from 1 Samuel 15:3: *"This is what the Lord Almighty says ... 'Now go and strike Amalek and devote to destruction all that they have. Do not spare them, but kill both man and woman, child and infant, ox and sheep, camel and donkey.'* "

What? She thought. Kill the child and the ox, the sheep the camel and the donkey. She'd lived all her life under the impression that God loved little children and the animals he'd created and placed on the earth and here he was urging someone to kill anything that moved. A God of love? Not this God, he was a vindictive, spiteful, nasty bastard from where she was looking in from.

She continued down the page, Moses again, this time his call to kill witches, in Exodus 22:18: *Do not allow a sorceress to live.*

Could this passage be what sparked the great Witch-hunts?

That holiday in America all of a sudden seemed like a very good idea. Sam couldn't explain the feelings she was experiencing but somehow sensed she was being watched and being a journalist her personal details weren't that hard to track down.

As she walked back through to her office she glanced at the computer screen. The red icon on Facebook notified her she had another message.

Lucrecia was back.

Reincarnation is a funny thing; it seems people either believe it or they don't. Once upon a time I was a little skeptical but not now. It was the little coincidences that cried out to me every day even right down to the duty like urges to write to you Sam. It was the voice I now know to be of Maven and her quest for justice from beyond the grave.

Reincarnation is believed to occur when the soul or spirit, comes back to earth after the death of the body. Some sects believe it occurs on the 49th day after death but the timespan is not set in stone. This phenomenon is also known as transmigration of the soul.

Druidism, Hinduism, Jainism, Sikhism, the Buddhists, Greek philosophers and Ancient Indians all believed in the concept of rebirth or "entering the flesh again". Many *believed that reincarnation was as natural as a flower or tree reseeding itself, a form of cyclic existence where a being is born, lives, dies and then is re-born again. No less a man than Plato argued that the number of souls must be finite because souls are indestructible. He agreed with many philosophers at the time and of course we've all experienced it. Some say reincarnation is the explanation of Déjà vu, already seen, when we experience flashbacks as if we have lived through a previous existence.*

Children in particular are prone to this strange phenomenon and seem to remember events in a life that had ended, particularly in a violent way, before the child was born.

In a study on 2,500 children conducted by Ian Stevenson psychiatrist-parapsychologist at the University of Virginia, he proposed that unusual behaviours, such as phobias, were a simple explanation to a violent incident in a previous life.

Mainstream Christian denominations have rejected the notion of reincarnation but what the fuck do the noble ones know? Why should reincarnation be so unbelievable, more unbelievable than the belief that a God in the image of a man sits on a cloud in a place known as heaven that you can't see? This God has never been seen or heard and yet he looks over the whole world and takes care of those who speak to him in prayer. He knows everything, speaks every language in the world and no matter if 20 million people pray at exactly the same time in a thousand different tongues he will hear them all and answer every prayer.

'Man cannot make a worm but he maketh Gods by the score.'

Sam wanted to reply but she couldn't find the words. As each minute passed she felt the killer drawing strength from her inability to act. It was round one to the opposition and she accepted that.

She highlighted the text of both messages and transferred them to a word document before printing them off and placing them in her overfull file.

She managed to Skype Eddie and his wife Corinne three hours later. They'd been having some lunch but had answered the call anyway. They looked normal; certainly no Fred and Rose West and Sam felt comfortable talking to them. Eddie didn't look anyway near his years and although his face bore the testimony to a lifetime policing the streets of New York she would describe him as ruggedly handsome. Corinne looked sweet, still very attractive for her age with naturally greying hair, gym slim and beautiful white teeth that had probably had a small fortune spent on them.

Sam made her mind up during that one and only Skype call; she was heading for America, trusting her judgement which had only failed her once before.

She was seventeen then and much too young. Her husband had beaten her to within a few inches of her life but she'd battled through and won the war. She swore no one would get to her again and yet here was someone she didn't even know testing that pledge to her. She wouldn't run away, wouldn't hide, but she felt she had an ally in the likable couple in New Hampshire. Eddie's house had an internet connection and she'd strike up a new dialogue with Lucrecia when she got there.

Thirty

No one does more harm to the Catholic Faith than midwives. For when they do not kill children, then, as if for some other purpose, they take them out of the room and, raising them up in the air, offer them to devils. Sam slept soundly on the early morning flight to Manchester, New Hampshire and arrived late afternoon local time. Eddie and Corinne were both there to meet her. They took the picturesque route, as Eddie explained, it took a little longer but it was worth it. They motored up through Pembroke and Belmont and as Sam and Corinne listened Eddie talked. He talked about New Hampshire and his favourite lake in the whole world and he talked about the Native Americans who first inhabited this beautiful part of New Hampshire and how a Reverend Wheelright had purchased a vast part of the lakeshore from them for 'just a few bucks then kicked their asses off his land.'

After a couple of hours the lake came into view. Eddie hadn't lied about one thing: it was a beautiful part of the world. As Sam stepped from the car the smell of nature overwhelmed her, pine trees and slightly damp grass and the beautiful but feint smell of a jasmine. And she was aware of birdsong and other small creature noises that she had never known in the places she'd grown up. It was idyllic and almost immediately she knew she had made the right decision to come here.

Over a typically American meatloaf dinner that Corinne had prepared some hours earlier they got to know each other a little better. This time Corinne managed to get a few words in edgeways and then Sam found herself talking in detail about her schooling and career and life in general. There were some things she didn't talk about of course and nor did the conversation touch on the very reason she was there. That would wait until tomorrow. Both Sam and Eddie kind of sensed that in a sort of telepathic understanding.

Sam called time just after ten. She explained that she'd been awake for almost twenty-four hours and she was desperate for a bed. She said her goodnights to Eddie and Corinne led her towards the rear of the large house to a bedroom clad in natural pine. A window was open and a gentle, warm breeze made the fine net curtains dance elegantly. As she walked over and peered out into the blackness she could see the full moon shimmering on the surface of the lake.

"A beautiful bedroom with a beautiful view," Corinne announced. "I do hope you'll like it here Samantha."

"I'm sure I will Corinne, I'm sure I will and thank you for your hospitality."

As Corinne turned and walked towards the door she stopped and paused. Sam watched as she turned to face her, hands clasped together fidgeting like a worried schoolgirl.

"What is it Corinne, what's wrong?" she asked.

Corinne was already shaking her head. "Nothing my dear, no nothing is wrong."

"Then what is it?"

Corinne walked towards her slowly. She held out her hands and Sam reached for them as she waited for her to speak.

"You seem like a nice girl Samantha."

Sam nodded, bit her tongue and waited for Corinne to speak.

"I have a wonderful husband."

"Yes."

"And we've planned our retirement for more years than I care to remember."

"I can see that," said Sam

There were tears in Corinne's eyes. "Make me a promise Samantha, please."

Sam nodded. "Anything."

Corinne's grip tightened around Sam's fingers, almost to the point of pain. "Don't let them take my husband away from me."

∾

The overviews of the killings started soon after breakfast. Corinne had made her excuses that she had to nip into town for some shopping and as soon as the car had pulled away Eddie produced his file of paperwork from a drawer in a large bureau in the lounge. He started by explaining that he'd had to pull the file together a second time as the Feds had taken everything associated with the case. He mentioned the computer glitch too, and said that he'd had his old PC into the best computer shop in New York but the old file was well and truly gone forever. The technician in the shop couldn't quite explain it, files just didn't disappear into thin air, they had to be removed deliberately, on purpose he said and it took quite an expert to remove it from a computer completely. Sure, it was possible to erase or hide it but there was always some sort of evidence on the hard drive that the file had at least existed in the first place even if it couldn't be retrieved or repaired.

Eddie had ditched the old PC in a rubbish skip on 5th Avenue West as he'd left the shop. He couldn't quite explain his actions logically, but somehow he felt that it was contaminated in some way.

Eddie told Sam he would like to discuss every individual murder but first he would start with the case he had been working on, that of Father O'Neil in New York. He clarified how even at this point in time the death wasn't being treated as murder.

"Just like the Bishops in Liverpool," she said.

Eddie shrugged his shoulders. "Exactly Sam, I've been a policeman for many years and sure we have hunches but this was more than any hunch. That boy was murdered, it was obvious to me and when I interviewed the Bishop of the Diocese I swear he pushed up the defensive barriers just as soon as I walked into that place."

Eddie paced the neat, tidy lounge area as he continued. "So many things don't fit and if I'd been given a little slack and a few weeks I could have proved my point." Eddie sighed as he continued to walk. "I'm not saying I could have located the murderer overnight but at least we could have made it a murder case and upped the manpower and man hours accordingly." He shook his head.

"Nobody wanted to know, nobody was interested, they just wanted it pushed aside as an accidental death case and buried for eternity."

"Which is where it is at the moment?" Sam asked.

Eddie turned to face her and nodded solemnly. "Finished," he said. "Just like me and because no one is looking into it, that's where it will lie forever and a day."

"Unless any further evidence comes to light." Sam said.

Eddie laughed out loud. "Which won't happen because I was the only cop willing to get my teeth into it."

Eddie's frustrations echoed Sam's. Perhaps she wasn't so paranoid after all. They had all ridiculed her suggestions even when the Vatican turned up. Jesus, the fact they'd flown in from Italy surely told them something.

Eddie's voice brought her back from her thoughts. "In the article about the four Bishops in Liverpool you mentioned a visit from the Vatican."

Sam nodded.

Eddie smiled. "Was that true Sam or just a journalist stretching the truth to make a decent story?"

"No," said Sam, "that was true; my boyfriend at the time received the delegation at Merseyside HQ. He told me all about it."

Eddie sat opened mouthed as he reached slowly for a pen and began to take notes. "Sweet Jesus H Christ," he said.

"What? Sam asked. "What is it?"

Eddie stood and began pacing the room again. He was beginning to annoy her and she wanted to tell him to sit down but realised she wasn't going to break the habit of a lifetime. It was Eddie's way of thinking, of solving little issues in his head and she could almost hear the cogs turning as he stared into space. She gave him a minute and he eventually spoke. He told her that he'd always suspected that the killings were linked and that the church was under attack but until this precise moment he couldn't be one hundred percent sure.

He turned towards her and spoke. "Ninety percent Sam, I was always about ninety percent convinced that my own theory was right but when even your own partner doubts you and your chief and the Bishop of the Diocese of New York you begin to have doubts yourself."

Eddie was grinning as he continued. "Not now Sam, not now, because now we know for certain that the Vatican subscribe to the theory too, otherwise why would a high ranking cardinal jump on a flight to the UK?"

"A Cardinal is high ranking?" Asked Sam

"You bet your bottom dollar he is."

Eddie started scribbling on his notepad. "A Cardinal is a prince of the Catholic Church and has to be appointed by the Pope himself, they in turn elect new Popes so have a huge political sway. I don't suppose your boyfriend gave you any names did he?"

Sam smiled as she reached into her folder. "He did. Give me a minute." Sam leafed through her papers until she found what she was looking for. "Here they are," she said, "two Cardinals, Barberini and Adams."

Eddie was already making his way over to the PC wondering why the name Barberini rang a bell. He reached for the mouse. The screen lit up immediately and he logged in and began searching.

Eddie located Cardinal Adams within a few minutes. "Holy shit, Adam's is the Papal Nuncio in the UK."

Sam was shaking her head. "What does that mean?"

Eddie eased back in his seat as he looked up at her. "It means, my dear, he's the numero uno Catholic in the British Isles, the Pope's bloody representative no less and it means that if someone as important as him makes his way up the country to Liverpool from London to investigate an apparent accident then we are onto something major."

Barberini took a little longer to find, a somewhat elusive cardinal who obviously wasn't comfortable in the limelight and didn't seem to fill any particular job role at all. They located him on a grainy 266 x 400 photograph on Google images alongside the

Pope and a description underneath. It appeared the photograph had been taken by a very knowledgeable tourist in St Paul's Square. It read 'The Pope accompanied by his close friend and confidant Cardinal Barberini.' They searched thousands of images of the Pope and sure enough every so often, every fifty or sixty photographs there was Cardinal Barberini in the background or slightly out of focus. Eddie clicked back a dozen pages until he found what he thought was the best image and pressed *print*.

As the printer warmed up noisily he eased himself from the seat and it came to him where he'd heard the name before. It was Barberini who had phoned the Bishop in New York to offer up his condolences for the priest who'd been impaled on the Judas Cradle.

"I don't quite get it Sam," he said. "It looks like the most powerful Catholic in Britain and the Pope's right hand man are in on this one." He removed his glasses and held them between his thumb and forefinger. "I think we've stumbled on something a lot bigger than any of us realised."

Over lunch Eddie talked quite freely in front of Corinne, which surprised Sam. It was as if the ex-policeman now had the bit between his teeth or had been given the go ahead to take it one stage further. He somehow felt vindicated and explained to his wife how he felt his early retirement had been as a direct result of digging too deeply into the death of the New York priest. Corinne showed very little reaction. She had obviously had a life time of Eddie sharing his cases with her when he felt the need for a shoulder to cry on.

He talked about the killings in Spain and in France and urged Sam to tell Corinne all about the four Bishops in Liverpool. Sam explained the role Kevin Howey had played in helping the two cardinals with their investigations.

Corinne looked up as she removed a fork from her mouth. "Your ex- boyfriend you say honey?"

"Errr... yes," Sam said. "We split up earlier this year."

Corinne reached across the table and forked a little more pasta onto her plate. "It wasn't working out for you?"

Sam was floundering; someone was asking questions that she wasn't comfortable answering. She'd always kept her relationships on the surface and didn't like going in too deep. Kevin tried and she liked him but she never felt like opening up and letting him see the real Sam, it was one of the reasons why the separation wasn't that painful for either party. She'd been in love before and given everything and it had landed her in hell.

"We were never that close," she answered honestly. "He was a boyfriend to go out with, nothing more."

"So no plans to marry?" Eddie quipped.

Sam shook her head and before she could stop herself she blurted out. "Been there, done that. Once is more than enough."

Corinne reached for Eddie's hand. "Don't let one bad experience put you off honey; if you find the right man, marriage is a wonderful institution." Corinne stroked Eddie's hand. "I know I'm lucky finding someone like this first time round."

Corinne's words drifted away as Sam crossed over to the dark side and suddenly she began to speak like she had never spoken before.

"I thought there was no one like him, he was a bit of a free spirit, tall, muscular and handsome and I fell head over heels in love with him. I was fifteen years of age."

Corinne and her husband somehow sensed that this was a time for listening.

"I was sixteen when I took him into my bed and a few months later I found out I was pregnant. My parents were furious but I didn't care and didn't listen to anything they said. Everything was still rosy and we were married just after my seventeenth birthday, we had a council flat with a scattering of second hand furniture but I was the happiest girl in the world."

Sam paused, reached for a glass of water and took a long drink.

"It was just a matter of weeks before he hit me for the first time. It was a shock at first and he begged forgiveness for what he had done and as they all do, he swore it would never happen again. The following week he punched me full in the face and this time there was no apology, no request for forgiveness, he said I had

179

deserved it and had to change. I was his wife he said and I had to make sure everything was just fine for him.

It was as if he didn't want to be in the same room as me," Sam smirked, "except when it came to sex. As soon as he'd finished work it was straight to the pub with his mates and when he'd had his fill he'd call me as he was leaving and woe betide me if his dinner wasn't on the table when he walked through the door. I'd run around in a blind panic preparing whatever I had in the house and if it was five minutes late or something he didn't quite fancy he'd kick the shit out of me there and then."

Corinne edged her seat a little closer and took her hand. She reached into her handbag for a paper tissue and wiped gently at the tears that were now beginning to streak Sam's face.

Sam looked directly at Corinne. "He kicked that child out of me and even when I was miscarrying he phoned for an ambulance, walked out the door to go to the pub and left me wallowing in my own blood."

Corinne was wiping Sam's tears and now her own. "You left him?" She questioned innocently.

Sam was shaking her head. "I couldn't, I wasn't strong enough at that point and he swore that if I ever did he'd hunt me down and kill me and I believed him. I had no money, nothing, and of course I hid it all from my family because I believed I must have been to blame in some way. I mean, he wouldn't beat me for nothing would he? That's the worst bit, not only does it affect you physically, it plays with your mind as well and you lose all your self-respect and when he tells you day in and day out what a worthless piece of shit you are you eventually start to believe it."

There was a short silence.

"It got worse as time went on. He'd punch and head butt me, one day he smashed a dinner plate into my face and on another occasion he almost drowned me in the kitchen sink. I lost teeth and he scarred me, I had more stitches in my head than a twenty five year old teddy bear. You become immune to the pain, once you've crossed a certain threshold you learn to live with it and it's really not that bad. You only fear death and the threats of death, it was always death that frightened me because I'd never been there and didn't know what it was going to be like. "

"And that's why you stayed?" asked Eddie.

Sam nodded. "I couldn't escape, I was trapped and I had nowhere to run. I only ever knew Liverpool and my husband was well connected, from a large family and he swore that if I walked out on him he would hunt me down, find me and kill me.

Corinne smiled. "But you did escape eventually."

Sam squeezed her hand. "Yes."

"Tell me," she said.

Sam took another drink.

"He allowed me to go to the Bingo once a week just as long as I handed over anything I won. He said he had friends there who would tell him if I was lying. Some nights he even battered me for not winning but as I've said you get used to it. I stopped going to the Bingo and enrolled in a self-defence class instead but of course I couldn't tell him. For the first few weeks I wondered what the hell I was doing there and knew that if I ever lifted a hand to him he would beat me twice as hard for daring to challenge him."

"But you persevered?" Eddie asked.

"More than that. I became obsessed with it and wanted more of the same. I started training in the house, I built up to a thousand sit ups one day then I'd do a thousand press ups the next and I'd practice the moves at every opportunity I had. He continued using me as a punch bag but my body was becoming conditioned and I noticed the change. It didn't hurt so much anymore. I asked him if I could start cookery classes and of course he agreed because he thought my cooking was the worst in the north west. But I never went to the cookery class in the community centre, instead I joined the Muy Thai class next door."

"Muy Thai?" Corinne said.

"Mixed martial arts fighting, known as the art of eight limbs because of the combined use of fists, elbows, knees, shins and feet. I threw myself into it; shadow boxed in the house for at least an hour every day and continued with my press ups and sit ups."

She laughed. "But my cooking was still as bad so I still got battered for that."

"The bastard," said Eddie.

"Shut up Ed," said Corinne, "there's a good ending to this story and I want to hear it."

Sam's tears had suddenly stopped but there was no hint of a smile as she focussed on nothing in particular, staring into space.

"Within six months I was holding my own against the best fighters in the club. It was time to face up to him; I wasn't afraid of him any longer."

"Stop." It was Eddie. He almost leaped from his chair and ran through to the kitchen, returning thirty seconds later with three tins of Budweiser. "I feel in need of something a little stronger." He popped the tops on each individual can and slid them across the table.

Sam gripped the ice cold tin and drank. "He beat me a few more times but I found I was unable to retaliate."

"Nooooooo..." cried Eddie.

Sam held up a hand. "Be patient Ed, it's coming." She took another deep breath. "I called round one day to see my younger sister. I could tell she'd been crying but she didn't want to tell me why. Eventually I managed to get her to tell me what had happened. My bastard of a husband had been round to see her and tried to come onto her. My sister was single and he'd obviously fancied his chances but she'd rejected him. For that rejection he gave her a slap across the face."

Sam drained the can of Budweiser in one. "I could handle everything he'd thrown at me for seven years but now he'd crossed a different line and attacked a member of my family and it was time. I ran home every inch of the way but the bastard wasn't in. I was pleased because when I did finally catch up with him my anger had subsided somewhat. My Muy Thai instructor taught me that it was better to fight with controlled aggression than a temper.

He drank in three or four local pubs, no more and I found him in the second one, a pub called The Feathers and by then I'd managed to control my breathing."

Sam looked up. "I was cucumber cool. His face took on an angry look as he spotted me. He was sitting with two of his mates, two of the biggest losers in Liverpool. He told me to get the fuck out and that I had no right to come into *his* pub. I stood my ground, said I knew that he had been round to see my sister. He laughed along with his mates, said she was a bigger cock teaser than I was.

"You hit her," I said to him.

"So fuck."

He stood up and walked towards me and I was aware of my legs starting to wobble but I started to concentrate on controlling my breathing as my instructor had taught me. It was an adrenaline surge and it was good if I could utilize it in the right way. We were nose to nose as he snarled at me that he was going to fuck me up good and proper like I'd never been fucked up before. I took a half step backwards and powered my right knee into the bottom of his ribs and as he lurched forward I brought up my elbow into the base of his nose."

She focussed on Ed this time. "The blow ripped the bottom of his nose from his lip, there was blood everywhere and I stood back to see how he'd react. He reached for one of the bottles on the table, smashed it and ran at me. I pirouetted on the spot, spun and jumped and the heel of my foot caught him squarely on the jaw. I managed to punch him four times in quick succession before he hit the ground. His mates had picked up a bottle each and decided to rush me. One of them was so pissed he could hardly walk and I kicked him so hard in the balls he just crumpled in a heap on the floor. His other mate managed to swing the bottle at me but his aim was poor and I caught his arm as the bottle flashed across my chest. I snapped his radius and ulna bone across my knee like two twigs. I spun him around by his broken arm and hammered the palm of my hand into the middle of his face. His teeth were swinging in his mouth like saloon doors."

Sam placed the empty tin of Budweiser on the table. "His friends were well and truly out of the equation and no one else in the bar seemed to have the stomach for a fight.

Corinne was shaking her head; Ed's mouth was open, catching flies, as Sam continued.

"I picked my fuckwit of a husband from the floor and made him stand. He was whimpering like a day old puppy trying to stem the blood from his nose and I taunted him to stand and fight like a man. He was looking around the bar for help or at least for someone to intervene. Eventually he swung a windmill of a punch towards me but it sailed harmlessly by and then it dawned on me what a shit scrapper he really was. He'd acted the tough guy for seven years but probably never won a fight in his life. He was a coward and his slip of a wife had taken him to the cleaners in front of the so called hard men of the local community, his friends, the drug dealers and local burglars, the men who had once looked up to him. I hit him four or five times, not hard enough to knock him over but hard enough to register the fact that I'd hit him. I split his eye and burst his lip as he tried to guard his face with his arms. In a desperate last effort to save face he kicked out at me but I deflected his leg and brought my knee up between his legs. He went down this time and started crying like a baby begging me not to hit him anymore."

Ed could contain himself no longer. "So what did you do?"

"I hit him some more. I took out seven years frustration on him until they eventually pulled me off him. I would have hit him until I couldn't hit him any more if they hadn't stopped me."

Corinne was grinning, rubbing at Sam's arm. "He deserved everything he got honey, I'm so very proud of you."

Eddie was nodding too. "That's my gal, just the type of partner I like to walk along the sidewalk with."

Sam shed a few tears when she finally stopped telling her story but the relief was immeasurable. She'd wanted to close this episode in her life for many years and found it more than peculiar that she'd only managed to do it with a couple of strangers at the end of a ten hour flight.

Thirty One

And this is the most powerful class of witches, who practise innumerable other harms also. For they raise hailstorms and hurtful tempests and lightnings; cause sterility in men and animals; offer to devils, or otherwise kill the children whom they do not devour. MM

Eddie was being practical; they had to face facts that perhaps the Vatican had caught the killer who had been terrorizing their organisation. After all it had been some months since the last killing.

Sam decided it was time to tell Ed all about Lucrecia and the Aberdeen connection with a girl called Marnie.

Eddie sat mesmerized as Sam told him about the Monsignor from Aberdeen and how she had discovered how he'd risen through the church ranks quickly but had been moved around the British Isles every two or three years before taking charge of the whole of the north of Scotland four years ago. Although she hadn't found any sexual indiscretions that could be the reason why he was moved around so much. She said the coroner had registered a verdict of suicide but also pulled out a newspaper clipping where one of his parishioners gave a brief interview to the Aberdeen Evening Post in which she described him as *a happy go lucky man, always smiling, with everything to live for*. This was hardly the description of a man who had just hung himself she said.

Sam told Eddie about the wedding of Marnie Wishart in Aberdeen Cathedral and how Marnie Wishart was now officially a missing person, allegedly kidnapped from her sister's house in London. She left behind her handbag and her mobile phone and has not been heard of since.

By now Eddie was taking notes, scribbling all of the names down.

He was chomping at the bit. "I have a friend in the Met in London, Steve Nichol, I'll give him a call and see if he can tell me anymore about that case Sam."

Sam had more. She told Ed about her sister, Celine Macarthur and how she'd reported

Marnie missing almost immediately. Sam had done a little investigating, Celine owned a very successful interior design business but despite numerous calls to her office and a mobile phone number she'd been given, she hadn't been able to get her. It seemed that Marnie's sister had vanished too.

Eddie sighed as he stood studying the notes he'd just written. "This is a complicated one," he said. "One door opens and two doors close. We've got nothing but one big dirty cover up."

Ed looked across at Sam. "Let me ask you something Sam."

"Sure, go ahead."

"Hand on heart would you take a guess that the Monsignor in Aberdeen was murdered."

Sam was already nodding her head. "I'm pretty convinced, he didn't sound like the type of man to top himself and he may have had a chequered past as did our victims in New York, Paris, Madrid and Liverpool, something we didn't know about but the killer did. Whilst his death wasn't so obvious or dramatic as the others they did hang witches back in the old days so it could be said the execution methods were once again copied."

"And the Bishops?" Ed asked. "How sure are you that the Bishops were killed?"

"One hundred percent," Sam answered without hesitation. "Again, a history of abuse, and the fact that Rome sends two of their top Cardinals to check it out leaves me in no doubt."

"Me too." Ed was nodding, waving his notebook in the air. "Me too, I'm with you on Father O'Neil in New York. He had a playmate that day only the playmate wasn't interested in playing just killing." Ed chewed on the end of his pen. "So we have six murders?"

"Correct." Said Sam

Ed waved his pen towards her. "Only they're not murders are they? They're officially accidents."

Sam knew exactly what Ed was getting at. They were up against the impossible, police forces in England, Scotland and New York taking the official approach that there was no foul play involved.

"I'll ring Steve Nichol now," said Ed, "he's a good boy, one of the old school and we have to start somewhere."

Sam wanted to tell Ed about Lucrecia. Despite her misgivings the time was right. She reached into her case and pulled out the print outs of the Facebook messages.

"Ed," she said, "sit down. Before you do I want to tell you about a girl called Lucrecia."

Sam handed Ed the first print out and explained as he started to read. She described how at first she assumed the girl was a crank but then she'd mentioned Marnie and Aberdeen and a little internet research had connected Marnie and Aberdeen together and then she'd asked the question of Lucrecia, 'who is Marnie' and she'd responded by saying 'ask Monsignor Campbell.'"

Ed sat in stunned silence as he read the second and third messages and Sam dropped the name Barberini into the conversation.

"When she mentioned Barberini my blood turned to ice. I knew then that I was dealing with the Real McCoy. No one other than a privileged few knew that someone called Barberini visited Police HQ in Liverpool."

Ed wasn't so sure. He was taking a more practical approach and suggested that her boyfriend could have been the prankster; after all he certainly had just cause to take out a little revenge.

"I thought of that," Sam said, "but it's not in his nature, it's not his writing style either and anyway we never discussed the Monsignor in Aberdeen. I don't think he would know anything about it."

"It's in the public domain Sam, it would have been easy to search for recent deaths of Priests and Bishops and even Monsignor's, after all that's what you did."

"Yes," Sam agreed, "but only because Lucrecia gave me the name Marnie and Aberdeen. It was her that made the connection not me."

Flynn was playing the Devil's advocate. He was trying to solve the craziest case of his career, six murders that weren't murders and yet he knew they were. But he had to be practical and work on the fact that someone was playing a great big trick on them. He looked over the messages again and focused on the name Desiro and Gianfranco. Lucrecia had used her victim's Christian name in one paragraph and his surname further down the page.

He turned to Sam. "Who is Desiro Gianfranco?"

Sam shrugged her shoulders. "I don't know, I typed it into the search engine and got half a million results. I trawled through the first forty or fifty results but couldn't find anything of any significance."

"And Lucrecia Mathren," he asked, "any significance there?"

Sam reached into her file, pulled out another piece of paper and read verbatim.

"The most famous Lucrecia in history, Lucrecia Borgia, was the teenage daughter of Pope Alexander VI, a young noblewoman immersed in all the glamour of the Vatican Palace."

Ed nodded, waved a hand signalling that she should continue.

"Lucrecia learned from an early age that a dark truth lay beneath the surface of the Papal Court in their ruthless quest for power. Her family were murderers, her father and brother more than willing to kill not only their enemies but their own friends and family for their own political gain. Lucrecia was a keen and eager student who took to poisoning anyone who stood in her way. Described as the biggest whore there ever was in Rome, an evil seductress, a femme fatale, a victim of the machinations of her father and brothers political needs and used and abused. When the marriage no longer suited her father, she found herself divorced and then later she was reputed to have given birth to her father's child."

"Good God no," Sam said.

Eddie nodded. "It's always wise to take another viewpoint my dear. At seventeen years of age she was married again, this time to a Spanish Duke who she was deeply in love with. The marriage was arranged once again for political gain but when that backfired her poor husband was attacked by hired killers. Lucrecia reportedly hated the Papal Kingdom and the Popes more than the Protestants who were trying to overthrow them."

"Then that would suit the killer just fine," said Sam eagerly. "If Lucrecia Borgia was used and abused by the Papacy then the name Lucrecia has great significance."

Eddie removed his glasses. "We're getting too hung up on that name, it might be nothing. It's her surname that interests me."

"Mathren?"

"Yes," he said.

"But it means nothing Ed."

"Precisely, so why has she used it and is Lucrecia just a little red herring to throw us off course."

Eddie walked towards the computer and typed Mathren into the Google search; he waited a few seconds before the results displayed.

"A very rare surname," he said, "and a third rate poker site. Like I said it means nothing."

Eddie had returned back to his notebook, sat on the sofa and started scribbling.

"But it has to mean something."

Sam walked over and sat down next to him. "And Desiro Gianfranco too, if Lucrecia is our

killer then she can't have made it up. We've found Marnie Wishart and the link to Aberdeen and she knows of Barberini so Gianfranco has to be a real person too."

She became aware that Eddie looked as if he was suspended in time. His mouth was open and he was scribbling the last few letters to the name of one that was familiar to her. She noticed that his fingers were trembling as she focused on what he had written on the page.

CELINE MACARTHUR.

Eddie was tapping the page. "It's her," he said, "an anagram."

It hit Sam like a bolt from the blue. Lucrecia Mathren was an anagram of Celine Macarthur. She looked in disbelief at Eddie.

"Her sister? Marnie's bloody sister is our killer?"

Thirty Two

The Devil states finally, that the witch is to make certain unguents from the bones and limbs of children, especially those who have been baptized; by all which means she will be able to fulfil all her wishes with his help. MM

Eddie had managed to catch up with Steve Nichol from the London Metropolitan Police. Whilst he hadn't been involved in the suspected kidnapping of Marnie Wishart, his colleague and good friend had been. Nichol phoned him back three hours later; he had caught up with his friend over lunch and had some interesting information for Flynn. They had held Celine Macarthur for ten hours, perplexed why she had telephoned the police in a blind panic only thirty minutes after her sister had gone missing.

It wasn't normal said the policeman. Although Macarthur had telephoned her sister's husband to see if she'd returned home unexpectedly, she hadn't called anyone else and was frantic with worry begging the police to act.

At one point the policeman was convinced she was about to tell them who had taken her sister, it was all rather bizarre. In the end they had released her realising she had nothing to do with what had happened. They told her not to leave London as they'd want her available at the drop of a hat to help them with their enquiries.

Steve Nichol, said the Met had not heard from Macarthur since despite trying to contact her several times. Marnie Wishart had not been found either. Both sisters had seemingly vanished into thin air.

Flynn found Desiro Gianfranco too, or at least a man called Desiro Gianfranco who had been buried in his home city of Bologna sixteen days earlier. A former member of the Italian Special Forces, *the Col Moschin,* the obituary said.

It all fitted in. If this was the Desiro Gianfranco Lucrecia referred to he was probably a member of the Vatican Secret Police on her tail and she had taken him out.

Sam and Eddie took an early evening stroll on the lakeshore prior to dinner. They'd made significant progress in just a couple of days and everything was falling into place, but they both knew their resources were limited.

Special Vatican Agent Capriotti, followed the couples progress through a powerful pair of Russian Red Star binoculars from a safe vantage point a mile across the lake. He'd been on the ground for over a week and felt the time was right to make the call to Barberini.

He removed his mobile phone from his pocket, located the number and pressed call. Barberini answered almost immediately.

"Cardinal," said Capriotti."

"Si?"

"The odd couple have been meddling more than you'd care to know."

"Tell me more."

"I read the data printout from Flynn's computer earlier this afternoon and for the last two days he's searched anything and everything to do with the our organisation and the killings in Madrid, Paris, Liverpool and New York."

Barberini let out a frustrated sigh.

Capriotti continued. "And the Monsignor in Aberdeen?"

There was no reply from Barberini but the agent could imagine what was going through the Cardinal's mind. He pictured him with a glass of his favourite cognac rooted to the spot gazing out over the Basilica di San Pedro.

"It gets worse Cardinal; he knows about Gianfranco's death and he's been browsing the Internet for anything to do with you, especially active on Google images."

There was another pregnant pause before Barberini eventually spoke. "It is time to go to work special agent."

"You want me to eliminate them Cardinal?"

"Yes. Make it look like an accident if possible." Barberini took a mouthful of cognac and shrugged his shoulders. "If not, it doesn't matter."

Capriotti smiled. He wouldn't tell the Cardinal but it would not look like any accident. Already he was planning the biggest fucking explosion Newfound Lake had ever seen.

"Give me a few days. I'm not in my own back yard and I'll need to pick up a few supplies."

"As quick as you can agent. I want those two out of the picture."

Barberini replaced the receiver and walked towards the drinks cabinet.

Thirty Three

We Inquisitors had credible full information from a young girl witch who had been converted, whose aunt also had been burned in the diocese of Strasburg. And she added that she had become a witch by the method in which her aunt had first tried to seduce her. For one day her aunt ordered her to go upstairs with her, and at her command to go into a room where she found fifteen young men clothed in green garments after the manner of German knights. And her aunt said to her: Choose whom you wish from these young men, and I will give him to you, and he will take you for his wife. And when she said she did not wish for any of them, she was sorely beaten and at last consented, and was initiated according to the aforesaid ceremony. She said also that she was often transported by night with her aunt over vast distances. MM

Ed Flynn and Sam sat at the picnic bench on the front porch. It was early, the sun barely climbing above the tree tops on the far side of the lake. Neither of them had slept well. Eddie poured two coffees from a small caffetaire.

Sam sat with her hands on her chin, elbows resting on the table.

"You don't look so perky this morning honey," Eddie said. "Lost a little of your sparkle if I'm being honest with you."

Sam sighed and shook her head. "If I'm being honest with you Ed, I haven't a clue where we should go from here."

Sam told the ex-policeman about her fears and how she almost regretted the discoveries they had made over the last few days. She confided in him that her blood had ran cold when they discovered the identity of the killer and that part of her wanted to leave everything to the Vatican and climb on a plane back to England.

Eddie let her ramble on; he listened intently, all the while making more notes. She echoed everything that Ed Flynn was thinking, though she didn't know it.

"Life is a storm my friend," he said. "One minute you will be basking in the sunshine the next you will be dashed on the rocks."

Sam looked up. "Nice words but not yours?"

Eddie smiled. "Well spotted; the words of Alexandre Dumas actually, his book, The Count of Monte Cristo and there's one more line to go."

"Tell me," said Sam.

Ed lifted his coffee cup to his mouth and took a generous mouthful. "The Count of Monte Cristo is without a doubt one of the greatest novels ever written. I can picture the scene with clarity as Dumas describes it so well. Our hero Edmund Dante is giving advice to a young man telling him that life is indeed a storm. What makes you a man, he wrote, is what you do when that storm arrives."

Sam felt a sudden warmth from the coffee cup that she hadn't noticed before. She knew exactly what the wise old policeman meant. Life was indeed a storm and whilst you can occasionally sit and watch from behind a window there were times you needed to be strong and face the wind and the rain. She could run back to England and carry on with her life but was it the right thing to do? Whilst she didn't believe they were in immediate danger, Cardinal Barberini undoubtedly was and also the man Lucrecia had named as Montserrat.

"Barberini and Montserrat," she said. "Lucrecia said she would catch up with them sooner or later."

Flynn remained quiet.

"We need to try and warn them, tell them what we know."

At that moment the sun screen door opened and Corinne breezed through. "Morning all," she said. "What's on the agenda today?"

Eddie stood and gave her a gentle kiss on the lips. "Nothing special my dear. Samantha is making a phone call to the Vatican, that's all."

Thirty Four

She said also that the greatest injuries were inflicted by midwives, because they were under an obligation to kill or offer to devils as many children as possible; and that she had been severely beaten by her aunt because she had opened a secret pot and found the heads of a great many children. MM

It had taken her more than 40 minutes to eventually be put through to Cardinal Barberini, he was indeed an elusive man and there was a stringent screening process in place to weed out the nuisances and the pests and those after favours from the Pope's right hand man. It was when she mentioned the name of Desiro Gianfranco that the Vatican telephone operatives seemed to pick up their pace a little.

"This is Cardinal Barberini," he answered. "How may I help you?

"Hi, it's Samantha Kerr here and it's a case of how I can help you. I believe your life is in danger from a girl named Celine Macarthur."

Barberini took a sharp intake of breath and reached for his Cognac bottle that now sat out on his desk. It had been a permanent fixture these last few weeks, why waste time putting it back into the drinks cabinet?

"I used to work for the Liverpool Echo and I wrote an article about the four Bishops that burned in the city. I know and you know they were murdered by Macarthur, I—"

Barberini interrupted her. "I know all about you Miss Kerr and your article was a fine piece of journalism, I read most things of any substance written about our organisation but now you are moving into the realms of fantasy. Just what is it you are trying to tell me?"

"She murdered Desiro Gianfranco who was buried in Bologna on the 4th of this month and Gianfranco told her that you and a man called Montserrat were on a mission to torture and kill her just like you'd tortured and killed her sister. She's out for revenge Cardinal Barberini and she's coming after you. I have more information I'd like to share with you, I don't want to see any more unnecessary killing."

In a few short, succinct sentences the girl had blown Cardinal Barberini away. He took several seconds to compose himself and two mouthfuls of Cognac before he could reply.

"Where are you now Miss Kerr?"

"America," she replied. "New Hampshire."

Barberini was thinking on his feet. "You will take a plane to Rome within the next twenty four hours, when you arrive call me again is that clear?"

"Yes Cardinal."

"I will cover all of your expenses and more, fly business class and try and get as much sleep as you can."

"Yes Cardinal."

"I look forward to what you have to say Miss Kerr."

"Thank you Cardinal."

As soon as Barberini hung up he picked up the receiver and made another call. The phone rang out only once."

"Sir."

"Rafaele, get me an immediate trace on that call you put through."

"I already have Cardinal. It was a strange one and I put the trace on as soon as I put her through."

"And?"

"Give me a second cardinal," said Rafaele. "it should be with me any time."

Barberini waited; glass in hand. He was aware of his assistant speaking on another line.

"Got it cardinal," he announced. "A public phone box in Cherry Hill Road, Plymouth, New Hampshire."

"Thank you Rafaele, you've been most helpful."

Barberini walked over to his computer and booted it up. He searched on Bing Maps for Plymouth, New Hampshire. He scrolled slightly to the right and moved the curser up an inch or two until he found what he was looking for. Newfound Lake, Pine Street North, the address Capriotti had given. He'd better make another phone call to Capriotti, make sure he wasn't planning the attack in the next few hours. Let the girl go he'd tell him and then he could do whatever he liked with the policeman and his wife.

Thirty Five

In the Duchy of Lausanne certain witches had cooked and eaten their own children. MM Barberini received the phone call two days later. It had been a long trip the girl explained; she had to wait five hours in London for a connecting flight. She had been travelling for over twenty hours but business class had been good to her and she had slept well and was ready for a meeting. She was calling from the airport.

Barberini explained they had booked her a room in the Intercontinental De La Ville and all her expenses would be taken care of. The restaurant Monte San Giuliano in Borgo Angelico was a short taxi drive away and if she felt up to it he would have a table prepared for nine that evening. The girl readily agreed and as they said their farewells Barberini picked up the telephone and called Montserrat.

She arrived fifteen minutes late carrying an oversized handbag "Samantha Kerr," she announced with a nervous smile.

Barberini held out his hand and introduced himself. "And this is Signor Montserrat." He studied her intently as she visibly reacted to the mention of Montserrat's name.

She then appeared to compose herself and leaned across the table to shake the Vatican Policeman's hand.

"Pleased to meet you," she said. "Glad to see you are both alive."

It was a little joke that at least deserved a smile thought Barberini as he gestured to her to take a seat. He turned to Montserrat. "So tell me Antonio how a simple journalist can appear to know as much information about our pursuer as your entire team of specialist professionals. She even knows the name of our killer, something it took twenty of your colleagues many weeks to ascertain."

Montserrat shifted uncomfortably in his seat. He offered no explanation to the question as they both focussed on the girl.

She smiled; she appeared to have lost her nervousness now that Montserrat had been put on the spot.

"First things first," she said. "We can talk business soon enough but you are going to have to get some food on this table because I'm famished, even first class airline food isn't fit for a dog."

Barberini smiled, called Luigi to the table and they ordered from the menu.

There was no talk of business during the meal, no mention of dead priests or cover-ups. It was a kind of 'get to know each other' session and Barberini liked what he saw. He wondered if his power and influence could tempt this young lady into his bedchamber and more importantly could she be discreet? As they talked and the girl smiled and laughed and he cast a roving eye over her beautiful form, those urges that the Good Lord instilled within him rose to the surface again. He reminded himself that there were more important things to think about and discuss but he remembered his grandfather's saying that he knew to be so true. '*A standing cock takes the thinking blood from the brain.*'

"Another fine meal Luigi," Montserrat said, as the owner of the establishment brought three coffees balanced delicately on one arm.

"My pleasure as always," said Luigi as he placed the cups on the table.

Barberini spooned a little sugar into his cup and stirred vigorously making eye contact with the girl. "I fear it is now time for you to enlighten us Samantha, I confess I have been unable to concentrate on the food Our Lord provided wondering how you know so much about what we are faced with. For example how do you know about Montserrat and me and poor Gianfranco?"

"And the name of the girl," said Montserrat.

The girl smiled and reached down for her bag, cleared a little space and placed it on the table.

"It's all very simple."

She reached inside and pulled out several sheets of A4 paper. "As you are aware I wrote the article on the four Bishops who burned to death in Liverpool and let's just say I was privy to some information that a high ranking delegation from Rome had visited Liverpool and were more than a little concerned over the deaths."

She looked up as she spoke. "So like any good reporter I started to rake around a little, the internet is without a doubt the greatest invention since the wheel. I discovered all I needed to know about the mysterious deaths in Madrid and Paris and of course New York."

Barberini bit his tongue. He was just about to say Aberdeen but of course Samantha Kerr wouldn't have known anything about Aberdeen.

"Your Church was trying to cover up the Liverpool deaths and of course Father O'Neil in New York but to me it was as clear as bottled water."

Barberini steepled his hands together and nodded. "I'm impressed, we may have a position for you here one day but answer my original question, how did you find out about me and Montserrat and Gianfranco?"

She looked through her paperwork and singled out a sheet of paper. "Lucrecia Mathren told me all about you and all about how she killed Gianfranco and how with his dying breath he said Barberini and Montserrat were on their way to get her."

Barberini and Montserrat were looking at each other in amazement. *Lucrecia Mathren,* who the hell was Lucrecia Mathren? Montserrat was shrugging his shoulders.

"Celine Macarthur," she announced with a grin. "Celine Macarthur is an anagram of Lucrecia Mathren, the killer is corresponding with me and this is one of her messages." She slid the paper across the table. "This is the one where she tells me about a girl called Marnie and Aberdeen."

"Aberdeen?" questioned Barberini with a look of innocence.

"Oh come on Cardinal, give me a little credit," she said. "Monsignor Campbell didn't commit suicide he was another one of her victims.

Barberini and Montserrat looked at each other in stunned silence. Barberini gestured the girl to continue.

"It wasn't difficult; Lucrecia fed the clues to me like a mother feeds her child. It was there in black and white. I found out about the kidnapping in London." She leaned forward edging a little closer to the shocked men. "I figured that was your doing Cardinal Barberini but you thought it was Celine Macarthur your boys had picked up." She grinned. "You fucked up Cardinal and you disturbed a hornet's nest."

Montserrat sighed as he leaned back in his seat, ruffled his fingers through his hair. "We sure as hell did," he said.

Barberini gave him a stern look and then turned to face the girl. "I'd appreciate it if you could moderate your language Samantha, remember whose company you are in."

The girl continued. "I'd bet my life on it that Marnie Wishart is dead, in fact I'd take an educated guess that her death wasn't very pleasant and orchestrated by the likes of Montserrat and other members of the Vatican Secret Police."

Barberini shifted nervously in his seat. Samantha Kerr was too close for comfort. Why had the killer picked her to communicate with and would it be possible to create a trap using the dialogue between the two girls. He'd sent the best Rome had to offer after Macarthur and not only had she escaped the clutches of Gianfranco she'd turned the tables and killed him. This girl could be stopped but it would take something or someone very special to do so. The plan was slowly formulating in his head.

Barberini picked up one of the messages and studied it intently. It was almost personal. He had no idea why Lucrecia had handpicked the journalist but she had and he had to make the most of it.

He looked up from the sheet of paper. "What was her last communication with you?"

The girl handed him another sheet. "This one on reincarnation."

"Reincarnation," Barberini repeated with a frown.

"Yes, she has a good old pop at Christianity and the Church and finishes with the line that man cannot make a worm but he maketh God's by the score."

Barberini didn't like the grin that had now pulled across the reporters face.

"You'd better face facts Cardinal that she hates the Catholic Church more than any other institution on the planet."

Montserrat shrugged his shoulders. "But why?"

The girl spoke softly. "Abuse of power, obscene wealth, the Crusades, the witch hunts, the inquisitions, torture, massacre, genocide, child abuse, take your pick."

Barberini was shaking his head as he reached for his coffee. "I agree there's without a doubt a hatred for our church in every message but I can't help feeling this is a little more personal. It's almost as if she feels she has been wronged herself."

"We did kill her sister," said Montserrat

"Silence," the Cardinal scowled, "are you stupid? She was on our case long before her sister became involved in this mess."

The girl sat in silence.

Barberini composed himself. "I know more than most men that my church has wronged the female sex Samantha, but revenge never achieves anything, just more bitterness and anguish, but I fear this Lucrecia will not listen to reason. We are talking about a psychopath who will stop at nothing to wreak havoc at the very heart of our organisation."

Montserrat caught the eye of Luigi with a click of his fingers. "I need a Cognac Cardinal if that's alright?"

Barberini sighed as he slowly nodded. "I fear I am in need of something a little medicinal too."

Luigi approached the table.

"Two of our usual Cognac's please Luigi, he said. "And Samantha... something a little stronger?"

"No thanks," she replied. "A strong black coffee would be great."

"And an espresso please Luigi."

Luigi gave a little bow and walked away.

"She must be stopped," said Barberini, "and quickly." He stared intently at the girl. "Will you help us to set a trap Samantha? See if we can reel the girl in."

"You want me to be the bait? she asked.

"In a way Samantha, Yes."

They talked for some hours, the cognacs were almost lined up towards the end of the evening and the conversation turned to Lucrecia Borgia.

"An evil woman," said Montserrat, "rotten to the core."

"Some would say not," said Barberini. "Remember Antonio, the history book is always written by the victor."

Montserrat frowned. "What are you saying Cardinal?"

"I'm saying Antonio that the record books were written by the men who succeeded the corrupt Borgia family and their writings would have done her or her family no favours. Some say she was an unwilling pawn in the Borgia game of chess and that her father and brother used her to advance their own political prospects. Are you familiar with the history of Lucrecia Borgia Samantha?"

She smiled. "I remember watching a documentary about her some years back. She wore a ring that contained poison if I remember right; she poisoned her husband's mistresses and others courtiers who stood in her father's way."

Barberini smiled as he raised a glass of cognac to his lips. His speech was slightly slurred, a little more relaxed. "Some say she never poisoned anybody Samantha, like I said, it depends on who writes the books."

The girl reached for her handbag. "I must get going it's been a long day but I think you'll find that Lucrecia poisoned at least two."

Barberini was past caring and past arguing about the legend of Lucrecia Borgia. He had the girl's room number at the De La Ville Hotel and tomorrow was another day. He'd made her feel privileged when he handed her his personal number and said she could call him any time of the day or night. Montserrat had assisted his cause when he'd explained to the young reporter that the Cardinal's private number was known to only a handful of people in the entire world. He'd work on her in the coming days; weeks if necessary and he'd show her just how much power and wealth he had. The female form was unable to resist power and wealth; it had been the same since time and memorial.

"Everything in the world is about sex except sex, sex is about power," he whispered quietly under his breath.

Barberini called Luigi over and asked him to call a taxi. "For the De La Ville hotel, Luigi, our pretty friend here needs to get some sleep."

There was a different sparkle in her eyes now, he hadn't imagined it, she was content and comfortable in his company and she was ready for what lay ahead. Barberini was pleased with the way the night had progressed and the fine meal with a handsome face had been an added bonus.

Barberini kissed her just once on the cheek when Luigi announced that the taxi had arrived and she stood to leave. He drank in her beautiful aroma like an intoxicating drug and wondered how long it would be before the beautiful smell would embed itself in his pillow.

The girl bid her farewells and climbed into the taxi. As it moved slowly away from the Borgo Angelico she settled back in her seat. The taxi driver was familiar with the Rome streets and before long they were outside the elegant façade of the hotel. Before she had a chance to reach for her purse the driver announced there would be no charge, the fare had been taken care of. She bid the driver goodnight and walked towards the doorway of the hotel and through to reception.

A stone-faced male receptionist nodded his head in anticipation of the question that would surely come.

"Can you order me a taxi for the airport. Immediately please."

Thirty Six

The witches met together and, by their art, summoned a devil in the form of a man, to whom the novice was compelled to swear to deny the Christian religion, never to adore the Eucharist, and to tread the Cross underfoot whenever she could do so secretly. MM

Barberini was more than a little perplexed at the stomach cramps that were by now becoming increasingly painful. It was not like Luigi to serve something up that didn't agree with him, he'd been eating there for many years and his establishment only served the finest cuts of meat and fish and was spotlessly clean.

He cursed Luigi as another spasm of pain ripped through his stomach. The bastard has changed one of his suppliers but it wasn't like him, he'd kept the same trusted suppliers for the best part of a decade.

Within twenty minutes Barberini had taken the decision to call the Vatican physician to his chambers, as the pain was more than he could bear. The doctor arrived within three minutes and disclosed that he had also attended to Montserrat who was suffering identical symptoms.

"That bastard Luigi," Barberini groaned as he lay almost doubled up on the bed realising that without a doubt the trouble had originated from something they'd eaten at the restaurant. The doctor administered a painkiller via a syringe and said that he would be a little more comfortable within a few minutes. He went on to say that he'd taken a blood sample from Montserrat but although he first suspected food poisoning Montserrat had not vomited nor had he had to run to the toilet which normally occurred within a few hours. Barberini looked at his watch, it was 4.15am and yes, simple food poisoning would have resulted in several trips to the toilet by now.

Barberini tensed up as he spoke, beads of perspiration clearly visible on his brow. "I want you to ring the Hotel De La Ville, we had dinner with a young lady, Samantha Kerr who is staying there. See if you can get a hold of her and see if she is poorly too. She ate the same food as we did and if she is ill I want you to get someone over there straight away."

The doctor said he would wait until Barberini was a little more comfortable and then call. Barberini dismissed him a little while later, Samantha Kerr had to be looked after, she was the lynchpin in bringing Macarthur to them.

Several minutes passed and the doctor returned. Barberini could see immediately that something wasn't quite right.

"What is it Doctor, you wear the look of a worried man?"

The physician shook his head. "Not some much worried Cardinal just puzzled." He looked at the piece of paper in his hand. "There is no one by the name of Samantha Kerr staying at the De La Ville Hotel, not now or within the last month. They have no record of any guest checking in named Samantha Kerr."

Thirty Seven

And when Peter asked one of the captive witches in what manner they ate children, she replied: "This is the manner of it. We set our snares chiefly for unbaptized children, and even for those that have been baptized, especially when they have not been protected by the sign of the Cross and prayers. MM.

She took the mobile phone from her handbag as she walked across the tarmac of the airport and located Barberini's personal number. It rang several times before the familiar voice responded.

"It's me," she said quietly, aware of the other passengers around her boarding the plane.

"Samantha?" Barberini replied.

The girl grinned. The Cardinal still hadn't put two and two together.

"Lucrecia poisoned two," she said. "Remember I told you that in the restaurant, now do you believe me."

Barberini managed to say her name just once before the penny dropped and everything clicked into place. The glass of water he was holding crashed to the floor and shattered. The physician rushed forward as the colour drained from Barberini's cheeks and he doubled up as another severe pain ripped through his abdomen.

"The poison is rare and by the time they manage to get an antidote into the Vatican you and Montserrat will be as stiff as boards." She laughed. "My only regret is that I won't be there to see you suffer." She looked at her wristwatch. "You have about another two hours of agony to endure and I warn you the pain will only get worse. Just before you die you will be begging your doctor to end your life."

Barberini subconsciously pieced everything together as the girl's tormenting continued.

"You checked to see if there was a photograph of Samantha Kerr but of course there wasn't because that's the way she wants it and that's why it was her I chose. Poor Sam has had a bit of a life Senor Barberini, even changed her name to stop her ex-husband and his associates catching up with her and therefore the only photograph in existence is contained in her human resources file at the Liverpool Echo which of course is confidential and not in the public domain. I'm figuring the only other check you made was the phone call I made from New Hampshire which of course stacked up because I was there watching over Samantha Kerr and her policeman friend."

She waited a few seconds to let the enormity of the disclosure sink in and then handed the final pieces of the puzzle on a plate. She figured it was the least she could do for a dying man.

"You had a man up at the lake and he broke in and bugged the house and checked out her passport and her photograph and made the call to you confirming that she was real enough and a simple trace on the call I made posing as Miss Kerr was good enough for you."

Barberini's muscles were starting to go into spasms as the physician rushed forward with another syringe in a vain attempt to stabilise him. In a mild panic now, he punched a number into his mobile phone and summoned more help.

"Very, very careless," she said. "I expected better from the Vatican."

Although confused, Barberini was piecing everything together. He had visited the toilet with Montserrat half way through the first course. They wanted to discuss something in private and gave the girl the perfect opportunity to add anything she wanted to their wine or their food.

"I've killed him by the way, Cardinal Barberini. The bastard Capriotti was buying enough ingredients to blow up the fucking USS Enterprise and I figured what his mission was. His body is hidden in the forest of Newfound Lake and I suspect the wild animals will be having quite a feast by now."

Barberini remembered now. The red berries; they were bitter and he complained to Luigi who said he'd have a word with the chef.

As if by divine intervention the girl gave a full explanation of exactly what she had placed on their plate.

"Rosary Peas are rather pretty and quite apt to give to two pious men held in such high esteem in the Vatican. They were so named as the beautiful scarlet berries were used to decorate the altar in days gone by. They contain a poison called abrin a close relative of ricin, one of the most fatal toxins known to man and death, when ingested, comes quite quickly especially with the amount you two took in. I'm guessing you are in severe pain now Cardinal and your internal organs are shutting down one by one, you have no control over your muscles and will be finding it difficult to string half a dozen words together."

Two more medics dressed in white garments rushed into the room and started working on the Cardinal.

"You body's safety valves will kick in within the next hour and you'll vomit and bleed from the anus. Your medical specialists will know by now that you have been poisoned but even if they had the antidote with them right there in the room it would be too late for you."

She laughed. "You're off to meet your maker Cardinal Barberini, do give him my regards."

Barberini could no longer hold the telephone to his ear and his hand flopped by the side of the bed as the phone fell on the floor.

The girl pressed *end call* and climbed the steps to the Boeing 747. She would be back in New Hampshire within 20 hours. Sam Kerr and Eddie Flynn would need to be looked after a little longer, she suspected that the Vatican may send out another agent almost immediately and she'd have to warn them that their lives were in danger sooner rather than later. After that she'd head back to Rome and finish the job she had started

Cardinal Barberini was trying to tell the doctors something but they were insisting that he remained calm and rested. He was breathing hard and coughing every few seconds.

"Blood pressure is dangerously low," one of them said. "We need to get him to intensive care right now, I'd no idea how bad he really was."

"This is no ordinary food poison," his colleague said. "And Montserrat is exactly the same."

At that moment the physician's phone rang.

He answered it, "*Si*," and simply listened. The phone call lasted no more than fifteen seconds and he flipped it closed in stunned silence.

"It's Montserrat," he said eventually. "They couldn't save him; he died a few minutes ago."

He took a look at Barberini who had turned a ghostly shade of pale grey. "We'd better call for a priest," he said quietly.

Thirty Eight

The witch said we secretly take the children from their graves, and cook them in a cauldron, until the whole flesh comes away from the bones to make a soup which may easily be drunk. MM.

David Perini's best men had been decimated in a matter of months but fortunately he had plenty more capable operative's to call on. He was quietly furious with Barberini and Montserrat for not even informing him of their meeting with the girl Samantha Kerr. Luckily Montserrat had made an official diary entry relating to their evening in the restaurant in Borgo Angelico otherwise he wouldn't have known anything about her. Furthermore Montserrat completed a side entry detailing as much as they knew including where she'd flown in from and the agent Capriotti who had been

assigned to watch over her in New Hampshire.

Perini perused over his new notes/he'd made and there were some things that had happened lately that didn't stack up. Capriotti for a start. Why wasn't he answering his phone and why were there no logs of calls made from it within the last three days?

Something had happened to him; that was the only explanation. Was it possible that the girl Macarthur had taken him out too?

Perini checked the telephone number of the retired policeman's house on the lake in Newfoundland. Perini didn't normally show his hand this early but it seemed the only option available. Samantha Kerr had not checked in the De La Ville hotel as she should have done nor was she listed on any flights out of Rome within the last forty eight hours.

Perini made the call to Newfound Lake late afternoon and his heart sank as the real Samantha Kerr confirmed she had not flown to Rome, nor had she stayed at the De La Ville hotel or had dinner with Barberini and Montserrat in the restaurant Monte

San Giuliano on the evening Barberini and Montserrat were poisoned.

Samantha Kerr seemed a little reluctant to talk at first but Perini decided the time for secrecy and undercover activities were well and truly over and eventually she succumbed to his honest dialogue and gentle persuasion. Kerr knew an awful lot about the multiple assassinations and Macarthur had clearly chosen her for a reason. Perini needed to know exactly why. Perini told her to sit tight and he would take the next flight over to Portsmouth, New Hampshire. He would be there in 24 hours.

Prior to leaving for the airport Perini called a meeting with his newly assembled team and they studied every conversation Flynn and Kerr had had since their coming together in Pine Street North.

Sam Kerr hid nothing from the man from the Vatican and for once a member of the Church seemed only too happy to call in a little outside help. Ed Flynn couldn't help himself at one point and said that if they had allowed Merseyside Police and NYPD in on the investigation earlier they may well have prevented some of the killings and even apprehended the killer.

Perini appeared to eat humble pie, agreeing with Flynn on more than one occasion. Sam Kerr explained how she'd tried to speak to Barberini by telephone in an attempt to warn him his life was in danger but she'd been blocked from speaking to him and eventually cut off altogether.

Perini shook his head and apologised. There'd been two Sam Kerr's trying to speak to Barberini that day and it had been the imposter who'd been the one who had persuaded the telephone operative to put her through to the man at the top of the Vatican's special investigation team. It was a mistake that had cost Barberini his life.

Perini told the policeman and the journalist all about the ruse Macarthur had pulled and how she'd administered one of the most lethal poisons known to man. He also told them how he suspected she'd taken another Vatican agent out, a man called Capriotti who hadn't been heard of for nearly a week. Perini admitted Capriotti had been sent to Plymouth to spy on them as Barberini was concerned that their interference may jeopardise the hunt for Macarthur.

Flynn shook his head in dismay. "That's a staggering admission Mr Perini," he said. "What is it that gives the Vatican that air of superiority that they think they can bring in a killer as good as this without the help of some of the biggest police forces in the world?"

Perini ruffled his fingers through his hair. He stalled for a moment and then a slight grin pulled across his face. "Because we've been doing it for two thousand years Mr Flynn and even you must admit it's been more than a successful approach up to now."

Perini was concerned but not worried for his own personal safety as he made his way back to Plymouth. Macarthur knew very little if anything about him and he'd taken a minimal role in the investigation so far, unlike Montserrat, Barberini, and Gianfranco Desiro.

The whole point of his trip to New Hampshire was to stick his head above the parapet and set the trap. Capriotti had swept the Flynn's retirement home and found the tiny spyware bugging device hidden in the base of a plant pot and rather than remove it he had been instructed to leave it there. Macarthur was back in Plymouth of that he was sure. They'd discovered the false name she'd flown under to Rome and that very same girl had flown back to New Hampshire via London Heathrow on a return flight.

His men were on the ground now, in position in the forest and in several locations in Plymouth. They'd flown in on the very next flight, via New York, just to throw Macarthur off the trail. There were fourteen of them and he was very much the live bait, the worm on the hook. They also had another two men on the airport to stop her flying out anywhere. The CCTV images from Luigi's restaurant were crystal clear and it was only a matter of time. He'd made sure that he told Flynn and Kerr that he was the main man leading the investigation and the buck stopped with him. Macarthur would have heard everything and she wouldn't be able to resist one last cast of the line.

Perini and another agent had talked long into the night. Despite the almost total surveillance cover of the area Macarthur hadn't been spotted.

"We just need to be patient," Perini said. "She's here and she wants to take the bait. We just need to make sure we offer her something too tasty to resist."

Agent Turano smiled. It was time to reveal his plan to his boss. Perini had explained the unusual relationship between the journalist Samantha Kerr and Macarthur masquerading under the guise of a girl called Lucrecia. It was clear Lucrecia had a soft spot for the young reporter and the agent wondered what her reaction would be if she was suddenly placed in danger.

It was five o'clock in the morning before Perini eventually agreed to give it a shot.

Turano was good, of that there was no doubt but he held his cards close to his chest and refused to give the exact details of what it was he was about to put in place. He had a motto, 'If you want something done ask a busy man' and Turano being Turano insisted he would be judge, jury and executioner, flatly refusing to involve Perini and any of the other operatives in and around Plymouth and Newfound Lake. Perini had no choice but to let him of the leash. He hadn't ever let him down and simply requested forty-eight hours to reel the killer in.

Ed Flynn had advised that Samantha no longer boot up the laptop and if she wanted to log onto Facebook she should do it via her mobile phone. Ed had lived on hunches all his life and when Perini had left he'd immediately disclosed there was something he didn't like about him. Sam had argued that he was the only man from the Vatican who had ever talked to them and some of the things he'd briefed them on were jaw dropping to say the least. Ed was adamant as he spoke.

"He didn't tell us anything we didn't already know."

Sam was standing with her hands on her hips. "I can't believe you said that Ed," she said. "What about the double poisoning? He didn't have to tell us about that."

Eddie shrugged his shoulders. "Okay, I'll give you that one but apart from that he spent his time telling us about the messages from Lucrecia which we knew all about anyway."

"And the meeting in the restaurant too."

Eddie was about to continue the argument and tell Samantha exactly what it was he didn't like about Perini when Samantha's phone let out an alert sound that told her a Facebook message had been received. She looked at Flynn and they both instinctively knew who the message would be from. Sam started to read the message out loud; the writing on her mobile phone screen was far too small for Ed Flynn's eyes.

Samantha — It's been quite an adventure I'm sure you'll agree but I suspect it is coming to an end, for me at least and I am glad Maven has chosen you to carry on my work. I do apologise for my lack of communication these last few weeks but I have been rather active as you will soon find out.

Sam let out a loud laugh. "Ha, now I know she's mental, she wants me to start killing the bloody clergy! Why stop there? Why not go for the Pope himself?"

Ed sat in the large armchair opposite, with his chin propped up on his fists. He didn't speak but instead made a rolling motion with his eyes that said continue. As she started to speak he reached for his notepad.

Barberini and Montserrat will interfere no more, they have been taken care of, Lucrecia enjoyed the sport ha ha and she was true to her word, truly one of the great femme fatale's, they did not suspect a thing. Careless indeed.
I have reigned in three of them now and only one man eludes me but the place is crawling with the bastards from Rome stopping me from working. I have overestimated my capabilities and fear there is no escape and made the

mistake of coming back here, I should have warned you from afar, no excuses, it was remiss of me. I will take out the man who poses the greatest danger to you but fear by getting close to him I may be preparing my own noose for my neck.

"She's here!" Sam exclaimed.

Flynn was nodding. "I thought as much."

"You did?"

Ed scribbled on his notepad and handed it to Sam. It read- *NO MORE TALKING LET'S GO FOR A WALK*

Sam's mouth dropped open as Eddie held a stiff finger over his lips and they both stood and walked towards the door.

They walked two hundred yards before Eddie spoke. "I've found three bugs in the house but two of them are only a few feet from each other. I figured that only meant one thing, and that was that two people were interested in what we had to say. The Vatican was one, that was fairly obvious and the other one is no doubt our killer. Sam's mind was in turmoil as she desperately attempted to put things together.

"But nothing is making sense anymore," she said. "Her messages are gobbledegook, the more she writes the less sense it makes. She writes like a schizophrenic. One minute she rants on about the church and then reincarnation and then she calmly describes how she's disposed of her latest victim." She waved her phone in the air. "And now she's talking to me as if it's my Mum dropping me a line about her holidays."

Sam let out a sigh. "I don't mind admitting Ed, the bitch is beginning to freak me out."

Eddie took a step closer and placed an arm around her shoulder. "Read on," He said.

You are in danger Samantha and you must run to Italy for that is where you will find him, the man who can change everything.

Maven will come to you Samantha, I know she will, she will point you in the right direction.

217

Eddie Flynn took her arm and turned her back towards the direction of the house. As she looked at him she was more than a little concerned at the worried look that had crept across his face.

~

Turano sat in the hotel bar looking at his watch every few minutes. His mobile phone lay on the table in front of him and he willed it to ring. He needed confirmation that the Flynn's and Kerr hadn't wandered out for breakfast; it was time to set the operation in motion. He smiled to himself. How fucking useless was that ex-policeman? His holiday cabin was positively crawling with surveillance devices a simple piece of spy software could have picked up in seconds. *Amateurs, the world is full of fucking amateurs.*

Turano's phone rang and he quickly snatched it from the table. It was the call he had been waiting for. He looked up at the woman standing in front of him shaking a charity tin. This was not the time and the place, he wanted to shout at her but looked around the crowded hotel cafeteria and decided the easiest way to get rid of *this fucking cripple* was to slip a few coins into her collection box. As he did so she leaned forward, smiled and pinned a cardboard badge to his crisp white linen shirt. *Fighting Cancer Together* the logo said. As she walked away he spoke.

"Talk to me Diego."

"They've gone."

"They've fucking what?" Turano said.

"They've gone Senor Turano, vanished without trace. Their car is still there but there's no sign of them. They normally take breakfast on the porch between seven and eight but -."

Durano was furious as he interrupted, oblivious as the other hotel guests looked on and listened in amazement at his foulmouthed outburst.

"And nobody saw them leave? What sort of fucking people are we employing?"

Diego was trying to pacify his boss saying they had the airport covered and men already in place on the highways.

"What fucking use is that you fucking cretin, we don't even know what car they are driving?" he bellowed into the phone. He was breathing heavily now as he tried to take stock of the situation. He'd need to pull his men together and hope that they had indeed headed for the airport. He banged his clenched fist against his chest in a fit of temper and winced in pain as the sharp point of the *Fighting Cancer Together* badge pierced his left nipple.

The men at the airport had been put on red alert but so far they had come up with nothing. They couldn't be far he thought, not without a car. One of his men had contacted the police at Plymouth and with a little gentle persuasion the chief of police had confirmed that no cars had been reported stolen overnight. They'd also checked out the local taxi firm and the rent a car companies in the area. He was fairly sure they hadn't left town. Had Flynn discovered the bugs and took refuge in another nearby lodge? That was it; that was the only logical explanation.

He telephoned Perini and explained that the situation was under control. They had men in Plymouth and in Grafton and New Hampton too and there was no way Kerr and the Flynn's could make it out of the area. He convinced Perini that it might even work in their favour. The disappearance could even flush Macarthur out of her hole.

Flynn was very well aware that every access road out of Pine Street North would be manned by an employee from the Vatican and so taking the boat was a logical choice. They'd rowed several hundred yards towards the middle of the lake before starting the engine and then cruised gently over to Wellington Forest and hiked the twelve miles to Grantham, just off Highway 89. He'd always enjoyed walking with Corinne and although Sam Kerr had moaned every step of the way they'd made it by lunchtime, booked in to the smallest hotel in town and decided to lie low for a few days. They studied the print outs of all Lucrecia's messages for the rest of the day, taking notes and making full use of the hotels Wi-

Fi internet. In the evening they took a little dinner in the small diner then retired to Samantha's room for more discussions.

Samantha frowned as she read the final message for at least the hundredth time. "She knows I'm not a killer Ed, so why would she say she wants me to carry on her work?"

Eddie handed the message to Corinne. "Any ideas honey?"

Corinne studied the message for no more than a few minutes. "It's as plain as the nose on your face," she said to her husband.

"It is?"

She nodded. "The killings were incidental, a necessary part of her grand plan and of course she took more than a little pleasure ridding the world of corrupt, egotistical child abusers but that wasn't the main reason why she killed them."

Eddie and Samantha had suddenly become more than a little interested.

"She had something bigger planned, something far greater than terrorising the church." She looked at Sam. "And that's what she means by you carrying on what she started. She doesn't want you to murder anyone dear, just finish what she's started."

Sam stood up. "But what?" she said in exasperation. "How can I finish something if I don't even know what it is?"

Corinne turned to her husband and smiled. "That's your job honey, you're the policeman."

"Ex policeman." he said.

"Work on it," she said. "The NYPD trained you for thirty years to work these sort of things out so get your pencil and your little notebook out and get cracking, it's hard to beat a person who never gives up."

The girl sat in a roadside café six kilometres from Plymouth. It was time to take out the man at the top. There would be no fancy stuff this time, the simulating killings from the days of the inquisitions and the witch-hunts pleased Maven but now it was all out war and it was dog eat dog. It would be nice, but not the be all and end all.

She'd slept well on the flight from London and Maven had come calling again. She'd said the job was nearing its conclusion and she'd been pleased with the way her sister had performed but the net was closing in and soon there'd be nowhere to hide. The girl felt it too, it was difficult to describe but she sensed her time was coming to an end, drawing to a close. She was running out of disguises and false passports and there wasn't enough time for more plastic surgery. She could lie low and change like she had in the past but the reporter was now in danger and therefore Lucrecia had to make sacrifices. Maven had explained everything. It was crystal clear.

She'd been severe, shaved her head and took to wearing a patriotic bandana. Her eyebrows had come off too; in fact every visible piece of her body had been shaved or waxed and she'd applied a slight amount of gothic white foundation to her face giving the appearance of a young woman undertaking significant amounts of chemotherapy after suffering from cancer. A pair of oversized sunglasses gave her the confidence that she'd be able to avoid detection but just to make sure she'd adopted a gait worthy of an old lady many years her senior and walked with a stick.

Perini was also staying at the Fox Park Hotel in Plymouth and was hardly making a secret of the fact he was there, making a point of wandering in and out every couple of hours. But his men were never far away and the bulges in their jackets told her they were armed to the teeth and ready for business.

But her disguise had worked once, why shouldn't it work a second time? She walked over to the girl at the counter and asked if she could be so kind as to phone her a taxi to take her to the Fox Park Hotel once again.

The stomach cramps were more than a little annoying but although Durano immediately thought of the Rome double poisoning he reminded himself he was professional and shouldn't jump to any silly conclusions. He'd only ever eaten in the hotel since he'd arrived from Italy and every employee coming into contact with food or drink had been thoroughly vetted.

Within thirty minutes Durano felt the saliva build up in his mouth and as a precaution had Googled on his mobile phone the biggest hospitals within driving distance. Barberini and Montserrat had been given a ricin like poison; he'd telephone ahead and tell the doctors if it got any worse. Twenty minutes later a sharp stabbing pain to his abdomen and a dribble of saliva that ran the length of his chin forced his hand and he lifted himself gingerly to his feet as he walked from his room, down a flight of stairs and into the reception area.

"Get me a taxi, as quick as possible, New London Hospital, Grafton. It's an emergency."

The taxi arrived and screeched to a halt as Durano climbed in. He handed the driver a fifty dollar bill and told him to break all speed limits possible. If the police intervened he had to explain that his passenger had been poisoned. As the taxi pulled away Durano reached for his mobile phone. The taxi driver was doing exactly as he'd said and Durano was sliding across the back seat as the car sped round the tight bends of the Ragged Mountain Highway.

As he rubbed at the annoying itchy pin prick scratch on his chest, it hit him like a hammer blow and he stiffened up in shock. His hands were visibly trembling and he was feeling nauseous but he managed to locate Perini's private number. He was barely able to speak.

Perini sat in the hotel bar with a glass of coca cola and pressed the green button as his mobile phone vibrated.

"Si."

"It's me, Durano. I've been poisoned. She's here, she's got me."

Perini sat bolt upright and covered the mouthpiece with a cupped hand. "Where, when, where is she?" he asked frantically.

"The cancer woman."

"The what?"

"The cancer woman." Durano repeated. "She looks as if she's had cancer; she's collecting for cancer research and carries a tin."

Perini could hear Durano's voice failing but give him his due, he continued despite being in obvious discomfort and pain.

"She is wearing a bandana, a stars and stripes bandana and she's pale as a ghost. Her pins Perini, watch her pins, they are poisoned."

As Perini looked across the crowded bar the woman Durano had described almost perfectly walked through the open doorway. He pressed the red button on his telephone and pressed another number.

It rang only once. "Get down to the hotel bar just as quick as you can, she's here."

Perini slipped the phone into his pocket and smiled as he picked up a newspaper from the table and pretended to read. He never took his eyes from the woman as she made a token effort in claiming a few donations from a few of the hotel guests. She turned to face him and shuffled slowly towards him.

The thrill of the chase, it was what it was all about. He remembered his time as a teenager in the Casentino Forest of Tuscany as his father taught him patience when waiting for the wild boar to make an appearance. His father would construct a perfectly camouflaged hideout that was more than a little comfortable with small seats and enough food and drink to feed an army and they'd wait. They'd wait for hours, sometimes all night and now and again they'd leave in the morning without ever seeing a wild boar never mind killing one. But more often than not their patience and skill at concealing themselves would yield it's reward and when his father gave the command the wild boar was despatched with efficiency and enthusiasm.

This was no different. Perini had been patient and his enthusiasm and his belief in his own ability had never waned and here she was standing right in front of him and he had her firmly in his sites.

She held out the badge, Perini smiled as he focussed on the pin then made eye contact with her.

"A small donation to help the fight against cancer sir?"

"Why certainly," he said as he reached into his pocket. "A most worthy cause."

Perini eased his wallet from his breast pocket. The wallet was level with the girl's eye line and in a well-practised and perfectly executed action he powered his elbow in an upward motion and smashed it into the girls chin as her head snapped back and she fell to the floor unconscious. He was aware of a woman's scream and more commotion as a barman ran towards him. He was halted by an agent who took out a Vatican Police ID card and told the startled man to back away.

Perini kneeled down and picked up the pin that was weaved through a cardboard circle that said, *cancer – together we'll beat it.*

The pin was wet, a globule of liquid balled at the tip and he smiled as he pushed it into the neck of the unconscious girl.

He looked up and ordered one of his agents to get the van and a rope. It took Montserrat and Barberini no more than six hours to die and they'd drive her around for as long as it took for her to breathe her last breath.

He'd tie up the formalities with the local police as he had done a hundred times before and the girl would simply disappear from the face of the earth and the Church would take a deep breath and he'd say a prayer and thank God Almighty for a more than satisfactory conclusion.

The four men stood in the White Mountain National Park Forest and watched the tormented, writhing figure take her last breath. It had taken an hour to drive north, another hour to find a spot deep in the forest far away from prying eyes and another three hours to watch Celine Macarthur die in agony.

Suffering was not something Perini overly enjoyed as his father had taught him from an early age to respect his prey and put it out of it's misery whenever possible. His father hated wounding an animal and seeing it limp away and one night by a camp fire in Casentino Forest as they'd chewed on freshly cooked boar he explained how every creature on God's earth had feelings and every creature on God's earth could feel pain but once killed they experienced nothingness. There were tears in his eyes as his father spoke and it was at that precise moment he realised that although his father had no reservations with killing an animal, a bird or a fish he had a clear affection and respect for them all. It was a competition, a survival of the fittest and a battle of wits that his father invariably always won but when it was over and the kill lay in front of him he displayed an enormous amount of respect for the dead creature.

This wasn't the case here, the poor creature in the back of the van had suffered and suffered terribly and even though he could have put her out of her misery many hours ago he'd had to follow Barberini's wishes. And strangely, although he could not afford her any dignity in death he did respect her in a strange sort of way.

The agents lifted Celine Macarthur's body from the car and tied her rapidly stiffening body to the tree. Diego loosened the lid on a huge jar of bloody fish bait and poured the contents over her head. It was a macabre spectacle as the red liquid oozed over her body making it look as if her head had exploded. The wild dogs, the boars, the pigs and the birds and the rats would come in at nightfall and within a day or two the flesh would be stripped from her bones and her internal organs removed and savoured. Every bone would eventually be removed and then the flies and the maggots would move in. It truly was the most undignified way a person could be treated in death and as Perini closed the boot of the van and climbed into the passenger seat he thought to himself that Barberini had been one warped, fucked up, sadistic bastard.

Thirty Nine

But no one who reads the histories can doubt that there have always been witches, and that by their evil works much harm has been done to men, animals, and the fruits of the earth, and that Incubus and Succubus devils have always existed. MM

The Vatican Agents caught up with the Flynn's and Samantha Kerr after three days. Perini took them out for dinner that evening by way of a de-briefing; they hadn't left the small hotel and were naturally quite nervous. Perini was annoyed that he'd no idea what they'd been up to for the duration of their 'hideout' but he would make sure he'd put the fear of God up them and that Celine Macarthur and her one woman crusade against the Catholic Church would be forgotten forever and never see the light of day. The Flynn's and Kerr were expendable and if necessary they could be taken out of the equation too.

"It was necessary to take Macarthur out," Perini said. "She had arrived at the hotel with enough poison to eliminate half of Rome and stood in front of me ready to kill me." Perini wiped his brow and sighed. "I had no choice, I'm not sorry."

The Flynn's and Kerr were somewhat subdued. Perini was a little puzzled as if they were kind of expecting the news he was delivering.

He continued; he wanted to leave them under no illusions what the Vatican was capable of.

"It was rather a tricky operation as the local police were called as soon as I hit her."

Corinne leaned forward, a look of consternation pulled across her face.

"You hit a woman?"

Perini frowned. "I had no choice she was about to kill me."

Corinne remained stoic. "You are sure about that young man?"

Perini nodded. "I am one hundred per cent sure, but even if I'd only been fifty per cent sure I would have done the same thing." He looked across at Samantha Kerr, made eye contact as he prepared to lie and prayed that she wouldn't see through him. "She scratched her neck on the poisoned pin as she fell to the floor and within a few minutes started frothing at the mouth."

Perini explained that they knew of the exact chemical make-up of the poison and that there was no hope for the girl.

He shrugged his shoulders and smiled. "Not that we were particularly bothered, after all she had killed out brethren en-masse with no compassion or feelings for them whatsoever, all good men, all law abiding, God fearing Catholics whose sole purpose in life was to help others."

"Where is she now?" asked Ed Flynn.

"Her body?"

Flynn nodded.

Perini frowned. "She has been returned back to nature, which is all you need to know."

Flynn displayed the first sign of rage. "Another victim of the Vatican Death Squad; I swear I'd heard the rumours but up until now I never knew teams like yours really existed."

Perini wanted to break out into a wide grin but decided discretion was the better part of valour. Her bones would be scattered right across New Hampshire by now but there was no need to go into detail. He would however drop a subtle hint.

He leaned forward and spoke in barely a whisper. "Mr and Mrs Flynn, Miss Kerr... we are a powerful and noble organisation and we will not be threatened by any individual or indeed any groups of individuals. We have weathered many storms and no doubt there will be many more to come. We are constantly under attack by the Muslims and the Jews and the Protestants and the atheists and of course lunatics like Macarthur, but we will never be defeated and must do what's necessary to survive. We may lose an odd battle but we will always win the war. We must do what is necessary for the greater good of the church so that we may grow stronger year on year." He paused for a second. "And yes, occasionally we kill or at least allow people to die as was the case with Macarthur."

"You could have saved her?" Sam Kerr asked.

Perini shrugged his shoulders. "Perhaps?"

"But you didn't try?"

Perini shook his head as he leaned back in his seat. "I had my orders and I obeyed them. My orders were to eliminate her and I took advantage of circumstances." A smug smile crept over his face. "And as always I carried out my instructions to the letter. Macarthur's mission failed, it's as simple as that."

The conversation was kept to a minimum for the rest of the evening and then the waitress returned with an array of tempting deserts on a trolley. All four diners politely declined. They took a strong coffee in the lounge, Ed Flynn's laced with brandy and just before midnight Perini bid his farewells. He was left in no doubt that he'd done just enough to curtail the amateur sleuths once and for all.

It was three in the morning when Samantha Kerr knocked on the bedroom door of Ed and Corinne Flynn. To her surprise they were fully clothed and as she peered over Ed's shoulder she could see that their bed had not been disturbed.

"We couldn't sleep," Ed said.

"Me either," she said as she walked into the bedroom uninvited. "He's lying, Perini was lying."

"In what way?"

"I've been looking up the poison on the internet, ricin he said didn't he?"

Ed nodded.

"It takes at least an hour or two before there's any sign of discomfort even if the poison is injected directly into the blood stream. And if he's lied about that, what else has he lied about?"

Ed walked over to the bed and sat down. "I don't think he's lied about her death."

"No?"

"I don't think so; he was altogether at peace with the world, a man whose mission had been satisfactorily concluded."

Sam nodded her head slowly. "I know what you mean, a real smug bastard. She's gone, there's no doubt about it."

Corinne stood with her hands on her hips looking over the two of them like a headmaster scolding two pupils."

"It most certainly is not over," she said. She stared at Samantha. "You, young lady, you have to finish it or have you forgotten?"

"Finish what?" cried Sam. "I've no idea what it was she was talking about, none of it makes sense. She talks about three victims when we know she has killed far more."

Corinne walked over to Eddie's ever growing pile of print outs and paperwork, picked up a handful and sighed.

"I don't know," she said. "But it's in here somewhere I'm sure of it."

Forty

And what, then, is to be thought of those witches who in this way sometimes collect male organs in great numbers, as many as twenty or thirty members together, and put them in a bird's nest, or shut them up in a box. MM

They'd studied and researched and talked for three days. Sam was fixated on Monsignor Campbell from Aberdeen. As much as she'd searched and researched and telephoned his known acquaintances in Aberdeen she could find no evidence anywhere of sexual abuse with minors or indeed any misdemeanours with the opposite sex. The church had moved him around quite often but otherwise he was clean.

"It's against her Modus Operandi Eddie," she said. "There must be another reason why she killed him."

What was it one of the newspapers had said, something about a meeting in Rome each year? Yes, that was it; the reporter had said one of his parishioners had said he was looking forward to his annual trip to Rome, to the Vatican. She flicked through a few of the papers and found a hand written note.

"Here Ed," she said. "Monsignor Campbell travelled to Rome on the first Monday in December."

"A vacation?" Eddie suggested.

"No, that wouldn't make any sense at all. If he was going for a holiday surely he'd want to go for Christmas."

Eddie paced the room; he hadn't sat on the bed or a chair for some time, his notebook and pen poised at the ready.

He turned to his wife; a half smile crept across his face as he spoke to her. "Corinne?"

"Yes dear."

"You're going to help us out here."

"I am?" She said with a puzzled frown.

"Yes." He walked over and knelt down beside her making eye contact. "What is the most important thing to the Catholic Church? I mean the most important thing."

"God?" She replied automatically.

Eddie was shaking his head furiously.

She raised her eyes to the ceiling scratching at the side of her head. "The Pope?"

"Perhaps, but I don't think Celine or Lucrecia or whatever we want to call her ever expected Samantha to kill the Pope."

Sam flopped back in a big armchair in the corner of the room and began to think. Eddie was on the right track, the Monsignor was in Rome for a reason and there was a connection between some of the other deaths, the other men she had killed.

"Charity?" Corinne questioned.

"No," Eddie said. "Definitely not, they spend less than five per cent of their income on charity; even most of the money Mother Theresa raked in year on year for her charity, the Sisters of the Poor, ended up in the Vatican vaults. She was nothing more than a puppet for their bank."

Eddie continued. "Their reputation is important to them; remember everything has to happen for the greater good of the church?"

"I'm sick of hearing that phrase," said Sam.

Eddie stood; he winced as one of his knees cracked loudly. "Power is what they crave ladies, wealth and power."

"Wealth," said Sam with a smile. "Money!" she shouted as she leapt from the seat. "That's the most important thing to them and that's where Celine Macarthur wanted to hit them."

Eddie turned to face her. "The bank? The Vatican Bank?"

"It's crystal clear Ed, don't you see? Monsignor Campbell went to Rome for some sort of committee meeting, something to do with finance."

"And so did two of the others," said Corinne. "Lucrecia said she had three of them and she only needed one more. There's a seven man committee meeting that takes place every December somewhere in Rome and it's about as big as it gets."

Eddie was smiling. "Holy fuck, I think you're right girls."

Corinne frowned as she waved a finger in front of her husband's face. "You won't use that sort of language in front of Samantha, Edward Flynn; you're not with your criminal friends in the South Bronx now."

Forty One

For a certain man tells that, when he had lost his member, he approached a known witch to ask her to restore it to him. She told the afflicted man to climb a certain tree, and that he might take which he liked out of a nest in which there were several members. And when he tried to take a big one, the witch said: You must not take that one; adding, because it belonged to a parish priest. MM.

Samantha Kerr travelled to Aberdeen within forty-eight hours and met up with one of the cleaners of the Cathedral of Aberdeen. Florence Mary Stanley had a slight fondness for Advocaat with lemonade, not forgetting the cherry on the top and after two or three she spoke quite freely. Sam discovered everything she needed to know over the space of four days. Florence was even persuaded to hand over a copy of the minutes from the previous year's meeting of the Vatican Charitable Donations Committee, hosted by The Institute for Works of Religion, commonly referred to as the Vatican Bank. It proved to be quite invaluable and very interesting reading. It transpired Monsignor Campbell, Cardinal Barberini and Bishop Mackenzie who burned to death in his Mercedes in Liverpool also sat on the committee. The final piece of the jigsaw had clicked into place.

Twenty four hours after she said her final farewells to Florence, Sam Kerr flew to Assisi, in Italy to meet up with Eddie Flynn.

Forty Two

The deeds of witches are such that they cannot be done without the help of the Devil. MM

The Institute for Works of Religion, in Italian *Istituto per le Opere di Religione* (IOR) had the power to influence the economy of more than half the globe and was run by a board of Superintendence made up of seven Bishops, Cardinals and Monsignors. The election period of each committee member was ten years and on the first Wednesday of December every year without fail they met in Vatican City to discuss and implement their charitable donation strategy for the coming year. Although the committee reported direct to the Camerlengo of the Holy Roman Church and t Institute for Works of Religion, as he was not commonly regarded as a 'Rome' man in the close confines of the Vatican. If that appointment came as a surprise, recent events had quite simply turned his head upside down.

Thon was ready. He'd never been as prepared in his entire life as he took a last mouthful of coffee, picked up his briefcase and headed for the meeting room.

Cardinal Aquila chaired the meeting for the first time in Barberini's absence; he tapped a small gavel on a beech wood plinth at exactly nine o'clock in the morning and the meeting commenced.

Before moving on to finance, the small group of men said prayers for three of their recently departed brothers who had sadly been taken by the Lord. Only Håkon Thon was aware that they had in fact been murdered. The Vatican Police had kept the truth from the financial men of the most secret bank in the entire world.

The worldwide charitable budget had been set at 4.5% the year prior and Aquila announced that with a spend of \$8.7 billion from an annual income of $170 Billion it had crept up to just over 4.7%. The accountants would need to be taken to task he said, possibly one or two suspended or even sacked. Aquila scowled as he said inefficiency would not be tolerated. He handed around copies of the accounts as he paused to give his six colleagues a chance to quickly browse over the final totals.

"Our reserves remain intact as always. We currently own fourteen per cent of the Italian Stock Market and if you turn to page six, you will see the varying percentages in the markets of London, New York and Berlin." He leafed over a page.

"The market share in the Far East and Africa can be found at the top of page fourteen, Bank liquid capital on page sixteen and gold and diamond reserves on page twenty."

Bishop Cortezi was the first to pose a question to the chairman.

"I see JP Morgan, Hambros and the Swiss Credit Bank of Zurich are still very active in our investment strategy Cardinal, are you still happy with their advice?"

Cardinal Aquila's reply was lost on Håkon Thon as he hung his head in despair. It was exactly the same opening to each Finance Meeting he had sat in and it sickened him to the pit of his stomach. He looked up slowly and gazed around at his fellow committee members dressed in their religious finery and sighed to himself. Even now he couldn't comprehend the enormity of the figures being bandied around; it was simply beyond comprehension. And he recalled last year's meeting as he was ridiculed and ostracised as he proposed a one per cent rise to the charitable budget. He was disillusioned; there was no other word for it. He massaged at the side of his temples with his thumb and forefinger trying to remember the exact moment when he crossed that line from a devoted God fearing submissive employee of the Catholic Church to a cynic... yes a cynic, a cynic whose eyes had been well and truly prised open.

While he had never questioned his faith as a young priest in Trondheim he'd had his doubts about the whole organisation and in particular the quite ridiculous rule imposed by the Vatican, that of celibacy. Surely it was of God's making to give man sexual desire, to allow him to procreate and continue the line of the human race, to evolve and better the world God had delivered mankind into? So it was with quite considerable regret at aged fourteen, some years after he had decided to go into the priesthood that he discovered what the word celibacy really meant. Although a virgin at the time he'd began to notice the female form and indeed the subtle changes in his body as he entered into puberty. Surely it would be just a matter of time before God magically turned those feelings off? But he hadn't and when Heidi, two years his senior had lured him into her father's shed at the bottom of her garden under the pretence of seeing some hens and lifted up her skirts inviting gentle exploration, he'd done just that. He tried to fight the exquisite sensation in the front of his trousers as his fingers probed the wetness between her legs and he watched in amazement, as she appeared to take pleasure from each subtle movement. It was the most natural thing in the world to take off his trousers as he lay down beside her and as Heidi eased him on top of her and guided him inside her he even praised the Lord for allowing him to experience this most beautiful act that surely couldn't be so wrong.

Håkon Thon fell in love that August morning in 1978 and even at eighteen years of age when he took the pledge to abstain from activities of a sexual nature and commit himself to the Lord he never stopped loving or dreaming about Heidi any less. Of course it broke her heart when he announced that their relationship was effectively over and he would be following the priesthood to Rome.

As he fiddled with a pencil on the desk in front of him he wondered what course his life would have taken had that decision been different. Thon took a sip of water from the glass in front of him and looked subtly over the rim. Cardinal Aquila was still talking figures and assets, interest rates and bond yields and it would be some time before they would set the coming years finance and then, possibly tomorrow, the worthy causes who would benefit directly from the generosity of the biggest charitable donator on the planet.

Thon admitted to himself he was more than a little nervous, normally calm and collected, unfazed by almost anything life threw at him, even his palms were sweating lightly this morning and yet he felt an inner glow as if God himself had appointed him specifically, appointed him on a mission that would rock the Vatican Bank to the core.

Forty Three

Whether the belief that there are such beings as witches is so essential a part of the Catholic Faith that obstinacy to maintain the opposite opinion manifestly savours of heresy. MM

"Our job is over Eddie, we can do no more."

Eddie Flynn lifted the coffee cup to his lips as they sat in a café situated in a small square in the centre of Assisi.

"When do you think the shit will hit the fan?" she said.

Eddie smiled, leaned across and rubbed her knee. "I do believe you are a little worried Sam, don't you think Håkon has it in him?"

Sam was shaking her head. "No," she said, " not at all, I'm just thinking there might be some way the Vatican Bank can stop it from happening, some way they can prevent Håkon from implementing his plan."

Flynn placed his cup on the table and wiped a napkin over his lips. "They can stop him before he gets into the room but there's no way they can stop him once the motion has been passed. They don't know anything about it so why would they want to stop him?"

"You're right," she said. "My only fear is that we were followed and they somehow got wind of our plan."

"Impossible," Flynn said. "Even if they were able to tail us to Assisi and put two and two together and even managed to bug Thon's house there was no way on God's earth they would have been able to guess the café we were going to meet in. Remember, we chose the café not Thon and he confirmed he had never set foot in the place before."

Sam was feeling a little reassured. Flynn was right... as always. They had been careful, meticulous in their planning and unless the Vatican bugged every table in every café, bar and restaurant in Assisi there was no way could they have found out exactly what it was they were planning to do.

Sam reached into her handbag and checked her airline ticket for the twentieth time. She wanted to be well away from Italian soil when the news story broke as it undoubtedly would. The Vatican Secret Police weren't stupid and after the bombshell Thon was about to deliver they'd investigate and pin point the coincidences that weren't coincidences after all. They'd assume that Celine Macarthur had 'got at' Thon before she died but if they happened upon Flynn and herself in Assisi, in the very place the perpetrator of the elaborate, carefully orchestrated scheme originated from there they'd be chased and caught and taken to task.

Flynn waived his hand at a waiter on the far side of the café. The man acknowledged him and walked over as he asked for the bill in perfect Italian.

"Quite the local," Sam said. "You seem quite at home here, any plans to stay on?"

Flynn laughed as he placed a fifty-euro note on the waiter's tray.

"No way," he said, "I don't think I'll ever set foot on Italian soil again. My grandmother was Italian and I love the people and their style and the climate and their love of good food and wine but we can't take any chances anymore and I confess I'll feel a lot more comfortable once my feet are back on American soil."

They sat in the late afternoon sunshine for another twenty minutes until the taxi for the airport finally arrived. They talked about the future and life and how it would never be the same again and they even talked about the possibility of going into hiding. And during the long drive to the airport they talked about next year's holidays and how they should all meet up in New York. Strangely, the elegant, pristine holiday home on the edge of Newfound Lake was never mentioned as a likely spot for a vacation.

Forty Four

"Stop the fucking meeting now," he said as he bellowed into the phone. "They were murdered because they sit on the IOR, the fucking bitch wasn't killing at random. She had a plan."

It had been nagging Perini for some time, ever since one of his colleagues had mentioned Barberini's death and how they had selected a new chairman for the board of the Institute for Works of Religion.

The person at the other end of the phone was an elderly Cardinal, quite unused to language of that kind. He explained that the meeting had already commenced but Perini was adamant he was driving into Vatican City and would stop it himself if necessary. After much shouting and swearing the Cardinal cut the phone dead and Perini made a bolt for the door, the drive would take no more than twenty minutes.

When Perini arrived in the Palace of the Governorate of Vatican City there was already a reception committee waiting for him. Early indications were good; Cardinals Forini and Dominguez were there as was Monsignor Botswuno and several lower ranking officials. They were taking his claims seriously and as if to demonstrate just how serious the situation was, soon after the Holy Father himself arrived.

Forty Five

It was Håkon Thon's turn to speak on the delicate matter of charitable funding. Cardinal Aquila had already proposed that the percentage rate remain the same as last year, 4.5%. Both Cardinal Francisco and Bishop Cortezi readily agreed and Cortezi said that if the Vatican income continued to rise year on year at the same rate it wouldn't be long before they were handing over ten billion dollars a year to worthy causes.

Aquila puffed out his chest proudly and smiled across the table at Cortezi.

"Ten billion dollars is more than impressive," he said with a smile on his face.

"I propose we increase the budget," said Thon. "It does the poor people of the world no good at all if we buy more gold and diamonds and stocks."

Aquila turned and scowled at Thon. "Didn't you hear Cardinal Cortezi, Håkon? Within a few years we will be giving ten billion dollars in charitable contributions."

"We can do more. Lot's more." Thon said. "We sit in our splendour and our finery with full bellies while the African and Indian child dies because he cannot drink clean water and we pontificate the laws of our church to the believers while they produce more children than their fathers can feed. We owe them more."

"We owe them nothing," snapped Cortezi. "Our funding is more than generous especially to Africa."

Thon reached into his open briefcase and pulled out a sheet of paper he had prepared the previous day.

"Our income from Africa and India last year was over seventeen billion, made up from church collections, business interests and rental income, sales and of course backhanders from third world dictators and despots who line the pockets of the Vatican on the promise of a Papal visit sometime in the future so that their underfed and undernourished downtrodden subjects have something to look forward to which will take their minds of their miserable pathetic existence."

Håkon Thon paused for effect as he looked out over the top of his bifocals. "Any of you gentlemen care to tell me exactly how much it was we gave back to those poor Africans and Indians?"

The room remained silent.

"I'll tell you shall I?" He held up the piece of paper and read from it. "We gave Africa the grand total of one point seven billion dollars in charitable aid and we gave India much less. In fact brothers we gave them less than three billion dollars in total which in my eyes means we stole fourteen billion dollars from the poor bastards."

"An outrage," screamed Aquila. "I will not tolerate that sort of language."

Cortezi was also on his feet. "We give them hope and faith and jobs," he said. "It's not just about money."

"He's right," said Aquila, "do you know how many people the church employs in the third world?"

Thon looked at Aquila square in the eyes. "Tell me Cardinal, how many?"

Aquila was caught temporarily off guard as he rummaged through a few papers faltering and stuttering.

"You won't find it in there," said Thon, "because no one knows how many children and cripples and slaves we employ in the backstreet sweat shops of Delhi and Calcutta and Mombasa. You won't find the answers on paper because they are hidden away, missed from official documents and statistics and the few dollars we hand them at the end of each month pales into insignificance with the billions we steal from them year on year."

It was Håkon's turn to stand as he leant on the table glaring at his three colleagues, his voice straining with passion. "We steal from them brothers... we take the bread from their families mouths and we sit and we gloat and we praise ourselves in the name of our Lord while they die by the million."

Aquila mopped at his brow as he looked at his watch and noticed that the lunching hour was now upon them. It would be a timely interlude as Thon had to be stopped. He was talking with passion and a strange confidence that Aquila hadn't ever noticed before.

~

The constitution of The Institute for Works of Religion had been copied and printed for the Cardinals and Bishops and Perini and a few secretaries and the Holy Father, the Pope, and they studied it in great detail.

"We need to stop the meeting and we need to stop it now," said Monsignor Botswuno as he looked at his watch. "They'll be having lunch. Perfect timing."

~

Thon noticed the sombre looking nun slip into the room unannounced. Her head was bowed in a gesture of respect as she handed a slip of paper to the chairman of the IOR committee. Thon noticed a look of worry spread across Aquila's face as he reached for a glass of water and drank rapidly. Soon after he stood and announced that the afternoon's session would be postponed until further notice. He gave no reason why, other than to say the Pope himself had approved the suspension.

Håkon Thon forked a small piece of potato into his mouth and chewed it slowly. The saliva in his mouth was non-existent but he persevered and eventually managed to swallow it. He tapped a spoon on the table to gain the attention of the assembled men.

"This meeting will continue." he said. "In the constitution, regulations and articles sub section four, page thirty nine the meeting can only be called off as a result of war, earthquake, fire or flood or the death or severe illness of a seating member of the committee."

Thon smiled. "So gentlemen, as you have all breezed through four courses of lunch and enough coffee to keep a small regiment awake I propose you are all more than fit to continue."

He removed a napkin from his shirt collar. "So come, let us go, we have some important decisions to make before darkness falls on this most beautiful of places."

The men filed slowly into the room and the door was closed then locked by a burly Swiss Guard from the outside.

Thon continued where he had left off with a stinging attack on the financial generosity, or lack of it of the Catholic Church, an organisation he had given his life too.

It was during a visit to a small church in the mountains of Tuscany when he had experienced the moment that opened his eyes and his mind to the mind-set of the masses that followed the Church from the cradle to the grave.

The lady was elderly, stooped in her walk with a wizened look and sun bleached skin. But nevertheless she was dressed in her finery that clearly bore testament to many years of use. She deposited a large amount of coins in the collection box and Thon suspected she could ill afford it. She would go hungry that week, he was sure; the story could have come straight from the Bible.

That evening Thon read the parable about the widow and the two small coins and analysed the passage word for word. It was man who had hijacked religion, manipulated the words and meanings from the good book to line their own pockets. The Vatican wealth was obscene, there was no other word to describe it and he wondered at what point in history it had all started to go horribly wrong.

Aquila cleared his throat. He looked a little uncomfortable.

"Brothers, during lunch I received an envelope from Cardinal Thon and he explained it contains an official proposal to increase the percentage rate of our annual worldwide charity contributions. Although rather late, it is within the timeframe according to the constitution and it must be discussed and voted on before the meeting concludes tonight. Tomorrow the agreed percentage and worldwide spreads will be discussed and implemented."

Aquila reached down for the envelope as Thon inched forward in his chair. Aquila read the seven line proposal and as he reached the final few words his face broke out into a broad smile as he turned to face Thon.

"Why my dear friend Håkon, I do believe you must be playing some sort of joke on us?"

Aquila's grin had now been replaced with a frown as his gaze pulled away from Thon and he looked at the puzzled expressions of his other committee members. He held up the paper and pointed to a figure at the bottom of the page. "Ha! Cardinal Håkon Thon has proposed that we increase our percentage from four and a half per cent to sixty two per cent."

The smirks from Cardinal Aquila and the other seating committee members soon turned into laughs and then finally loud guffaws.

"I'm assuming this should have read six point two per cent Håkon?" Aquila said, as he faced him again.

Thon wanted to smile; he so much wanted to smile as he looked around the table at the laughing grinning sheep who followed everything their chairman said. This was the trouble with the so called independent, unbiased gathering. They were glove puppets in the last chance saloon to make a name for themselves before retirement. Honour, glory and a large stipend were their reward if they kowtowed to their paymasters and took guidance from their chairman. Aquila, Barberini before him... Rome men, Vatican marionettes, Thon wanted to reach across the table and shake some sense into them. They had lost their way; it wasn't their fault, a lifetime of Vatican indoctrination, bowing to the company line.

"There's no mistake Mister Chairman, it says sixty two per cent."

Aquila's mouth fell wide open as he removed his glasses, the sheet of paper still suspended in mid-air. "And praise the Lord where did you pluck that figure from?"

Thon reached into his briefcase and pulled out three bound pamphlets as he handed it across the table to his stunned colleagues. Their laughs were no more, their smiles wiped from their faces as they realised that Håkon Thon was deadly serious.

"The figure was calculated by an independent accountant in Milan. Thirty eight per cent represents the annual running cost of the Catholic Church worldwide, together with all of our employees. Sixty two per cent is surplus to requirement."

"Surplus to requirement, are you out of your mind?" said Aquila

Thon reached into his briefcase and pulled out three more pamphlets that he cast across the table.

"I wish I was Cardinal, I wish I was. Last year we gave less than five per cent to charity as you well know. Eight per cent was earmarked for church and cathedral restoration, five per cent paid out in sexual abuse compensation and a further three per cent on lobbying various governments around the world persuading them to keep current statute of limitation in place." Thon looked up and smiled. "After all we wouldn't want to lose our rather generous tax free status would we?"

Cardinal Cortezi had started to shake his head as the gravity of the figures and the realisation that Håkon Thon was serious started to sink in.

Thon continued. "Another nine per cent was spent on clergy retirement contributions, conferences, overseas trips and conventions, funds for cemeteries and the education of seminarians. The final proportion of the thirty eight per cent was spent on salaries and wages worldwide, including that of the three thousand employed in Vatican City itself."

Cortezi was the first to speak. "Then what was the rest spent on Håkon?"

"In a nutshell Cardinal Cortezi, reinvestment. Last year the Catholic Church spent one hundred and five billion on the purchase of diamonds and gold bullion, land, art and property, stocks, shares and bonds and of course multinational and conglomerate take overs which adds to our already considerable wealth."

"But that's business Håkon," said Aquila, "that's the way of the world, the way a big business works."

Thon nodded. "I agree Cardinal, but I'm proposing we have a year off investing, trying to make our church even richer and more powerful and put something back into the world by helping and re-educating the poor, building health centres and schools and water wells. Building more churches is not the answer."

Cortezi looked at Aquila. "Håkon has a point Cardinal, it would be nice."

Aquila rose from his chair and placed his hands on the table. "Are you out of your mind Cardinal, sixty two per cent?" He raised his voice slightly. "Have you taken leave of your senses; you want our organisation to donate over a hundred billion dollars to charity?"

Aquila flopped into his chair. "You are mad, stone cold crazy."

"Think what it would do for our reputation," said Cortezi. "The detractors, the Vatican bashers, would be made to eat their words."

"I think Cardinal Thon is beginning to sway you," said Aquila, "and you Cardinal Francisco, you have been rather quiet in this last round of debate, what is your opinion on giving sixty two per cent of our annual budget to charity?"

Cardinal Edmund Francisco laid the last pamphlet Thon had given him onto the table. He appeared to breathe deeply before he answered, looking Thon directly in the eyes. "I fear you are a noble man Cardinal Thon and your warmth and generosity has not failed to move me since you came to sit on the committee of the IOR, but I fear you are forgetting one thing."

Cardinal Francisco continued. "Our organisation is indeed a business and we have controlling interests in more companies that any other establishment in the world. The international pension and insurance fund managers and bankers and private investors look to invest in the same companies as we do because they see us as a secure and shrewd player."

For the first time in a while a smile began to draw across Aquila's face. He knew how the voting strategy worked and knew he only needed one man on his side for a null and void conclusion to the proposal, which would mean last year's financial contribution would automatically be implemented and Thon's plan would be dashed on the rocks. He eased back in his seat as Francisco concluded his summing up.

"Imagine what would happen if we suddenly gave away an amount like that to charity. It would be a disaster Håkon, an unmitigated disaster and it would take our church decades to recover because everything we invest in would be halved in value and we may even need to dig into our reserves."

Cardinal Håkon Thon was in the mood for an argument. He spoke with passion for several minutes stating the wealth of the Church was a startling contradiction with the direct teaching of Christ is too glaring to be tolerated or even ignored he explained and with over two thousand years of wealth accumulation it was time to make a change.

"We can make that change," he said. "The men in this room can make that change."

He looked at Aquila and then to Cardinal Francisco who was slowly shaking his head.

"I won't do it Håkon, I won't. The church has been my life's work and I won't risk it."

Cardinal Francisco spoke equally as passionately as Thon and when he eventually signalled to Aquila that he was finished the chairman called for an adjournment. During the short recess he explained to Perini and Monsignor Botswuno that everything was under control. He agreed with Perini that some unknown person or persons may indeed have unduly influenced Cardinal Thon but the situation was very much under control. He'd had a word with Cardinal Cortezi too and explained what the Papa himself had asked of him.

It was just after six o'clock when the four committee members walked into the room and the door was locked. Aquila appeared relaxed, looked at his watch and announced it would be the last piece of business concluded today.

"Cardinal Thon," he said, "as it was your proposal can you start the ball rolling so to speak?"

The leather sack and a row of small black and white balls lay in the middle of the table. Thon picked up the rack and offered it to Cortezi who took a black and a white ball and then passed it to his right to Aquila who in turn handed it to Francisco and finally it came back to Thon.

"It will be a white ball that shall signal agreement to implement my proposal." Thon said. "A black ball signifies disagreement that the budget should remain as it was last year."

"Is that clear?" Aquila asked.

Francisco and Cortezi nodded in agreement.

Thon took the sack from the middle of the table and slipped his hand inside depositing his ball. He handed the sack to his left and eventually all four men had placed the ball of their choice.

The chairman requested the leather sack and Thon handed it to him. Without hesitation Aquila reached inside and pulled out the first ball. White. A good start thought Thon, but by the look on Aquila's smug face he was sure of the final result. A black ball followed and then Aquila pulled out a white. He glared at Cortezi who he felt sure had betrayed him and his suspicion was confirmed as Cortezi appeared to hang his head in shame unable to make eye contact with the chairman. Thon remained relaxed and watched a look of joy pull across Aquila's face as he pulled out the final ball. Black.

Thon had studied the constitution long and hard and knew exactly what the tied vote meant. Aquila was on his feet quicker than he had moved all day announcing that a tied vote meant the previous year's contribution would be implemented for the coming year.

Thon cleared his throat and spoke quietly in barely a whisper. "You are jumping to conclusions Cardinal Aquila. You are clearly not familiar with regulations relating to the voting rights of deceased members."

Aquila smirked and reached into a pile of papers. "Ahhh Håkon, I'm afraid you are wrong, because I am more than aware of the rules relating to our dear departed brothers." He located the section he was looking for. "In that they are null and void."

"Read on," said Thon.

Cardinal Aquila drew his finger under the sub section and strained as the small writing became a little more difficult to read. *"Unless they have specifically requested their voting rights be passed to sitting IOR committee members."*

As soon as he read the sentence he knew Thon was about to spring the bombshell.

Thon reached in his case.

"I have here; two signed and witnessed statements from our deceased brothers, Monsignor Campbell and Bishop Mackenzie. We talked long and hard after last year's committee meeting and met again several weeks later. We came to the conclusion that the time was right for change and because both the Monsignor and the Bishop were in failing health, decided it would be prudent if we covered all eventualities. We knew our decision might not sit well with certain individuals within the city." He looked up. "Let's just say I am wiser than the next man when it comes to the responsibilities of the Vatican Police."

Thon handed the two sheets of paper to the chairman of the IOR.

They were simplicity themselves, three lines giving up the dead men's IOR voting rights on the amount of charitable contributions to Cardinal Håkon Thon on the event of unexpected death. Both were independently witnessed by acting Barristers in Liverpool and Aberdeen, both stamped with official wax seals from legal headquarters in London and Edinburgh respectively.

Aquila was lost for words as Thon reached into the centre of the desk for the rack of balls. In full view of everyone he dropped two white balls into the leather pouch and announced that the formalities were now complete and the charitable contribution for the forthcoming year would be sixty two per cent. He stood and walked towards the door knocking three times before he turned.

"Thank you gentlemen," he said, "it was a pleasure doing business with you and I look forward to a very special meeting tomorrow morning."

Forty Six

Africa. Eighteen months later.

The Democratic Republic of Congo is the largest country in Sub Saharan Africa and the eleventh largest country in the world with a population of over seventy five million; it is also universally regarded as one of the poorest nations on earth. It has the second-highest total Christian population in Africa, mainly Catholic; there are six archdioceses and 41 dioceses.

Ancient religions within ethnic groups are widespread and witchcraft and sorcery beliefs are not uncommon. US inspired Pentecostal churches have been in the forefront of witchcraft accusations particularly against children who when accused of witchcraft are sent from their homes and family. These children are known as *enfants sorciers* and suffer from physical violence and death. There are even some church organisations that capitalize on the belief by charging exorbitant fees for exorcisms. One of the worst affected areas for persecution and accusations of this type is Kikwit, three hundred kilometres east of the capital Kinshasa.

For Cardinal Håkon Thon it seemed like a good place to start and spend some of the Catholic Church's enormous wealth. He had been there six months and had witnessed an enormous change. There was full employment for a start and unknown to the powers in the Vatican he'd even started to distribute condoms quite freely advising the locals that the Papa himself had made an exception for this most deprived part of God's world.

The health centre was now complete with over seventy nurses trained to support the dozen or so qualified doctors who had been persuaded to up sticks from Kinshasa and relocate. At a cost of over twenty six million US dollars, a desalination plant had been built at the port of Boma in the east of the country together with a 600 kilometre pipeline that brought fresh water right into the heart of the town and towns and villages around them.

Without a doubt it had been the biggest single factor in stabilising the region and bringing a modicum of prosperity to the people who had suffered for so long. The outlying farms grew crops and employed farm hands and markets flourished as the fruits and vegetables were brought to town.

Schools were built and classes started and teachers and assistants and cleaners paid directly from the funds provided by the church. Thon insisted that a weekly allowance was paid direct to a cooperative organisation that provided over two thousand children with a freshly cooked dinner every day. There was no greater sight, he thought, than a smiling child with a full belly and friends to play with. When he saw a group of small boys kicking a football around it reminded him of his happy childhood in Trondheim, Norway, though the climate was altogether different.

Håkon Thon was the happiest he could ever remember, despite the heat and the flies and the lack of air conditioning and cold beer. He hoped his guest who was flying into Kinshasa airport would take to the conditions as well as he had, she would be landing just about now, a dangerous ten-hour road journey ahead of her.

Samantha Kerr's bus pulled into the village of Kikwit just after 11 o'clock the following morning. Her pretty white face, as she stepped from the bus, caused much excitement among the children. It was nice to see her again and as she made her way towards him he took her outstretched hand and kissed her gently on the lips. It was a spontaneous gesture, one that he could have and should have stopped himself from doing but he couldn't help himself, he owed this girl so much.

Never would he have guessed when they first sat down in a small café in Assisi, the mountain they would move together. The plan had been relatively simple as she explained about a female killing machine called Celine Macarthur and blackmail and how the girl had a plan to distribute a large proportion of the world's wealth a little more fairly. It transpired that two of the deceased members of the IOR had one or two skeletons in the closet that they would prefer to stay behind closed doors. Sam Kerr had explained what was expected of Thon and how it could be achieved. He had sat in stunned silence as Sam went into the intricate details of Macarthur's insight and forward thinking and planning and realised it was incredibly well thought out and almost fool proof. Somehow Macarthur had managed to get hold of the minutes from the meeting of the IOR Thon first sat in on, where he had been quite vociferous and had made his opinions on charitable contributions quite clear. It had been the final piece of the jigsaw, Thon the human lynchpin.

Macarthur's plan had taken nearly four years to perfect and by bringing in Sam Kerr she had implemented a more than capable insurance policy. Macarthur knew just how powerful the Catholic Church was and guessed they would catch up with her eventually. As he stood almost motionless and looked at the slip of a girl from England with admiration and great affection, he hoped with all of his heart that she would escape the clutches of the men from the Vatican with revenge on their mind.

Thon took her hand. "Come Sam," he said, "I'll give you a little tour and show you what we have achieved."

Thon took her to the school where they sat in on the last ten minutes of a geography class. She counted over forty, enthusiastic children, over keen to answer the teacher's latest question. *What was the capital of Norway?* Sam wondered if Thon had had a little input into that one. Afterwards he took her to the kitchen at the rear of the school where two plump women prepared a typical Congolese stew. One of the ladies invited Sam to take a taste, which she did. It didn't escape her notice that the stew was well packed with vegetables and meat and the type of consistency her old grandmother would have been more than pleased with. The village was prospering and on the way up, the atmosphere in the school one of hope and contentment.

As they walked from the school Håkon turned to Sam. "Don't let anyone tell you that money is the root of all evil. If you'd seen this place a few years ago you wouldn't have believed it."

Sam was nodding her head; she spoke quietly. "I can imagine."

As they sat taking a coffee in the local street bar they spoke in whispers. There was a certain nervousness, perhaps a little fear.

"I don't regret a bit of it," said Thon. "I was happy to carry out the final piece of her plan and while I don't condone what she did to the Priests and the Bishops she has undoubtedly left the mark she wanted to leave."

"She's left an amazing legacy," said Sam, "but I can't forget she's a cold blooded killer. Part of me didn't want to get involved in her plans but the more I looked into it the more I felt it was the right thing to do."

Håkon lifted the plastic cup to his mouth as he smiled and took a sip of sweet coffee. He'd wrestled with the same guilt for many days but when he'd managed to carry the vote at the IOR it was as if he'd been cleansed and he'd never been so sure of anything in his life. Looking around the villages and towns at the schools and health centres and shops his chest swelled with pride.

"And Mr Flynn. We can't forget his part in all of this."

Sam nodded. "And Corinne too, she was an absolute diamond, a real rock."

Sam said she missed the Flynn's, they felt like her adopted parents and she hoped it wouldn't be too long before they got together again. There were risks involved of course and they both knew it. Even now it was as if their conversations were being listened too, someone possibly watching from the dense jungle that surrounded the town. They both felt it but they kept their thoughts to themselves.

Håkon stood. "Come, my housekeeper Heidi has prepared us a pleasant lunch. She's a great cook and I'd love you to meet her. We go back a long way."